YEAR of the TURNIP

YEAR of the TURNIP

JOHN DOBSON

Published by Mercury
an imprint of Burnet Media

•

Burnet Media is the publisher of Mercury and Two Dogs books
info@burnetmedia.co.za   www.burnetmedia.co.za
Facebook: Two Dogs / Mercury Books
Twitter: @TwoDogs_Mercury
PO Box 53557, Kenilworth, 7745, South Africa

•

First published 2015
1 2 3 5 7 9 8 6 4

•

Publication © 2015 Burnet Media
Text © 2015 John Dobson

•

•

Distributed by Jacana Media
www.jacana.co.za

•

Printed and bound by Tandym Print
www.tandym.co.za

ISBN 9780992194994

Also available as an ebook.

John Dobson is a rugby coach, LLB grad and author. This is his second novel, after *Year Of The Gherkin*.

To Bubbles.

SUNDAY 8 MAY 2011

I feel a bit like Keith Richards the morning after a triple-header on tour. On a massive downer, mouth tasting like Malema's underrods, a worse loser's complex than the white guy running against Usain Bolt, more anxious than a dried-out Betty Ford in the wine aisle. The difference between me and Keith is that I didn't wake up next to last year's Miss Venezuela. And the year before's. Plus Keith probably had access to more 'products' than 12 Hansas, 12 Hunters and a bottle of Cape to Rio to get him where he needed to be.

I wake up to my mother.

No, not like that.

To my mother bringing me a steaming cup of Earl Grey. In my 'temporary' accommodation in digs (at my folks), I haven't got a bedside table. She knows that and hands me that cup of shit making me sit up to avoid scalding myself. Her way of forcing me to wake up and get to the golf club. Tragically not to tee off.

'Mine's a Bell's, Jason. Pat here's having a Dewar's. And Geoff a double White Horse and soda. With a twist of haste in all, chum.'

I never thought that I would be pouring drinks to Cliff Saunders and his mates after 18 holes at Port Alfred Golf Club (the one course without hot promo girls). It's not *the* Cliff Saunders, the one who used to be on SABC with Jacques Pauw filming oil tankers on the rocks and Trevor Quirk. This is another Cliff Saunders. From Zim. And looks a bit like Nikki Lauda – *after* the accident.

Have none of these jokers ever heard of Chivas, Jammies or Johnnie Red? They all drink whiskies they feature on promotional ashtrays.

'And whatever your old boy's having. He's just in the bogs.'

Whatever your old boy's having? What is my old man *not* having would be a fairer question. I know he hates First Watch because he says it's South African and not real Scotch and that it's aimed at the 'emerging market'. And it's a cheapo; more, he says, in demand among the parking attendants than the parkers themselves. So I pour him a large First Watch.

He comes back, zipping up the fly on some checked pants so wide at the bottom you could pull them on over your rugby boots. I blush. More so when I see the wet spot that shows his drip drying isn't what it once was. And those awful two-tone glasses – the ones that change colour when outside.

'Jason.'

'Dad.'

'Large low-flyer, please.' Why can't he just say Famous Grouse?

I slide him the First Watch. 'Here you go, Dad. Poured already.'

'Your lightie knows his old man,' pipes up the dick called Geoff from their fourball who lost a lot of money in O'Hagans. I don't know if they meant as an investor or as a patron. Dad slurps his First Watch. And lets out a melodramatic, satisfied 'aahhhh…' What a vegetable.

They call him T-Rex at the golf club. Stands for Thirsty Rex (Brydon). That's not going to make any son's bosom burst with pride. Not sure men have bosoms, but I read in the *You* that men can lactate. I hope I never do. Besides, I would not produce much cos there is no real gym in Port Alfred (well not one without a nurses' station and with a dumbbell over 2.5kg) so my pecs have faded a bit. Kim Kardashian on the other hand could supply the whole of Parmalat. Plus the *You* also tells me men can get breast cancer. That must be sooo blind. It's a bit like a chick getting gout.

Cliff is banging on about his favourite subject. Zim. 'Listen, guys. I am not moving again. This is as far south as Cliffy Saunders goes. This is my last stand.'

Fuck, you would think he was Lieutenant General Custard or whatever his name was from the way he speaks about a last stand.

'Nope – Salisbury to Joburg – too many Dutchmen – then to Durban till they stuffed that up. Port Alfred and no further. No point in moving down to the Western Cape, that's even more fucked. They think they are alright there because they have all those coloureds as a buffer, but I am telling you they count for nothing. Never have.'

Dad adds value: 'Would be nice if they made some contribution.'

Cliffy is unrelenting. 'So what if we move to Agulhas – next thing we will have to buy flippers if we want to go any further south. Jason, same again please.'

To Rex Brydon this talk is a sweet lullaby.

'No, I am telling you the kak is coming. Malema is coming for us. Look, I'm pleased I got out of Zim when I did, but no more running. A lot of my mates were duped by all the reconciliation kak Mugabe spoke when he took over, just like Mandela did. The stayers accused those of us who left of doing the chicken run. Well, where are they now? All living in mates' garages in Harare eating post toastie boxes for lunch, that's where.'

T-Rex takes another slurp of the First Watch.

'That's my boy.' He winks. He thinks he's something out of *The Sopranos* cos he fixed me this job through his mate Cliff, the vice-chairman.

It wasn't meant to turn out like this. Barman at the Royal Port Alfred and staying with my folks, sleeping in a single bed with a Formula 1 duvet cover. Never.

Mind you, a sign of how things would turn out was probably when I must have been the only 14-year-old not in an institution to get a cap gun for Christmas.

Dad still sends fan mail to Jody Scheckter. Someone said he looked a bit like Nigel Mansell, but that was probably cos they both had moustaches that hosted bio-cultures. Saying they're alike is a bit like saying, apart from the assassination, Jackie Kennedy enjoyed her drive through downtown Dallas.

MONDAY 9 MAY 2011

Getting back into this diary thing. Can't see why I stopped it actually. Following in the footsteps of Anne Frank and Bridget Jones (thinner diary, fatter person).

What a start to the week. I get a letter. And it's not from Edgars accounts.

Hayley is threatening maintenance court unless I sign the order. Again. What a cow! Sapphire is not even born yet and she's behaving like this. Imagine what she's going to be like when she has to buy its first school uniform. I know what the order is, but a barman's – sorry, deputy club manager's – wage, relying on members tips and watering down some of the J&B, does not exactly fill the coffers. In fact my basic salary just covers the car repayments and my Old Mutual debit, which I'm trying like buggery to cancel. The fellow called Zane, who sold me the policy and who used to call me three times a day and virtually sucked my blood out himself for the blood test, is now nowhere to be fucking found.

My mom paid off my credit cards from Gran's inheritance, but we're not allowed to tell my dad cos he would do his nut.

Apparently I am expected to go and see Sapphire after she is born. That's a drive to PE then Kulula to Joburg (R40 for a ham-and-cheese croissant that is potentially more of a weapon than any Swiss army knife) to spend bucks I haven't got to visit something that will have no clue who I am and whose mother, quote, would rather blind herself with a hot poker dipped in faeces than see me again, unquote.

Morale check: lower than a coelacanth's cellar.
Time to becoming a dad: 1 month.
Available cash: R223.35c.

If I invested that at 7% through some pleased-with-themselves pricks like Allan Gray who make all those ads about the world coming together or adopting a tiger (that presumably goes on to eat a whole village), I would get R15.63 a year or R1.30 a month. Would it be fair to say my portfolio, like Amor, is looking slightly anaemic?

TUESDAY 10 MAY 2011

Don't want to bang on about it, but why's it my fault that Hayley was moronic enough to fall pregnant? As she told her folks herself, it was an accident. Then, I ask you, if it was an accident, why is it my fault?

Accidents, tweeps, don't have faults. That's why they're called accidents. So why am I going to be paying R2,500 a month 'for now'? For now. Apparently because it will escalate.

Condoms are nowadays about AIDS, not pregnancy. That was the '70s.

From: Jason Brydon <Jasebrydon069@gmail.com>
Date: 10 May 2011 at 12.12pm
To: 'Slug'
Subject: Class Action

Howzit Slug

Hope all's lekker in Cape Town and the legal world. And with Lettuce. I miss you buggers. I am thinking of coming back to Cape Town to join the real world after my gap year here on the Wild Coast sampling the local Transkeian Scooby-doo.

Listen, quick one, with this whole Hayley stuff-up that could actually work out lekker for both of us. I know you said we have to assume she took the pill and that I was one of the very very unlucky 0.8% and that the goalie was fast asleep but is there any way we could sue Bayer or Adcock Ingram who makes the pill?

We could sue on behalf of all the countless dooses who have been stitched like me. I think you call it a class action like that movie with Julia Roberts, Ellen Brokovich, where she actually looked quite kak, and we do it like you get like 25/30% if we win and me the rest but if you lose then you get nothing. But I don't see how you can lose cos it's like crystal clear. If I buy a crash helmet and I fall off my Kawasaki and my helmet breaks and I die or become a vegetable then of course I can sue the okes who made the helmet. They do it in America all the time. And class actions are like millions and millions, you can sue for everything from their future school rucksacks, matric dance dresses and tampons to my loss of earnings and lifestyle discomfort.

And it's cool cos you sue the pharmaceutical company which is cool because they have very deep pockets and much better for the Jason brand than suing Hayley herself (tempting as that is).

We can sue them in the Western Cape High Court and we can meet before at the Brazilian coffee shop and I can wear those black Pradas I got. And maybe be in the Cape Times. Channing Tatum could play me if they ever make a movie about it. And my accent is not too South African.

Himme back.

Shot
Jase

SMS to Hayley:
> Hi Hayles this new Super Rugby format is bullshit hey? Hope you OK, not long now, I am sure we can sort the maintenance order no worries. Listen quick one, just out of interest, which company made your pill? X

No reply. Odd.

WEDNESDAY 11 MAY 2011

I made R42.20 in tips today which works out to exactly R4.69 an hour. And I got a packet of Balsamic Lays. Am I destined to shop at Mr Price for the rest of my life? At this rate I am!

I am not sure I am ready to be a father.

THURSDAY 12 MAY 2011

Mom phones while I am on duty during the Nashua Golf Day. Apparently Dad has 'skinned' Rascal. Rascal was/is (I am not sure) the mutt they got from the animal welfare place in Grahamstown. Dad thinks it was the same animal shelter in the film *Disgrace* (so boring I could have screamed) where Weird John Malkovich has sex on one of the operating beds with the human beach ball who ran the place. Anyway, Rascal was a very fluffy, cheerful cross lots of things, but mostly Maltese Poodle and Jack Russell with liberal spurts of Township Setter. They thought it would provide companionship in their 'golden years'. Rascal's case would have been helped were he not incontinent. Leslie thinks Dad frames Rascal for some of the urine smell in the house when it's Dad being 'inaccurate' after a night at the club.

One of Dad's only jobs is to walk Rascal. Mom is too scared – she says Rascal is not a watch dog and that he could not stop her being raped by blacks. I am not going to say Mom has completely lost her looks, but any would-be rapist would have to be quite far-sighted.

Dad was obviously in a bit of a hurry or a bit lazy or a bit boozed (probably all three) and took Rascal down to the bottom of the road,

14

let him out and then drove the kilometre back home so Rascal could run following the car and tire him out. I know Rascal likes that. But when he got back Rascal had no fur left and was half dead. Dad had let him out on his lead, but closed the lead in the door and basically dragged Rascal home. His legs are about 2cm long so the poor thing was dragged behind like a ball. Rascal is in the vet's ICU. Dad says it's going to cost a 'bloody fortune, but your mother wanted a dog'.

T-Rex is still smarting after Muffin, Mom's last rescue dog. Mom loved Muffin, who was ¼ Maltese, ¼ Jack Russell, ¼ Mamelodi setter, ¼ collie and a ¼ five other breeds of hound. Muffin went missing for five days and Mom was beside herself and made Dad post flyers everywhere, issue a R500 reward and buy ads in the *Argus* classifieds which cost him almost R700. Some gardener in Pinelands (poor Muffin) found him and brought him to the house. Dad accused the fellow of stealing him for the reward and Leslie had to remind him that the oke did not know there would be a reward, especially for a tatty rag like Muffin. He paid and Mom boiled a whole welcome-home chicken for Muffin that afternoon, who promptly caught a chicken bone in his throat and choked to death in the kitchen. Dad is still bitter about that.

FRIDAY 13 MAY 2011

I wonder what could possibly go more wrong on Friday the 13th?

I am insolvent, nothing technical or provisional about it. You can quantitative ease all you want – it is what it is.

I am 93.3kg which BMI-wise makes me obese, but I do know that I do have heavy bones.

American Express have handed me over to some attorneys with the requisite name like Levinsohn, Levinsohn, Shapiro and Mdlala.

Leslie, my sister, is getting married to Carol on Soweto Day and I have to go and my dad does not know yet. I suspect, though, when he finds out that it's a same-sex union, he will be very happy to give Leslie away.

In about 3-4 weeks I will become a father.

As far as 2011 goes, the Pope has had more action than me.

Most first-years would not do my job as a vac job, let alone a career.

My mom makes me lunch – mostly apricot jam and cheese sandwiches.

What else could possibly go wrong?

In some ways I feel for a rat. And maybe in some ways I feel *like* a rat. Rats must be so bleak and sit there thinking if only we had furry tails (like squirrels) instead of rubbery ones people wouldn't spend their lives throwing bricks at us and shrieking *'O vok, dis 'n rot'* loudly. If I was 5kg lighter and maybe 6cm taller and my hair two shades less red…

SATURDAY 14 MAY 2011

I get 'tazered' at Numbers in East London. Far, far from ideal.

It goes something like this. I go up to East London cos my best (only?) mate Stevie is in Slummies for a friend of his new chick, Mel's, wedding at Beacon Bay. He had called in the week: 'J, you won't believe this, but I am in East London this weekend. Pull in.'

'Awesome, what for?'

'It's some friend of Mel's fucking wedding, but I promise you not even David Blaine could get out of it. I like tried everything, but one, she's paying and B, I thought we maybe could hook up for a few petrols.'

'Flat-out, china, flat-out,' I told him as I calculated how much the fuel there and back would cost me, and whether I would in fact have the cash to go out with Stevie in East London. Gents, I promise you, in an ideal world you don't want, aged 30, to be going up to your old lady to ask for some cash to go out with your mate. So I lifted a lazy blue one or two out her purse. Be that as it may, it would be nice to drink with someone who's under 60 and doesn't have red veins all around a bulbous nose. And who, unlike the rest of those Cape Town pricks, doesn't judge me.

Stevie has a plan. As always.

'I have already told Mel that my mate Jason lives up there and that I haven't seen you for yonks. We're just up for the one night, but she says I can leave the wedding after the speeches.'

'Shit, Stevo, that's good of her.'

'Yip, told her you had cancer.'

Gulp.

'Had to, boet, or she would never let me leave. Plus she doesn't know any of the gang and I'm going to fire her before the end of the Super 15 anyway, so don't stress.'

'What cancer do I have?'

'Liver.'

'Shit, that's the one that they cannot fix.'

'Precisely. That's why she is letting me leave the wedding. You haven't got long. Plus it's better than ball cancer.'

Awesome. But I could see his point about the liver given T-Rex's abuse of his and maybe it's genetic. Mind you, if Dad hasn't got liver cancer by now, then, like Pik Botha, he is never going to get it.

Anyway, we go to Numbers which is a complete vibe. Firstly the shaven-headed doos at the door does not want to let me in cos I am wearing slops. I point out that they are Havaianas. 'Probably worth more than your jeans and top, pal.' Probably getting things off on the wrong foot (pun).

We get round it by Stevie producing from his car a pair of white socks that he ran to Nahoon and back in this morning (15km). Image and hygiene wise, far from ideal, but I get in.

It's wall-to-wall punda in there – as the Slumtown locals say, 'the shad were running thick, boet'. I am in the True Religions I bought in Sandton City last year and an Ed Hardy T. There is more chance of finding alluvial diamonds in PE or Slummies than an Ed Hardy T.

They say East London has the highest female-to-male ratio in SA and they were all at Numbers, maybe cos that self-satisfied prick Gareth Cliff was 'playing'. Playing? I can also put a CD in and push play. Learn a real instrument, you knob. Oh yes, and why don't you put your headphones on properly instead of holding one to the side. You're not David fucking Guetta.

One female is talking to me. I'm the first to admit she's not off the showroom floor, but she is friendly. And has two arms, two legs, breathes, etc. Stevie's mate Choppie walks past, looks at 'my one' and chirps 'throw that one back, boet'.

There is an Indian guy dancing, probably about 43kg, looks like something out of *Slumdog Millionaire* with biceps like a famine victim. He could probably split a molecule before breakfast, but he's out of his depth in a club.

Anyway Stevie is spading a cheerful number that has probably seen better days, but in that light she's fine. You would probably need turps to get all that base off, but she seems fun and her barriers to entry seem particularly low. I, of course, am lurking like an over-enthusiastic Indian waiter. I'm standing with a Jack-and-lime near this fire escape door. Stevie thinks it's funny to push me through it. Problem is an alarm goes off and this massive light shines through it… So obviously some big knob in a black suit with sloping shoulders and an earpiece, very closely related to Cro-Magnon man, comes up to me.

'That's one, bru'

'One what, BRU?'

'Warning.'

'OK, cool, but he pushed me,' I explain, pointing at an amused Steve.

We carry on partying. Jäger bombs, slammers, Aftershocks, Patrons – then Stevie pushes me through the door again. Music stops, alarm rings, light on. Yay. The rest of the club are looking at me and shaking their heads. The Friend of Neanderthal Man is more aggressive.

'Last warning.'

He waddles off, shoulders sloping so steeply you could ski off them. Stevie enjoys the show so much he treats us to some tequilas. I don't know about you, but these days I almost kotch just smelling a tequila.

'Listen, Stevie, can I sit this one out?'

'Brydon, don't be a complete wuss. Besides tequila is an upper.'

No it's not, it's a down-and-blackout-er. My gills are twitching at the smell. Armies of bile are assembling on the plains of my tongue. But I take it and as Stevie calls 'crouch-touch-pause-engage', I lift mine, but as the others drink I throw mine over my shoulder. Straight into the face of Neanderthal Man. He actually staggers back, a bit theatrically. Come on, pal, it's Jose Cuervo, not hydrochloric acid.

Steve and his squeeze are beside themselves they are laughing so much. I put my hands up, do the decent thing and start towards the door like Adam Gilchrist, not even going to wait for the umpire to give me out. Thing is he doesn't just let me leave. Next thing I know I'm on the floor in a heap with a very large and spreading wet patch in the True Religions. I have been tazered.

Out of interest, the only thing a girl says to me tonight is 'So, do you always stalk?'

SUNDAY 15 MAY 2011

Caster Semenya is preparing for the World Champs. I'm not sure where I stand on the whole issue as I have mixed feelings… pardon the clever pun. The point is wouldn't you rather have a hot thing representing your country than something out of *The Cosby Show*?

You know when I was repping at 2Dye4 Paints, which I now kinda miss (even though my boss told me I was as 'useful as a turnip'), I didn't want my gravestone to say: 'He sold paint'. I didn't really… sell much, that is, and thus the turnip moniker. But my point is that there is more to life. Likewise I don't want my tombstone to read now: 'Here lies Jason. He served Cliffy'.

My job's also not gonna pay little Sapphire's maintenance and I read now you get named in the papers if you don't pay maintenance. Like for drunken driving. If they focus on those two categories, I got a feeling I could become quite well known.

> **@jasonator069** East London going downhill faster than 5FM #stoptherot

Stevie isn't very nice, but am not sure this tweet is directed at me:

> **@steviewunda:** Steve Jobs was born out of wedlock, put up for adoption at birth, dropped out of college, then changed the world. What's your excuse?

Answer: Sexy Rexy.

MONDAY 16 MAY 2011

Tonight's weekly inspection reveals definite signs of recession on the cranium. That is two consecutive inspections of negative growth, just on the sides, especially on the right where my school side parting used to be. Definitely thinning, which means only one thing. Propecia. Those bloody pills cost almost R600 a month. But, hey, they seem to work for Gareth Cliff so why not?

I find another worrying ear hair. Out it comes but I wonder if I was the first of the Born Frees to have an ear hair? This redeployment of hair is becoming an issue.

Top three hairs to pluck:
1. Ingrown on chin (more popped than plucked)
2. Inner ear hair
3. Long nose hair

I think I'm a Born Free – 11 when Nelson Mandela was released (I was at cricket) and too young to vote in 1994, but saw it on the news. And in 1999 I was in Hermanus so couldn't vote. Voted in 2004, but in '09 the weather was awesome and when I got back from the beach they were closing so I missed out. But I put a koki mark on my thumb because I had to go to a braai at Dawesy's with his self-righteous mates.

TUESDAY 17 MAY 2011

Update my status. Haven't been on the 'book' for a while:

Jase is enjoying his chill year kicking back, cruising up and down the Wild Coast, sampling the local jumbo…

Mich posts:
   Thought you were staying with your folks…

That chick. Really. I know Port Alfred is not exactly the Wild Coast, but it's only a couple of bridges, a few burnt out taxis and three KFCs away.

   Thanks Mich. Nope, just over the corporate shit for a few months. Will head back to civilization soon, or when the money dries up.

Then Muggs posts:
   So Thursday then?

On duty today, ladies fourballs. Spot the under 70 (age not handicap) and win a Samsung Galaxy. Where the fuck do they get those shorts from?

WEDNESDAY 18 MAY 2011

I want to be described as 'gaunt'.

THURSDAY 19 MAY 2011

It is time to head back to Cape Town. Or any city. Even Bloem. Just need to find a job there. Or anywhere. Come on, Jason.

Fuck Mumford & Sons.

FRIDAY 20 MAY 2011

Dad comes home from the club tonight as tight as a tick that's fallen in a bottle of Cutty Sark. It's my night off so am lying on the couch watching TV with Mom. SABC3 (who do have a little left for white programming). It's *Isidingo* so Mom says we should try etv, but I could not watch the fireman get it on with the aerobics instructor with Mom saying 'Oh no, really, this should not be on television. These days…' They don't have DStv. Dad says it's only for the sport and he can get that at the club, thanks very much.

A few points on that:
• It works well because then he has an excuse to go to the club. Lesotho playing Southern Gabon at beach volleyball is enough of an excuse to get down to the club – any club – to watch.
• Mom wanted to have it for the BBC Knowledge, food and entertainment, but Dad hates Jeremy Clarkson because he is an opinionated pom. Err, Dad, that's why they hired him.
• Some shacks in Nemato (one of our two, yes, reader, *two* townships) have DStv. Their 'houses' are made of Heinz cans, some corrugated iron and some old Sunlight soap bottles, yet they have the non-stop magic. The Brydons don't. Awesome.

Anyway, Dad comes back from the club, fries some eggs on toast and asks me to get him a Steve Hofmeyr CD. Seems he's the new hero because, according to T-Rex, he has balls. Apparently he has said he was 'sorry to emphasise the colour, but I'm struggling to spot the terrible whites who climb over blacks' walls to do that to their children'.

And then Stevie Wonder makes himself even more popular in the beer halls of Port Alfred: he's had a go at Malema who has, according to Steve, 'yet to admit to the fact that they have yet to give this continent anything that makes the world sit up'.

I pipe up: 'They invented the necklace.'

Dad guffaws so much that some HP sauce lands on the settee.

SATURDAY 21 MAY 2011

Slug's tweet:

> **@slug:** great news, we expecting our first. Fiona is 3 months!!!

> **@jasonator069 @slug** awesome slug, thats rad, send best to lettuce

> **@slug @jasonator069 @slug** jase, i have asked you not to call her Lettuce, please boet

Slug is excited yet I haven't told them about the impending arrival of (our) Sapphire. I don't want to steal their thunder.

SUNDAY 22 MAY 2011

We start rehearsals today. Thanks to my folks, I am to be Inspector Maine in the Port Alfred Dramatic Society (PADS) production of Agatha Christie's *And Then There Were None*. Don't ask.

And what's more, Rex is the prompt. He is not allowed a speaking role, which may have something to do with his propensity to slur after lunch.

I hate plays and opera and all that shit. I mean, what's the point? Nobody watches, nobody cares. And if you asked the good citizens of Nemato if they would rather have funding for the arts or toilets that flush, I can tell you the answer. Unless they were a homo.

My only dramatic experience so far was exactly that. Dramatic.

It was the school nativity play in the hall. The Sub-As had to lay it on for the whole school right up to the matrics and including the First XV. Hectic in other words. Miss Ferris had given me the prime role of Joseph. Some okes thought it better to be one of the three kings who bore gifts of gold, frankincense and myrrh because they had the most insane velvet robes and fuck-off big crowns. Joseph was cooler than Kanye West cos he had a donkey and was the first guy to enter and had a talking role. The plan, which we rehearsed at big break every day for the whole term, was that I would enter the hall with my pregnant wife Mary (Ricky Shaw, a boarder) with a pillow up his dress sitting side saddle (like the Queen and Elton John) on a donkey (Worm's bike with training wheels and a cardboard donkey head made by the Sub-Bs).

(Interjection: I wish Sapphire was just a pillow.)

We then had to go down the middle aisle of the hall and turn left to the first inn – a cardboard mini-shack made from cardboard boxes with a sign saying 'Inn', then back across to the right to a similar construction called 'Inn number 2' and then we had to go up on the stage – Ricky had to dismount and Miss Ferris would carry the bicycle up the stage stairs and then we would go to the waiting manger with straw in the ground and some stars hanging from the ceiling and some arb shepherds lurking around waving at their grandparents in the audience.

In my case my folks were there, and my sister – I was too young then to realise what a total embarrassment she was – and Rex's dad, my grandpa, who must have left a whole trail of brill cream on the N2 in from Gordon's Bay, and my mom's mom, who had sewn a dress especially for it, and my other grandpa who hated crowds, people, children, coloureds and Martin Locke.

In we go, me and Ricky Shaw. More than the odd flash going. Down the middle and left to the first Inn. I 'knocked' on the 'door' with the knocking noise being provided by a somewhat out of sync Miss Ferris hitting a tray with a ruler behind the inn. And I knew my lines, boy, did I know my lines.

'Greetings, innkeeper.' (Reggie Bamford from number 47.) 'I am but a humble carpenter Joseph and this is my wife Mary, who is with child.' Although I do think the pillow up Ricky's dress was a dead giveaway. 'Do you have any room in the Inn?'

There was a slightly stressful pause, but then Reggie got it right. 'Sorry, sir, we are fully booked.'

Perfect. The plan then was to walk across to Inn Number 2 and once rejected there get up to the manger for baby Jesus to get born.

Across we go. I can see Grandpa Brydon fast asleep three rows back. I get to Inn Number 2 and again a mistimed knock. The innkeeper, Trevor de Kock, whose parents were divorced, appears.

'Greetings, innkeeper, I am but a humble carpenter Joseph and this is my wife Mary, who is with child. Do you have any room in the Inn?'

Silence. And then it came.

'Howzit, Brydon, plenty of room, pull in.'

Silence. A long silence. Then I could hear some twittering in the audience which was increasing. There were some out-and-out laughs, but I was in a panic. I stood there, knowing full well that I had to get to the waiting shepherds and three wise men by the manger. But how could I when Trevor had just invited me into Inn Number 2. I don't think anybody in the whole hall was not laughing now. Except me. I was crying and holding my winkie in case I weed in my pants.

Luckily Miss Ferris reacted, came and grabbed me by the hand and pulled Mary and the Donkey onto the stage and hissed to Trevor that she would 'deal with him later'.

It turns out that Trevor's brother in Standard 9 had coached him what to say as a joke. He got four jacks for it from Mr Wiltshire the headmaster, but it's not the point. The damage was done.

MONDAY 23 MAY 2011

Dawesy posted this shit on Twitter:

> **@dawesman** Selebi: Quem custodis custodent, sed custodis ipsis

It seems Jackie (what a name) Selebi has been found guilty, *finish and klaar*, largely based on evidence by a mobile grease ball called Agliotti.

> **@jasonator069 @dawesman:** @Dawesman tweet in English not Spanish so rest of us wolf pack can understand

> **@dawesman @jasonator069 @dawesman:** its Latin you fool. It means basically who guards the guards themselves?

Whatever Dawesy. Nobody speaks Latin any more except the pope and then he must talk to himself cos it (and he) is virtually dead. Hate it when Dawesy tries to show off. But I kind of see his point. Like what he means and like he should have tweeted it as, like who checks on the guards? Like who checks on the ADT guys? If they start stealing nobody thinks it's them. But who checks on guards – more guards? But who checks on *them*? You get my drift? That's what Dawesy should have said.

TUESDAY 24 MAY 2011

Seems a bit late, but Rex is getting ready for Rascal's wake (I can hear the ice bucket being filled and 'Valerie, I could swear I asked you to buy blitz'). Ronnie from the Boat Club is coming round for an (imitation) Weber. I have met Ronnie once. He is an ex-cop who took 'the package' after he was accused of racism because he told one of the new constables he had been given to work for him in PE, who could not even spell constable and had put his cap on back-to-front, to dress properly and that he was a policeman not the Fresh Prince of Bel-Air.

He used his package not to open a Seven Eleven, but to get into the private security game and had got the contract to help with security at the Grahamstown court, which he lost when one of his German shepherds bit Magistrate Mayosi. Ronnie says it was because the dog, ironically called Dingaan, had mistaken the magistrate for disgraced Judge President John Hlope. Ronnie says he is now thinking of moving to Zim cos their 'shit' was over and ours was still coming.

His son is a supernatural investigator in Utah.

WEDNESDAY 25 MAY 2011

I get so wasted at Caprice in PE that I puke through my nose.

THURSDAY 26 MAY 2011

Rehearsals start. I get a lift with the prompt.

'Dad, I am sure you don't have to come. We haven't even got our scripts yet, so I'm not sure how're you going to prompt.'

'Jason, it's important that I am part of this from the start.'

Anything but a night in with Val. Which is SABC Afrikaans news with Riaan Cruywagen because they 'can trust him'. I think seeing him makes them feel that the country has not completely gone to the dogs.

When we arrive at the hall, the prompt has an announcement to make to those who will listen.

'You know, when Agatha Christie first wrote this play, it was called *Ten Little Niggers.*'

Rex on a roll. 'And the island it was set on was called Nigger Island till they changed it to Soldier Island. Yes,' he guffaws, 'there's lots of soldiers in the Eastern Cape.'

Cliffy (aka Sir Thomas Legge) finds this quite amusing. 'Eeny meeny miny moe, catch a soldier by his toe.'

This is all a bit awkward because Mr Dumphrey, the director, one of those dreadful theatre types who wears a cravat, has cast Phumeza, the receptionist from the hotel, as Vera Claythorne.

Dumphrey is unmarried and has started a scholarship for some of the township kids and takes them on hikes. That should tell you all you need to know. His arrest must be imminent.

FRIDAY 27 MAY 2011

Five missed calls from Hayley's dad. Really, the chick is about to have a child, she is old enough and big enough (especially in the thigh area) to fight her own battles.

Her *ballie* does not scare me, not at all, but I'm still not answering his calls. What for? To get abused by some vegetable high up at Bidvest? I listen to the voicemail. Seems he wants me to put Sapphire on my medical aid. Oops.

SATURDAY 28 MAY 2011

We are black, we are white, we are, we are DYNAMITE!

Sharks beat the Waratahs at the Shark Tank to stay in the hunt and the Stormers lost! The only downside to a great sporting Saturday was that Barcelona gave Man U a klap in the Champions League Final. I will take two out of three

Maybe if Sapphire comes out around 11 June I could meet her and see the Sharks v Lions at Ellis Park at the same time. There's a plan. Rex is on my side. Says that Hayley's dad should cover the medical aid as that prominent Jew Brian Joffe probably pays her old boy plentsh at Bidvest.

SUNDAY 29 MAY 2011

I have to get out of this town. Spend this afternoon at rehearsals. Rex is dozing off in the props room (sulking too because nobody agreed it would be 'fairer on Agatha to call it by its original name, it's not her fault the world has gone PC-*verskrik')*. But Mr Dumphrey pointed out it got changed in 1940 because even then people were upset.

Rex persists. 'But why're they allowed to call each other nigger and we can't?'

My part only comes on in the last few minutes of the whole play so I have to watch the rest read their words. I must say Phumeza is very good at her role. And thin.

MONDAY 30 MAY 2011

Q: How do you know ET was a feminist? (ET the alien, not Eugene Terre'blanche.)
A: He looks like one.

TUESDAY 31 MAY 2011

T-Rex reminds us over his Maltabella that today used to be Republic Day.

I have a long chat to Phumeza at rehearsals. She went to DSG in Grahamstown and I promise if you were standing backstage and heard her speak you would not know she was black. She's one of those. Like the one from the DA.

I know it sounds crazy, but I think there is a bit of a vibe between us. Not that... *not ever*.

WEDNESDAY 1 JUNE 2011

This is the month that I become a father. And iPad 2 hits SA.

OMG! Coldplay are playing Cape Town in October.

> **@steviewunda:** I am gonna buy tickets NOW, who wants?

> **@jasonator069:** please Stevie, jase will be in da house

There are some things in life that you just don't tweet. Not right.

What is it about Chris Martin? He could probably have any chick in the word, including Pippa Middleton, but he chose Gwyneth Paltrow? She looks like two broomsticks with a bit of *fynbos* in between.

I wonder when Steve is going to want me to pay him by. You cannot use the budget facility on a Visa card to pay a mate.

THURSDAY 2 JUNE 2011

On duty this afternoon at the bar. Cliffy is spouting forth. About rugby.

'The best referee in the world, by a mile, is Jonathan Kaplan. You know, Jews make very, very good refs. But there not many left.

'You see, they dig rugby but they are too small to play. And it's not regarded as cool any more. They would rather be in mobile software.'

Some other oke with him pipes up.

'They're quite stocky.'

Cliff is adamant: 'Name a Jewish lock. You can't.'

Other oke thinks. 'But they say every great Bok side has a Jew in it.'

'OK, when was the last one?'

'Joel Stransky in '95.'

'That's my point.'

'2007 didn't have one and they won a World Cup.'

'Yes they did,' asserts Cliffy. 'Percy.'

'He's not Jewish.'

'Yes he is. His name is Percy and he lives in Camps Bay.'

FRIDAY 3 JUNE 2011

Almost suggested meeting Phumeza for a drink. Not in that way, but just because she's a mate and makes me laugh, but where could we go in PA?

In Joburg it's almost cool; Cape Town you choose where you go carefully (and never in the suburbs); and if you're German it's essential of course. But in Port Alfred? Tricky. Even if we're just friends.

We could get away with it in Grahamstown. Maybe when the students are there. Or even better at the time of the festival. When all those freaky types are there nobody would bat an eyelid if I had a parrot on my shoulder and an Eskimo boyfriend called Errol.

SATURDAY 4 JUNE 2011

Hardly had time to think the club was so busy. Ate two burgers, the Dish of the Day (bobotie) and helped myself to four packets of Willards, a peanuts and three pieces of droëwors. No wonder my belt no longer serves a functionary role but is purely for aesthetic purposes.

I am following Richard Branson on Twitter. It really is him cos it's a verified account. He has 1,572,610 followers. That makes him 150,000 times more famous than me. He manages to run like the world's biggest company and kitesurf and hot tub with models and still be married and own his own island. One day, baby...

SUNDAY 5 JUNE 2011

After rehearsal today, looooong talk to Phumeza in the car park. Not often a chick can make me laugh. (They're generally not funny.) She is also so understanding and not judgmental like all those up-themselves Cape Town and Joburg and Durban chicks. She doesn't care that I haven't got a degree, got a verbal warning at the golf club (shhh – a 'shrinkage issue'), stay in a house that has a golf-ball letterbox and a settee on the stoep – with my parents – or that I hold the record for the least sales by a rep in a calendar year in the history of 2Dye4 Paints (since the merger).

MONDAY 6 JUNE 2011

T-Rex comes into the bar, at what he calls 'beer 'o clock' for a post-golf snort. Not that he has played, not with his 'pesky disc' from when he put his back out when he had to help the movers because they would not get off their (African) backsides. He has slipped into a pair of stokies with Tommy Bedford's old Natal rugby socks (when they were still Banana Boys) bought at the Hospice Golf Day auction, a pair of short, short blue Judrons, a red tropical shirt from his Magnum PI phase and a floppy green 'Forever Protea' cricket hat. I do not know where to look.

But he does share with the bar that he is relieved that Gary Kirsten and not Peter de Villiers has been appointed as national cricket coach. 'They're not fools,' he knowingly assures Cliffy (white Crocs, the first pair of light, light blue Emme jeans ever produced with a nipple-high waist, and a white shirt with sleeves rolled up to the shoulder). 'They appoint Gazza so the team will keep winning so they can keep their hands in the till, Majola and them.'

'And Bacher, too.'

TUESDAY 7 JUNE 2011

I think I am partly to blame, but I read today in the *Dispatch* that SA is in the top 3 in the world in obesity and in the top 6 for drinking. I would rather that was top 3 for rugby and top 6 for standard of living or easy chicks.

Tweet of the Day:

> **@camerondiaz:** Feeling a bit lonely today.

Does she know help is in the Eastern Cape, the adventure province? She must be in her forties now, but I would still smack that.

WEDNESDAY 8 JUNE 2011

From: Murray Godwin <mgodwin@RMB.co.za>
Date: 8 June 2011
To: 'Slug'; 'BADGE'; jase – wild coast; Dawesy; Mich; 'Hotdog'; Stevie; reg@hobson.com and 53 others
Subject: Muggsy on the Move

Howzit Buggers

Hope we all awesome.

Just to let you know, I am leaving RMB. Me and some Joburg corpfin big hittaz are going on our own in a little private equity/hedge play. We have about 1.3 under management and are looking for, unfashionable I know, b2c techs in about phase II, so if you guys know of any, hit me back. Def not playing in the mobile space though.

Be working from home and probably in Joburg a day or two a week but definitely part of the play is to kick back a bit and spend some more time with Sands and the kids.

Call it semi-employment if you want.

So if you up for some more golf or the odd sneaky surf, you know who to call.

Cheers
Muggs

Fuck me. Firstly I don't understand the first paragraph. Secondly, how is this? This oke, he is kicking back in his career whilst I am a barman at RPAGC trying to start one? So that I can support a kid I don't want to have.

I mean Muggs is a good oke, but he is a little bit (very) pleased with himself.

Dawesy replies with a 'Congrats, you deserve it' to Muggs. Puke.

I SMS Muggs:
> Muggs, awesome bugger, welcome to semi employment! Will be back in CT soon and we can hook up. JB

THURSDAY 9 JUNE 2011

Phumeza is my third black black (i.e. African) friend on Facebook (after my old maid and small Lotto winner Delicious's daughter, who is at a Model C school, and an oke I was at school with). I know it's only 0.7% of my friends, but it's better than most okes.

SMS to Phumeza:
> Hey, P, wot u up 2?

> Chillin. Listening to some John Legend Learning my lines!!! Lol

John Legend – problematic in many ways, but I bite my tongue.

> OK, wanna hook up for a drink sometime? There I said it. haha

Reply in nanoseconds. I know I am not climbing Everest in terms of goal-setting here – it's only Kilimanjaro (LOL), but it's still good for the ego.

> Sounds awesome.

OK her reply was a bit quick, but the stock here is so limited. I have to fish in the other pool. The big one.

Here goes: space, the final frontier.

But it has to be an away match – this place is far too small.

> Listen, there is no place to hook up in this coffin. I have to be in G/Town tomorrow to meet my masters supervisor & I know u go up there lank. Does that work 4 u?

> Awesome, where and when?

> How about 8 at The Skull

> Cool, c u then. xx

Oh my god, what have I done? As Caesar said, the line is cast. At least I chose the Skull. Won't know anyone and it's a goth dive so black is in, haha.

And the x-es?

FRIDAY 10 JUNE 2011

I pull her at the Rat and Parrot during Aerosmith's *I Don't Want To Miss A Thing*. In front of everybody.

She is not a bad pull but now I may as well move to rural Central

Abyssinia or tattoo 'I've crossed to the dark side' across my increasingly flaccid chest.

SATURDAY 11 JUNE 2011

Hungover like Jack Parow. And it's a year since the Soccer World Cup started. I really don't think 2010 paid off for us like they promised it would.

SUNDAY 12 JUNE 2011

Bit awkward at today's rehearsal. I keep thinking every other cast member is talking about me and Phumeza. And then she tries to rub my shoulders (I am sitting).

I pull her to one side 'Listen P, what happened Friday was awesome. Awesome, awesome, awesome. But now we must be very professional in front of these okes. We obviously got to perform with them and they are small town closed-minded fucks'.

I think she got the point.

And I know I am right. I am talking to P in the kitchenette and am about half-a-second late for my part and I hear Mr Dumphrey having his period as he minces up and down the stage.

'Jason! Where is Jason? Jason?'

Now the mincer gets really worked up.

'Jason, I really am going to *punish* you... I want to punish you. Geez, did I just think that or did I actually say that?'

You're not coming near me, pal.

I hear the helpful Sir Thomas Legge (Cliffy) say, 'Jason is in the toilet, practising his *lines*,' and I see him rub his nose and sniff and give Humphrey Dumphrey a knowing wink.

Look, I know I am the Bright Young Thing of Port Alfred and the trendiest oke east of Vredehoek, but the one thing I am not doing here is coke. Firstly, there is just *no* budget. Secondly, where on earth could you buy coke in PA? Bacardi Breezer? Sure. Dagga? By the bakkie load. But coke?

Besides the last time I enjoyed a line or three was at Stevie's 'Two Years of Sobriety' party.

MONDAY 13 JUNE 2011

I want to write to Bono but I cannot find an address for him. I can for 'his people', but they are not going to pass on something critical, are they?

I try test the six degrees of separation rule, but cannot find him on Facebook. But this is what I would say.

Dear Bono

Lose the welding glasses, china, and focus on the music, bru. I know you want to save the world and you come for Desmond Tutu's birthday and you worried about AIDS and Mount Everest melting, but first and foremost you are a musician.

Go back to the old days of *Pride (In The Name Of Love)* and *I Still Haven't Found What I'm Looking For* – but what sort of kak is this when you write rubbish about living like a mole and excavation and going down in a song called *Elevation*. I have asked a few okes and they also think it makes no sense. 'At corner of your lips' would get you failed in English second language, standard grade!

I mean *puh-lease*. What on earth does that mean?

If you really were that worried about the poor you would not have charged so much for tickets like you did here in Feb. You would make the tickets free. *People* magazine says you earn over four million dollars a day before you get out of bed.

Forget the Dalai Lama, Sudan and Tracy Chapman and get back into the studio and get the U2 vibe back.

Point taken?

Tjeers, tjom

Jason Brydon

TUESDAY 14 JULY 2011

CSI Miami tonight. Must be the only time where a short receding red-headed oke in a Hummer is surrounded by Miss Bikinis. It is amazing that the chicks with their lab-coats cleavage can analyse

DNA, abseil and shoot bad people. I suspect our CSI may be a little different. CSI Khayelitsha… that's where a moustached, disillusioned, about-to-take-the-package bonehead with a boep and over a thousand dockets arrives in a white Tazz in a short-sleeved shirt with epaulettes and a tie, a tape measure, a bucket, a thing of Handy Andy and a mop.

WEDNESDAY 15 JUNE 2011

Stevie tweets this.

> **@steviewunda:** I hear JB is really mingling well with the locals, loving life on the '#Wild Coast'

Shit, shit, shit. He knows. About Phumeza. Life altering.

Besides, surely that should be an SMS, DM or WhatsApp or a BB, not a tweet? What a knob.

You know what they say – what goes on Twitter, stays on…

THURSDAY 16 JUNE 2011

Public holiday – Youth Day.

The old boy can hardly believe it's 35 years since the Soweto riots, seems like yesterday he says. 'The country has hardly been the same since' and 'T'was the end of the age of innocence.'

44

If I was working in a normal job this would be one of those great big long weekends, piling into somebody's Jetta with a tog bag, cooler box with 24 Heinekens, three bottles of the Boschendal and a bottle of Jameson's, heading off to so-and-so's place. Unfortunately this no longer applies to those in casual employment.

I think it a bit 'obvious' to be seen with Phumeza on Soweto Day, nice as she is.

FRIDAY 17 JUNE 2011

Two things arrive in the post in handwritten envelopes, unusual these days, but not it appears in Port Alfred. There's one addressed to Mr Jason Brydon and another one to Mr and Mrs Rex Brydon. Thank Mandela, the old boy's out, down at the neighbourhood watch car-boot sale. My mom and I open our letters simultaneously and there it is, written in a nice Helvetica font, a wedding invitation. My mom goes whiter than the Ventersdorp bowls team.

'Leslie Brydon and Carol van der Walt are delighted to invite you to their wedding ceremony and commitment tea to be held on Saturday, 20 August 2011 at Hog Higgidy Hog's Hideout and Lair, Hogsback at 3pm. Regrets no children. Donations, in lieu of gifts, to the SPCA in East London.'

I try not to laugh. Until I realise my mother may actually faint, 'I don't know how I am going to tell your father.'

Christ, Leslie, you could have warned the *ballies*. And, I am instantly sure, the date is a Tri-Nations Saturday – genius my sister. Rule 1 of weddings: check out www.supersport.com/fixtures.

45

Not only that, do I really want to see my once semi-normal sister swapping ribbons, spit and matte-silver-entwined rings with the female Bakkies Botha?

Not even the arrival of mom's Royal Wedding pair of coffee mugs, one with Kate and one with Will, can restore any colour to her cheeks. Nor does the fact that our post office predictably has broken one of the handles seem to even register. I guess it shouldn't – it's already a miracle the mugs made their way here and didn't end up in Alexandra.

She didn't order them online. Dad says it's too risky. A relative from Swansea in Scotland sent them.

SATURDAY 18 JUNE 2011

Rehearsals today and tomorrow so I miss the Sharks *klapping* the Bulls!

Something came over me after this afternoon's rehearsal, I'm not sure what, but I blurt out to P:

'Do you want to go and grab a bite after this rubbish?'

It's one of those questions that as you ask them you hope the answer will be an immediate and clear no.

'That would be awesome, Jase.'

Someone called Ma Sisulu has died, yet another mother of the nation, but thankfully she doesn't come up in conversation.

SUNDAY 19 JUNE 2011

The following really happens at the dress rehearsal to which the Old Age home has been invited.

Cliffy as Sir Thomas Legge has this line: 'Let's reconvene in the drawing room at 9am prompt.'

Rex, the prompt and razor sharp, thinks this is him being called on. From behind the curtain he bellows out '9am prompt'.

'Rex, that's what I said. Prompt.'

'9am prompt.'

'That's what I said. "Prompt" is in the script, it's not calling you.'

'Stay focused, Cliffy.'

MONDAY 20 JUNE 2011

I see you can do an MBA on your iPhone or your iPad. Now there could be an option. I wonder how much data you would use. Probably need an uncapped contract.

TUESDAY 21 JUNE 2011

Still, thank fuck, no news on Sapphire. Apparently Hayley could pop any second. We are into referee's optional time. The hooter has sounded and the SuperSport clock on the screen has turned red.

Other than Cliffy's farting, the opening night of *And Then There Were None* goes well enough. Some people have even bought tickets.

WEDNESDAY 22 JUNE 2011

Phumeza and I go for a long walk down East Beach in the late afternoon. Luckily it's the middle of winter and the world's shortest day so nobody sees us.

She tells me Kader Asmal, one of the Indian ones, has died. They called him Biggles apparently because of the way he spoke. The old man's take was different: 'I don't care what they call him, we are going to be paying for Outcomes Based Education for years to come.'

There is no news from the maternity wards of Gauteng.

THURSDAY 23 JUNE 2011

If you were to look at my Facebook info page you would deduce the following:

That I am single; that I live in the adventure province; that I am in the hospitality industry; that I have 396 friends; included in my groups are: big wave riders, Sharks rugby, kite surfing, no more Malema, house music and Hurley clothing.

Overall not too bad, hey?

I cannot put Phumeza as my girlfriend. I leave that kind of PC-ness to Dawesy and his soya latte types. Besides, I'm not even really seeing her. I post this:

> The 3rd night of our production tonight, I must say live Theatre is much more of a rush than I ever expected it to be.

That imminent lesbian Mich posts straight back:

> ha ha ha ha. Jase please put it on YouTube. Pretty pretty please.

FRIDAY 24 JUNE 2011

I am following 363 people on Twitter and am followed by 43. One day followers will exceed the followed. I am determined.

Joost is bullshitting. There is no way he has Motor Neuron Disease. But I know where he's coming from – if I was married to the daughter of the Sopranos and I had done that to his daughter, you need to play a big card to get yourself out the kak. Not only get out the kak, but get everyone to feel sorry for you. #MND #masterful

Mistake: I tweeted the above. The nicest reply I got was

> @jasonator069 you sick insensitive fuck

It's the last night of *And Then There Were None* and the front 2½ rows are almost full.

I do not go to the after-party for a few reasons. Party and your own father should not go together, it's awkward like when you see your class teachers dancing on holidays.

Secondly, the whole Phumeza thing.

SATURDAY 25 JUNE 2011

Hayley:
> Congratulations and for what it's worth, Jason you r now the father of a 3.1 kg baby girl called Sapphire. Hayley.

Gulp.

There I was hoping Hayley would break the world gestation record. I know I can never say it and I know I should never think it, but if it was to save another couple the heartache and pain, I would not have jumped into the Kowie River ballsack first if ours had been stillborn.

I know I wasn't there for the birth. Robbie Williams watched his wife have their first. Someone asked him what that was like. Great response from RW: 'It's like watching your favourite pub burn down.'

Know what you mean, Big Guy.

On the same day the Sharks Super Rugby challenge effectively ends.

I do not tell my parents. My dad has a hangover from celebrating the best amateur production ever on the Sunshine Coast and my mom is sitting on the time bomb that is Leslie's selfish 'wedding' invitation.

After 4-balls are in, I take P to supper at the Red Apple in Bushman's. When I phone to book I book on behalf of 'my colleague and I'.

I tell P everything about this whole Sapphire fiasco and she is very understanding, but then again their culture is much more open-minded, if you look at our president, on matters family-related. It's all very French.

SUNDAY 26 JUNE 2011

Talk about Sunday blues.

MONDAY 27 JUNE 2011

I cannot put it off any longer and I go online to book my flights to Joburg. I know online bookings are meant to be so much easier and the way of the future and all that crap, but honestly I would rather go to a presentable 5.5 out of 10 girl called Sandra in a travel agency and, while she finds me the cheapest flights to get to Joburg at the times I want to fly, have a browse through brochures of people skiing like something out of those old Peter Stuyvesant ads.

Now it is complicated. God I am sick of drop-down boxes. And registering.

My session on Kulula.com times out whilst my Mango session freezes while I am on 1time. 1time is the cheapest, but then I also have to look at SAA from East London as well as British Airways out of PE. Then there is SA Express. Three hours on the interweb eating my data. It seems the best option is flying up on Kulula from PE and back to East London – that means T-Rex is driving me to PE and fetching me from East London so that almost rules that out.

Conversation will run out by the Spar.

R1,700 later, excluding a crapload of taxes, and am flying to Joburg to see Sapphire on Thursday.

TUESDAY 28 JUNE 2011

Hayley is getting hundreds of congratulations posts on Facebook, I am not going be able to keep the lid on this lose-lose 'situation'.

I tell my parents that they are grandparents, I'm not sure they know what to think. I can see Rex is not sure whether to say 'bad luck, old boy' or 'congratulations, old chap'. So he pours us both a 'stiffener'.

But the folks were expecting it. The problem is that I may not have told all my friends.

This is *not* a Facebook issue – rather good old-fashioned email.

From: Jason Brydon <jasebrydon069@gmail.com>
Date: 28 June 2011 at 11.25am
To: 'Slug'; 'BADGE'; Muggsy; Dawesy; Mich; 'Hotdog'; Stevie; reg@hobson.com;
Subject: Oopsie, one past the goal keeper

Howzit Okes

Hope we all awesome.

Just to let you buggers know something. Remember that chick Hayley I was kind of seeing in Joburg last year? Well, it seems I made her pregnant – if nothing else that should shut up some of you doubters about the Jasonator – and she chose to have/keep the baby. We are all stoked. OK, well maybe not her *toppie*.

There's nothing I could have done about that but have agreed to support her in that and, believe me, that is not gonna be cheap.

It is a decision that Hayley has taken and she has decided to pursue this life. Baby's name is Sapphire and right now my daughter comes first.

There's not much else I can say other than unless you sure you really really want lighties, wear a jiffy!

Cheers
Jase

That is the official position, but it just seems incredibly harsh that because of Hayley's selfish decision, I end up paying through my nose for the next 18 years. It's like paying for a car every single month, wham bam off your current-account, and you don't get the car or you write it off before you've had time to call Outsurance. In fact, because I will be paying for 18 years, it's almost like a house bond. Just that you get nothing to show for it.

I'm also not sure why I'm bothering to go to Joburg given that I'm not sure what my reception will be like and I'm pretty sure little Sapphire will have no clue at all who I am.

WEDNESDAY 29 JUNE 2011

I realise today, to my horror, that the scale in the men's cloakroom (members only) puts me at 3.5kg heavier than the one in my folks' bathroom. This is potentially devastating. There I was thinking that I was cruising merrily along maintaining, like Duran Duran and this country's infrastructure, in the early 90s. But I know the cloakroom scale, one of those fuck-ass big ones, is correct.

So it's back to the old diet, with immediate effect, but with less than three cheat days a week.

THURSDAY 30 JUNE 2011

Drive myself to Port Elizabeth 'international' airport (apparently it was international when you could fly to Umtata when we had the old Transkei). Only after I park do I realise I have nothing for Sapphire, other than the booties knitted frantically over the past two days by Val B. Luckily there is a Sneakers so I buy a 'Springbok in the making' green-and-gold babygrow.

There is such a vibe between me and the one air hostess it's scary, like there is so much electricity we could sell it to Zimbabwe.

She is a bonehead, but one of those hot ones. Blonde and still looks hot even with her hair tied back. Sure, she's not the brightest kettle in the fish, but then again I'm not asking her to enter the *Weakest Link* with me. Her name is Sanmarie. Her one 'ouma' was a Sandra and the other a Marie. Why do they always go in for these combos? But right now I do not care about her grans. I care about right here, right now.

She brings me two Castles and a Hansa and I know I'm not making up the vibe. In fact, we stand in the galley chatting until we get interrupted by some Muslim asking for a sparkling water. Gets the fright of his life when he realises he has to pay for it.

We, I think, are not far off a quick snog when Captain Miller comes up with, 'Right folks, we are about to start our descent to OR Tambo International.' And that was that and in no time Sanmarie is telling us on the PA system to return to our seats, ensure our tray tables are stowed and return our seats to the upright position.

After we land, she calls me over. We chat more in the galley. I think bugger this, its not every day you stare the proverbial gift horse square in the chops. And a trolley-dolley has always been on top of JB's Most Wanted.

'Are you doing something later?'

'Nah, I am free,' Sanmarie purrs.

'Shall we do something?' I know I must not sound desperate cos once chicks smell that, and believe me they smell it like dog shit on a shoe, then they lose interest.

She is keen, she tells me, she just has some flight admin and then we agree to meet at her spot. Back of the net, Jason, my son.

I am almost stuttering when she asks if I want her address.

'P-p-p-p-p-l-l-l-ease.'

'It's Acasia Road 13, Blomhof, in Randburg. Number 2 in the complex.' She writes it down on a napkin, just like something out of a Bond movie and I am Daniel Craig.

'Give me an hour and I will see you at mine' – and she plants a peck on my cheek.

Hayley and Sapphire and admin can wait. I use what's left on the card which somehow goes through, and hire a Tazz, devour a pack of Stimorol, change shirt in the Tazz having drenched my armpits in Adrenaline by Ego. Basically, Jason, you are as stoppable as a Super Tanker sailing downhill.

I strike a luck and drive right past a Keg, almost too good to be true, so stop in there for a quick Kremlin, which is a refreshing Castle draught with the tot of vodka added in as soon as space allows. Nerves are now a thing of the past.

I find Acasia Road thanks to the hired Tom-Tom. It's not a bad complex, at all. Facebrick, shade parking, standard issue. I ring the bell at the gate but there is no response. She must still be folding seatbelts. Some freak comes out in a one of those crappy weird half-Jeep half-Hummer new Toyota 4x4s so I slip into the complex past a friendly security guard, Elias, who greets me as if I live in number six and give him a Christmas box, and dutifully park in visitors.

I wait outside for 20 minutes. I don't have her cell, just her address. I double check the napkin. I am at the right place and I notice under Randburg is written. *Hurry up and come f(ind) me... xxx...* Clear enough... I look down the side of the house. There is a pool at the back with the Kreepy chugging away and some garden furniture and a real Weber. There is a sliding door and I look through.

Being a highly secure complex, there is no Trellidoor, which we know can withstand the impact of a wrecking ball or a Sam7, according to the ad. Tired of waiting, I decide to get a bit more creative. How classic would it be if when my Sanmarie comes back she finds me inside, beer in hand, golf-shirt off? Well, maybe not the latter. I know the fish is on the hook, but she's not on the boat. We don't want to scare her.

With a little bit of *rukking* and *plukking* I open the sliding door and in I go. I must say things are very neat, but still there is no sign of her. And I wait. I figure I'll help myself to a nice beer from the fridge and catch up on some SuperSport Blitz. The first three Amstels hardly touch sides and disappear down my gullet like scalded rats down the drain. Still no sign of my hostess. I should've got her bloody number. And now things start to complicate themselves: I need to go.

Like *go* – for a number two, because those beers went straight through me. I now feel a bit like Goldilocks, but there is something purer about blonde little girls and porridge, rather than rotund golf club barmen and pooh. And what if she arrives in the middle of my movements? What if she arrives in the 10, somewhat fragrant, very pungent, minutes after that? That may put a dampener on this fledgling romance. But as my old boy says, only a fool would stand between a Brydon man and his constricting bowels.

Fact that the only reading material I can find is *Men's Health* should have triggered a warning. I enjoy an article on how to make myself look seven years younger without surgery and am halfway through one called 'how to have killer winter abs' when it is wipetime.

The toilet gods smile upon me and it all ends peacefully with a hearty spray of morning dew. Then I treat myself to a little tour of the facility. It goes something like this: when I see the child's room, I think to myself there's something she's not telling me; when I see the pictures on the wall of the room are of Justin Bieber and Michael Bublé, I think I'm confused. Did she have the lighties in grade 4? When I go into the main bedroom and see two distinct bedside tables, one with a *Huisgenoot* on it and the other with a Wilbur Smith on it (people do still read him), I know there is trouble.

I go through all the bedside photos. There is nothing vaguely approaching a resemblance of my air hostess. Then it hits me. I may have got two dummy numbers at last year's Durban July and the last four J&B Mets, but this is my first experience of a fake address. Sanmarie does not live in this house, a random family do. I am calm at first until I realise I have broken into a house, stolen liquor and left my prints all over the shop and a good dose of my DNA somewhere in the plumbing. I see myself doing time. I cannot risk taking a nanosecond to dust off my fingerprints, clear away the empties or turn off Blitz.

I run.

When I get to the car, I accurately estimate my heart rate at around 11,000. Honestly, think I could be going to jail.

FRIDAY 1 JULY 2011

Phumeza:
> good luck today J in meeting Sapphire. Really thinking of you and miss you XXX

Easy. Easy.

A plate of Cajun calamari at the Red Apple and suddenly we're new-age husband and wife…

Hayley is already at home and her parents Jeff and Georgie are up from the Midlands to see her through this process. In retrospect to visit while they were there is a mistake. To say my reception is frosty is like saying there is a nip in the North Pole air.

I get stony silence and, from Georgie, 'You had better come in.' I'm not sure what I ever saw in Hayley and certainly the rigours of childbirth (came out the sunroof I think) have done absolutely nothing for her; in fact, I hardly recognised her without make-up, hair scraped back and in Os du Randt's old tracksuit.

All that Jeff said to me as I was waiting for him to open the gates when I was thankfully (for all concerned) leaving, was 'Don't hurry back.'

And then as I was beeping open the Tazz, he followed up, right in my face so that I could almost taste the Nando's (lemon and herb) he'd had for lunch, with, 'If you don't honour all *your* commitments with respect to *your* daughter I am coming after you, pal.'

What, with your hanky? But I don't say anything, I just leave and enjoy four well-taken Castle draughts at the Keg and Aviator at Walter Sisulu International in Joburg to settle my shot nerves.

SATURDAY 2 JULY 2011

Stormers get a nice klap from the Crusaders in the semis. The whole of the Cape Flats apparently is going mad for Sonny Bill Williams and the Crusaders. Apparently because of apartheid. Never mind that the New Zealanders shot most of the Maoris and threw them into the sea before anyone caught them, which is far worse than making someone sit on the back of a bus like PW made them do.

It makes me think, though. That this bloody country can never move beyond race. That we have all laughed off what Mandela said about no race dominating another. It is in everything we do. If I tell Boswell, who clears the empties and glasses behind the bar, that he is slack or slow or fat (all three in fact), then I am being a racist. No, errrr Boswell, you're bad at your job, doesn't matter if you are fluorescent lilac.

It's clear to me this Phumeza thing is not going to work, is it? In fact I think it is really sad – a poor reflection on our sick, bigoted society – that it isn't going to work. She is a really nice girl who is great fun and probably has the nicest chassis in the area that used to be known as the Ciskei.

But what can I do? I cannot change the world.

But how do I tell her? Just be honest and tell her how racist the world is? I guess she knows that.

I don't want to stereotype, but how can you have a 'girlfriend' who sends you a 'Please Call Me'?

And then, to make the day worse, I turn on my cellphone and type in my PIN without concentrating. Code incorrect, one out of three attempts, so I type in again and it says code incorrect, two out of three. By now my heart rate spikes, I think clearly 2125 and type it in. Phone blocked. It now wants my PUK. How did I get that wrong? I think in my troubled mind, with all the Sapphire and Phumeza stuff going on, I used my autobank PIN. Now it wants my PUK. Where, where where on earth do I find that?! Who on earth keeps their PUK? And why do they make it so long? Call-centre time.

SUNDAY 3 JULY 2011

A long chat on the phone with Stevie which makes me feel much better. He says it's time for me to come back to Cape Town and I know he is right. But how is me going back to Cape Town going to keep baby Sapphire in nappies?

Did have one lag though – if you sleep with a really ugly girl and you don't want to wake up when you leave, she's called a 127. From the film 127 hours when the rock climber falls down a crevice and gets stuck and saws off his arm with a Leatherman.

Five missed calls from P.

MONDAY 4 JULY 2011

I am going home home home…

From: Greg Dawes <greg@askarimedia.com>
Date: 4 July 2011 at 08.34am
To: Jase
Subject: and don't mess it up, Bond

Hi Jason

What is this new Jason Brydon I hear about? With a baby daughter, and an isiXhosa girlfriend. Who would have thought? But we can catch up when you back here JB. I'm sure I'm going to live to regret what I am about to write, but here goes.

My mate, Costa, has had to go back to Cyprus and Greece for the rest of the year at least.

He has this awesome house in Tamboerskloof and he is looking for someone to look after it. He has two French Bulldogs, Ferris and Gary Cooper, that are *the* most precious things in the whole world to him and need looking after. They don't need long walks or anything (but you must walk them a bit) so not too much can go wrong there unless you manage to starve them to death, and given how they're shaped now he would probably be back before that happened.

You would have free use of the house and *possibly* cars, even though I will – in the interest of our friendship – argue against the use of them. It is an awesome spot with a pool, great deck and on a clear day you can see all the way to Rio!

From what I can work out you are not overly committed in the 'Transkei', and as your mate I must say your long-term future and career prospects (sic) are probably more here than there.

It is available immediately, and he kind of needs an answer sharpish because he needs to leave soon so let me know what you think.

Every year you and the Proteas let me down. They have already this year – prove me wrong JB.

Cheers
Dawesy

RESULT!!!!
It is Independence Day, after all.

TUESDAY 5 JULY 2011

From: Jason Brydon <Jasebrydon069@gmail.com>
Date: 5 July 2011 at 11.15am
To: Dawesy
Subject: RE: and don't mess it up, Bond

Howzit Dawesy

Shot for this, bru, it sounds super awesome.

Just got a couple of questions, but one thing first. I have actually got a couple of business interests here in the Eastern Cape, but I agree, its time for me to head back to Cape Town. A little bit small and slow here for JB Inc. But I really needed the time out and I'm good to go now. Ready to fly.

OK those questions.

One, is this the oke who iced Lolly Jackson? Why else is he fleeing to Cyprus and Greece? I don't want the Hawks busting in on me busy with Miss Cavendish Square or have Derek Watts or Debora Patta knocking on the front door.

Two, is this oke gay? Two French Bulldogs? That's kind of the dead giveaway isn't it? Does he have funny underfloor coloured lights to attract the gerbils?

Three, what type of cars are they??? Year and model pse.

Four, will I get paid??

Shot, bru, I really really appreciate this and I won't let you down, buddy.

Later
JB

From: Greg Dawes <greg@askarimedia.com>
Date: 5 July 2011 at 11.57am
To: Jase
Subject: RE: RE: and don't mess it up, Bond

J

To answer your questions:

No. he is a Greek bond trader and if you ever, ever watched the news you may realise that, like you, they have a few issues there around debt.

Grow up. Married with two kids at Reddam.

Don't know, don't care, gonna tell him to hide the keys.

Really, Jason, really?

Cheers
Dawesy

I must say, sounds awesome and I tell Dawesy I will tie up some loose ends here and be there by the weekend, ready to Rage Hard. Now I just need to find a job.

WEDNESDAY 6 JULY 2011

I am back on Career Junction, jobs.co.za, bestjobs.co.za and every other website I can find. But every single one wants experience. 'Experience essential.' I don't get it, how are you meant to get experience if they won't give you a job? Where are the dooses who do not need experience? Does that mean that if you are a coffee percolator repairman that's all you can be for the rest of your life? You cannot go and become the dog kennel repairman because you've got no experience in it?

Anyway, CV updated and sent to absolutely everybody.

SMS to Cliff Saunders:
> Hi Cliff, its Jason here from the club, I hope you dont mind I included you as a reference!! If they do call, could you just confirm that I was in a management position at the club, which I was when Mr Jacobs went to PE for that course. Shot. Jason.

I'm not sure if the vegetable can SMS, but eventually a reply comes:
> Sure Jason, no problem. Sexy Rexy said you may be heading back to CT. I will know what to tell them but maybe it would help more these days to change your name to Jason Bruintjies or Jason Brydikhize. See you at the bingo evening. Bye bye.

The only, really the only, condition that I put on my CV is that I am unwilling to do a job that requires a name tag.

THURSDAY 7 JULY 2011

It goes like this:

I get a call from an unfamiliar number, an 082, and I think it might be one of the recruitment agents so I answer. It's not.

'Hello, Jason speaking.'

'Jason, it's Jeff, Hayley's father.'

Heart rate spike. 'Howzit Jeff.'

'Jason I just want to confirm one thing as I sincerely hope it's not true.'

I cannot see an upside here so I think about pushing the red button. In retrospect I should have. 'Jaaa?'

'Jason, when you came to, in inverted commas "visit" Hayley and she was talking to you in private about your failure to offer any emotional or financial support or show any interest in the pregnancy and subsequent birth of my granddaughter, you said to her, "Oh for Christ's sake get a Kleenex" and "You chose and made your bed, now get under the duvet." Is that true, Jason, because if it is then I think I think less of you now than I did before, which would baffle scientists as to how such a thing could be possible?'

You know, really, Hayley should fight her own battles so this makes me properly the *moer* in. For once I'm going to tell DJ Jazzy Jeff where to get off.

'Easy, Santa, easy.' He doesn't like that.

'Don't Santa me.'

'Listen, before you preach to me, *dominee*, I know for a fact you had

66

that affair with that lady client of yours from SA Nylon Spinners when Hayley was only four, sucker fool.' Chew on that. 'She told me herself and when she did she was actually crying.'

After that, well, it seems Jeff really has anger management issues. I did well to dodge having him as my father-in-law. It's a whole family of fruit loops.

FRIDAY 8 JULY 2011

From: Jason Brydon <Jasebrydon069@gmail.com>
Date: 8 July 2011 at 11.05am
To: Dawesy
Subject: RE:RE:RE:RE: and don't mess it up, Bond

Dawesy

Shot for all this, bru, I think we have a deal, but as is often the case with these things, the devil is in the detail.

Can we just tick off the following boxes please:

The maid: how many days a week; does she feed the dogs?; would looking after JB be included in her job description?; like not just laundry – say I am out and about could she, if I phone, roast me a chicken... and ideally take the skin off if it's a non-cheat day? And most importantly who funds her?

Is there an alarm? Linked to armed response?
DStv? Full bouquet?

I would prefer a gardening service rather than a fixed gardener. Don't want to have to help with the deposit on a lounge suite, make him lunch, have to work out which is his mug, or end up paying another kid's school fees.

Is the gate automatic?

Is there a nice indoor/outdoor entertainment area?

I trust this is not 'the renovators dream'!

Tick these off and I think we have a deal!!

Shweeeet

JB

SATURDAY 9 JULY 2011

Sniff. No Knysna this year. Sniff.

Stevie has a new chick and she is working at Sexpo in Cape Town (I kid you not), but apparently in 'marketing', (errrr, which, Stevie, does not clear anything up). And Muggsy isn't allowed to go to Knysna after last year. And Dawesy, surprise, big wank surprise, has 'outgrown' it. Says he no longer wants to avoid stumbling on passed-out people at Crabs Creek. Preach for yourself, padre!!!

But in some ways it's a relief: it's not in this quarter's budget.

But still it's Super Rugby Final (scrambled egg and super rugby promotion for brekkie at the club) and Charlene, the unheard of swimmer from Benoni, is marrying Prince Albert of Monaco today who, I think, would rather be marrying Elton John. Or Nathaniel.

They say the only reason is that she can produce an heir. If only I had known, I would have put Hayley's name forward.

Mind you she shouldn't have too much trouble. Sir Elton and David Furnish managed to.

SUNDAY 10 JULY 2011

I run 7km out on the Bathurst road in my new Nikes and a vest. Also wear those new try-hard long, like rugby, socks. Fuck knows what they do, but wore them just in case somebody drove past. I need to get into shape for my Cape Town return – I cannot, pardon the very clever pun, let them think that JB has gone to pot on the 'Wild Coast'.

With all the stress of fatherhood, my hairline is retreating like the Italian Army up the two sides. I know I cannot afford it, but we are going to have to look at that Propecia. Before it's too late, I'm going to have to make plans about the budget for those pills. It's now or never, because once it's gone, unless you are Jacques Kallis, it's gone!

These are things that need addressing urgently before I can give Dawesy the green light. Well, these and a job.

69

MONDAY 11 JULY 2011

I wonder what Mandela is costing us to keep him going. Can't say it publicly, but I wonder.

TUESDAY 12 JULY 2011

I'm going to have to fire P. Not going to be easy, especially when she brings me a plate of lasagne for lunch while I'm working over ladies' club champs. She's an awesome chick and gives me no gears at all.

Give me strength, especially if she plays the race card.

Folks got DStv today. Dad wanted the dish on the front of the house so the neighbours could see, but it has to face in a certain direction otherwise you don't get signal. It did remind me:

> Dawesy, just doublechecking – obviously there is DStv there, hey bru? Full bouquet?

> Yes, Jason. Costa will give you a ring, but I think it best to remember he is doing you (and thus me) a favour.

Well, Costa could just lock up and go and when he comes back there'll be street kids with HIV and PhDs in sodomy living in there with a whole roomful of faeces, the floorboards burnt for warmth, tadpoles living in the bath and the French Bulldogs' livers on their winter menu.

Zip, nada, niente, nil, vokol on the job front. I may have to go out on my own.

WEDNESDAY 13 JULY 2011

Apparently Mom has made her famous cottage pie this evening and I am to be home. Famous where, I'm not sure, maybe among the bingo halls of Port Alfred West? Dad has opened a very special bottle from his collection, a 2005 Meerlust Rubicon (RB likes odd year reds), saying 'it's not often we eat as the family any more'.

I chip in with, 'But Les's not here.' Silly me

Gruff response from T-Rex. 'We will get to that.'

This may sound petty and unappreciative, but I don't think Jamie Oliver, Gordon Ramsay and any other celebrity poof/chef with teased hair as well as Deloitte's finest culinary forensics could discern the difference between Val Brydon's famous cottage pie and the plastic microwave Woolworths option that always steams my fingers. The Rubicon, on the other hand, was another level and well wasted on this trio of misfits, especially when my mom dilutes hers half-half with Port Alfred's finest E.coli-laden tap water. Dad says nothing but his look says 'your mother'.

Rex brings it up first. 'Your mother showed me the invitation from Leslie,' as he guzzles four centimetres of Rubicon and replaces some of it in his glass with some floating mince.

'I told your mother we should not have sent her to Westerford.'

'I'm not sure it's their fault, Rex.'

'Well, whose fault is it then, Valerie? It's certainly not mine. I invited each and every boyfriend in for a beer and could not have been more encouraging.'

I can see the remaining gears in Rex's mind engaging. 'Maybe it was those jerseys you knitted?'

'Never, Rex. Maybe it was that camp you let her go on in standard 9 against my better judgment.'

'Mom, one netball camp did not make a lesbian of Les. Nor did those jerseys. Look, I don't think they filled her with confidence, but I'm sure there are other reasons.'

'But it was a Christian hockey camp.'

'Ma, that is not going to make her a lesbian. Maybe she was just born that way.'

This upsets Rex-dog. 'Born that way? How is that possible? Well, where does she get it from? Certainly, my side of the family is clean… Valerie?'

'Mine, too.'

I point out that it could be a recessive gene. Rex isn't having any of it.

'I can trace the Brydons back to the day the *Dorchester* docked in Algoa Bay in 1820 and there is not even a hint of it since then.'

I ask about his cousin Ossie, the scoutmaster, who left 4th Berea under a cloud.

'He never actually did anything.'

'That they could prove.'

'Shut up, Jason.'

Val is not altogether subtle in changing our tack: 'I could have let the potato go a bit longer.'

'Nonsense, love, it's delicious, but I am still not walking her down the aisle.'

'Rex, I don't think she's asking you to,' Mom points out.

For some reason this seems to cause umbrage.

'Well, I am not actually sure if I am going to go at all.'

Silence.

Then Rex is back at it: 'Who wants to see two dykes waddling down the aisle like arthritic ducks?'

'It depends what they look like,' I offer.

'Rex, she is still your daughter.'

'Not in my eyes. It's not how we brought her up. For Christ's sake, I even bought her a Patrick Swayze poster… In retrospect, I think she would have preferred a Brooke Shields one. I know I would have. I suppose that sums up the problem.'

Dad is now on a roll.

'Ja, Dad, I don't think I'm going to go either… it's lank embarrassing.'

'She still is our daughter,' Mom whines.

'Valerie, do you know that they actually strap things onto each other to replace the parts that we have? Think about that, picture it, now tell me you still want to go and watch them swap spit in Hogsback?'

I nearly wet myself laughing.

Shouldn't have.

'And as for you, Jason, what on earth are you going to do in Cape Town? No, let me phrase that more accurately – what are you going to do workwise to earn an income in Cape Town, Jason? Let's face it, if it wasn't for Cliff, you would be selling blackbags, Bafana shirts and *Funny Money* at traffic lights... So what are you going to do?'

'Jeez, old boy... That's a bit harsh... I am actually thinking of going on my own.'

'On your own? You are not Raymond Ackerman.'

'Do you prefer it with peas?' This is Mom's only and ignored contribution.

'You know I read an obituary in the *Dispatch* yesterday about this chap who passed away in Gonubie. He was ex-Standard Bank, high up, like properly high up, his one son played for Eastern Province before they were kak, his other son is something like number 5 and a bit in Investec and his daughter won Miss Matie when she was there. And then married a wine farmer. The point is: how is it possible that I actually am jealous of another guy who has just died of cancer?'

The *Sunday Times* carries a report saying that the Australian government has apologised for forced adoption back in the day. Why couldn't that have happened to me? And Sapphire.

THURSDAY 14 JULY 2011

Reflecting on yesterday's conversation, I realise that had Rex known about Phumeza, they would have had to send an ambulance from Grahamstown.

I've come to this conclusion: life is something like a DVD player and I suspect I should be ejected.

But chin up, Jason, that's not gonna help, so I tweet:

> **@jasonator069:** Dawn patrol boardies surf followed by some boerie and scrambled eggs. Loving this #mzansi magic

Follow-up by:

> **@jasonator069:** Cant wait 2 get back 2 the mother, back 2 @ VidaeCaffe, HZee & a city who knows what True Religions are & dont think its just funny stitching!

Mind you, I see Kurt Darren has a pair of True Religions... if they've reached Menlyn Mall, well then maybe they are last month's jeans.

FRIDAY 15 JULY 2011

After a fun game of tennis with P (she won quite comfortably... on merit) and a nice lunch, I sit at the dining-room table at home before I have to go on duty at the club because tonight is the Monthly Draw. I have a foolscap pad in front of me and a Parker jotter and I write the heading:

Reasons to fire Phumeza

There is only one I can really think of. Look, it's a helluva important one, but I can't bring myself to write that down.

Tonight is not only the monthly draw, it turns out. It's also my second-last night behind the bar at Royal Port Alfred, but because most of the committee are in the monthly draw, it doubles as my farewell. I get a club golf shirt, an embroidered club towel, a club ashtray (apparently they still make them) and four new Titleist balls.

I don't think I am overwhelmed.

Cliffy, who says he single-handedly grew the Rhodesian tobacco industry as he has smoked since he was nine, speaks on behalf of the club:

'We are obviously very sad to say goodbye to Brydon Junior, he has been a real asset to this club. Whilst we would not call him the human dynamo, he certainly knows how to unwind and also make the members feel very welcome.

'With his background and knowledge of some of the big city hotspots, he has brought in some great new ideas like introducing Tequila Thursdays, Flaming Sambuca Saturdays, Jägerbombdrops, and who would forget the Patron and pizza evenings as well as his own cocktails, 'Gatskop' and 'Sex on the roof of your mouth'? None of these may have worked out.'

Rex gets defensive and interrupts: 'Yet.'

Cliffy ignores him. 'But that is probably more of a reflection on us in this sleepy hollow than Jason. I am sure with time he will be proved right. Jase is leaving us to go to a fantastic new opportunity in Cape Town so we wish him well. Don't worry, Mr Treasurer, Rex is staying right here so we needn't worry about our turnover.'

Fair laughter. So proud: Dad raises a beer-filled glass and toasts 'Charles' the never existent alchemist who SAB invented to have invented Castle Lager.

SATURDAY 16 JULY 2011

I end up last night at Barmuda in Van der Riet Street. I do not even remember arriving I was so torn by the time I left the club. I absolutely transmogrify myself on Aftershock and vomit off the bridge into the Kowie, which seems to me to be an entirely fitting and appropriate end to my stay in the next next Knysna, watching my regurgitated cocktail sausage rolls, pieces of cheddar and gherkin and mini meatballs float down to the Indian Ocean.

Not even mom's famous full English can make me feel any better and while none of the fogeys say anything as regards my impending departure, there is an atmosphere of 'good riddance to mediocre rubbish' floating around the sitting-room. I hope.

I hog the newish DStv remote and watching PDivvy's team of Bok embarrassments getting pumped by Australia only increases the nausea.

I am pleased the folks have DStv. It was embarrassing that they didn't – that's almost as bad as those who don't have a maid. I rate the embarrassments, in ascending order of shame:

11	No armed response
10	Neither DStv nor M-Net
9	Use Capitec
8	No DStv, only M-Net
7	Mow their own lawn
6	Bunny aerial TV
5	Low fence
4	No maid
3	Only one car family
2	Use state hospitals/clinics
1	Take the odd bus/train

Or whites sending a 'Please Call Me'.

SUNDAY 17 JULY 2011

My second-last day in PA. I am pleased I kept my CA plates – they are even cooler here than in Jhb, but now the cool Capie is heading home. I have to still tell P that I am outta here, that it's over. Today. Definitely. Just not right now. A little bit later. For sure.

As a farewell I take the folks to Guido's, where Dad depletes their Bellingham Rosé.

Dad reads in the *Dispatch* that Bisho Airport is regarded as a 'white elephant', but they're looking at refurbishing it.

'Why?' I ask more cos it's the source of some potential conversation at a complete hack of a dinner than any interest on my part. Besides, I could not endure another 'so what *are* you going to do in Cape Town, son?'

'Well, the Nats built like a massive airport there that you could land 747s on because they wanted to make the Ciskei and Transkei seem like real international countries so our lot could be citizens of them and not SA. They could still work on the mines here, but they wouldn't be SA citizens. Then we could, once that box was ticked, have our own elections here where everyone could vote and the UN could do fuck all about it.'

'Rex, language!'

Rex is not the type to get deterred. 'I am just not sure why they would bother to refurbish it. Bisho isn't far from East London.' He takes a glug, if a glug is bigger than a sip, of his Bellingham and reflects: 'It's not far from East London, not far enough.'

'But if that airport is a white elephant then the Mbombela and Cape Town and Peter Mokaba Stadiums as well as Coega, are black elephants.'

Mom chips in: 'What about the Gautrain?'

It appears that open-minded Rex does not have a position on it yet. He is going to give it some time.

I have to use the budget facility on my Discovery card.

> **@jasonator069:** one more surf on the Wild side, then hitting C Town on Tuesday, straight to Planet Bar, tweeple #ready2rockthemother

If 10 percent of those following me turn up there will be 4.3 of us.

MONDAY 18 JULY 2011

Last day on the Sunshine Coast and my vegetable, clinically braindead mother signs for a traffic warrant of mine – 140 outside Coega in a 120 zone – not like I held up a building society or castrated an orphan, is it? Jesus, mother. How dense can you get? I suppose it's one way of getting me to visit. For my appearance in the Grahamstown Magistrates Court on 4 November.

I must say, and I did not tell my mother this, I was relieved it was a traffic offence and nothing from the maintenance court, because that, my bru, is coming.

I try to tell Phumeza that I'm out of here, but my phone freezes. I'm sure that's what happened. And when it unfroze I was out of reception. And then it wouldn't turn on. Going back to Blackberry when I'm back in civilisation.

Hitting the road at 4am as I have to meet Costa at his/my new spot in CT in the afternoon. The golf is packed with all my stuff, but there is, depressingly, still enough room for a couple of passengers. Including my golf clubs and surf board.

I must say I expected to be surfing every night in boardies while I was here, but I don't know, it just felt really sharkey here. But definitely going to in Cape Town.

TUESDAY 19 JULY 2011

Before I get to PE, two missed calls and an SMS from Phumeza. It's not good for my heart rate. Not at all.

I stop for a Coke and a four-bar KitKat just to get the blood sugars up to deal with this high-pressure system that's rolling into my car.

She deserves an explanation and a bit better treatment and, I think, I will genuinely miss hanging with her.

She calls again. Which is a stuff-up because I was just about to SMS her. SMS:
> sorry P can't chat now just driving x

Phumeza:
> So it's safer to SMS is it?

I feel quite kak about this.

Another SMS. Phumeza:
> Have you really left Port Alfred?

> Kind of, just come down to do some shopping at Greenacres in PE then back in a couple of days

> Really?

> Really

> You have a lot of time to SMS while you driving

I pulled over.

> Not true I almost got cleaned by a Shell tanker on the N2

> Well then why can't you call?

This bullet is a heat-seeker like out of *Top Gun* that follows the plane until Maverick (Tom Cruise) does a manoeuvre that no-one has ever seen before and Cougar says is lank dangerous.

Phumeza calling… Phumeza calling… Phumeza calling…

Basically I am strapped in the chair, the tubes are in my wrist, the padre is there with the Bible and the Governor ain't calling on the red phone…

I answer. Blood pressure about 2,000 over 2. Heart rate 890bpm.

'Howzit P.'

'Jason.'

She never calls me Jason. What is it about chicks, of all colours apparently, that as soon as you have done *anything* wrong, from leaving a wet towel on the bed to having sex with their sisters, that the first thing they do is address you formally? 'Jason.'

'When were you going to tell me that you were moving back to Cape Town?'

'I am not.'

'You are.'

'I am NOT.'

'Jason, I spoke to your dad.'

'Before or after lunch?'

'I stopped by your folks' place.'

Oh Ker-ist… I hope they did not think she was looking for work.

'They both said you had left. In fact your mom showed me your room. She said you had even taken your *Men's Health* calendar.'

I hit the red button. Let Vodakak take the heat for dropping this call. I need to regroup.

In the old days I could have just said it was illegal and that I was not the kind of person who breaks the law.

Phumeza calling… Phumeza calling… Phumeza calling…

Here goes.

'Howzit, Phum, sorry don't know what happened there. Kak reception here.'

'Where?'

'Just past Coega.'

'Plenty of signal there. They're not going to build a deepwater port with no signal, are they?'

This was going well. But I see the gap. 'P, I been a thinkin'. Do you think those masts cause brain cancer? Do you think this call is growing tumours in our heads?'

She doesn't bite. 'Are you or are you not on your way to Cape Town?'

I am going to have to man up.

A very quiet 'ja.'

Silence.

Longer than the Iron Age and Bronze Age put together.

'So when were you going to tell me?'

'Yesterday.'

'Yesterday? Only a minute ago you told me you were going shopping at Greenacres. Nice. Today?'

Crikey Moses. They really do pick on the smallest thing and hammer it home, don't they?

'Sorry... I just didn't want to break up with you so could not face up to it. I was too scared, still am, to lose you, and this really great awesome opportunity has come up in Cape Town.'

'Jason, you don't get it. Do you not think as your girlfriend I am entitled to know?'

Girlfriend... my word... Not how I would have phrased it.

'Do you not think, Jason Brydon, you owe me a bit more than that? Do you also not think that I would not be happy if my boyfriend got a great opportunity? Even if it's in another town. Any normal couple would celebrate this.'

Boyfriend, girlfriend, couple... I kind of regret what happens next.

'You see, P, that's just the point. Are we any other normal couple?'

Industrial silence.

'Look, I really really really like you, P. Too much. That's why it's so hard to leave.'

'Jason, what do you mean we aren't any other normal couple? What are you saying?'

Oh dear. 'I just meant that I am leaving town.'

'Jason, that happens to normal couples, except the one tells the other.'

'Izzit?'

'Yes, Jason, it is. You don't get it, I am happy for you, for this awesome opportunity. But just tell me. Let me in.'

'I am sorry. Just didn't want to lose you.'

'I can come to Cape Town every second weekend.'

Backfire.

'Listen, P,' and now JB Inc is in a corner and straight shooting back.

'It's not going to work for us.'

'Huh?'

'Long-distance relationships don't work.'

'It's Cape Town to PE, seven hours away. It's not Mars. Besides I can get a job at the Holiday Inn tomorrow in Cape Town.'

Oopsie.

'Sorry, Phum, it's still not going to work.'

'Huh? What do you mean?'

'Well, there's something I should have told you…' I said that last bit without knowing how I was going to complete it. Clutching at straws does not begin to describe it. 'I am a recovering addict.'

'No, you're not.' This chick is bleak – and far from dof. 'What do you mean it's not going to work?'

'Well not really, like not long-term. Like not the whole way. Like it's fine for now, but it's not gonna work and that's just gonna mess you around, why waste your time on an oke you are not gonna get married to? Thing is, what I need more than anything is the chance to be the best dad I can.'

'I beg your pardon?'

She sounds somewhere due south of sceptical.

'It's true,' I defend.

'Jason, you have seen Sapphire once, and you just posted her a *Pirates Of The Caribbean* cutlass and a *Star Wars* T-shirt that was about seven sizes too big.'

'She will grow into it.'

Phumeza snorts. That is not the most attractive feature in a woman. Especially one trying to squirm out of Death Row.

'She *may* grow into it. In grade 2.'

P was *not* doing herself any favours with this sarky *houding*. In fact she was turning herself into a walking break-up stat. Really, maybe this chick is not as switched on as I first thought she was. She may have a degree, but she was making it easier and easier for me to axe her.

'I didn't ask you to get married, Jason, I asked you where you were going... but, pray tell, why would it not work "long-term"?'

'I don't believe in lobola.'

I regret it the second I say it.

She screams. Really loudly. The sort of pitch that can burst an eardrum. Got to red button her. That's life-threatening.

Doesn't stop her: *Phumeza calling... Phumeza calling... Phumeza calling...*

Lucky escape, Jase. That was poes close.

Treat myself to KFC in Knysna to get over that drama. Rounder, Streetwise5 and a Coke Zero, which I eat in the car. I use the inside of my Guess jeans and the very bottom of the back of the passenger seat to get the mayo off my fingers. The crocodile on my blue Lacoste looks like he has just vomited as a blob of mayo got there when I had to swerve for two dooses on roadbikes by Brenton-on-Sea.

I know I shouldn't be eating whilst driving, but next you won't be allowed to listen to 5FM while driving. Likewise Phumeza should not be screaming at me knowing I am on the notorious N2. I understand that she may hate me at the moment and that she hasn't been brought up with the same anger-management control tools that we are bred with, but what if she screams at me, I get a fright and swerve into the oncoming lane and hit a family of four on their way back from the Spur? It's just irresponsible of her. #arrivealive

I must say cresting the rise of Sir Lowry's Pass to see Cape Town and the Peninsula in the distance does put a lump in the throat. I was going home to The Mother.

'Mom, Jason's home,' I tell the city.

You couldn't actually see the mountain that clearly cos of all the smog. It's from the Cape Flats where they burn all the Port Jackson (which T-Rex says may be an alien, but Cecil Rhodes brought it in to stop the flats being so sandy) and the smoke is also from shack fires when they knock over paraffin stoves and have to move to church halls.

In a funny way Cape Town lies across these flats much like an oasis, because before you get there you have to cross places like Somerset West and Khayelitsha. I am not sure why they didn't tidy up the shacks by the airport for the World Cup. Doesn't create a very good impression, does it? Imagine what Herr Mueller from Switzerland, where the police answer their phones and a cat in a tree is a crime stat, must think when he leaves the airport en route to the One&Only.

They could have just put houses in for the first few rows. Or built a high vibracrete wall with some nice Soccer World Cup murals.

I stay with Slug as I am now only meeting Costa tomorrow (he 'pushed back') and there wasn't exactly a clamour to host me when I sent out the mail. One at a time, gents! No, Slug was the only response, but the okes are lank busy now and got kids and shit (including me, if you count the Sapphire gem) and people don't really stay much with each other these days. I think Slug only said yes to dilute having to talk to his freaky wife, aka Lettuce.

In the old days you always used to stay with people, now it's a nearby B&B or the Garden Court. As Dawesy says, there are a million more ways of communicating, but it's very bad form just to pop round.

I remember Slug's bachelors. We were all so excited as a bachelors is a justified and justifiable chance to enjoy some Ukranian Sly. But when Lettuce found out that Stevie had us heading to the House of Rasputin, she put her birkenstocked foot down and all he was allowed was a freak with a kombi and a chunky pullover making balloon animals. To be fair the guy made an amazing giraffe which I would like to have taken home, but you cannot get home from a bachelors with a balloon. So I popped it.

Slug really should grow some balls.

Point is: JASE IS BACK.

WEDNESDAY 20 JULY 2011

Meet Dawesy at Vida half an hour before we're due to meet Costa. I had Slug's maid Prudence iron my Polo striped long-sleeve shirt with a red horse as I really want Costa to like me cos I need a pozzie. Cannot see Lettuce being keen on me for another minute. Especially after I used the kids' loo this morning, a visit so long I read a long article about John Smit v Bismarck for the upcoming World Cup and a review of the Proteas' latest abortion at the World Cup in *Sports Illustrated*.

Dawesy thinks he is funny as we do an awkward hug.

'Nice to see you, bugger. Nice shirt.'

'Shot, bru. It's Polo.'

'What colour is it?'

'They call it salmon, china.'

'Whatever they call it, it's the same colour as your hair.'

Haha.

I meet Costa. I don't care what Dawesy says, he is as straight as Chapman's Peak. One of those metrosexual Euro-trash types with the requisite stubble and gelled greasy hair and smells like the perfume counter at Edgars. Seems nice enough, even if slightly pleased with himself. No socks with Sebagos and some linen pants.

He is leaving for Greece this evening. And you're telling me he's not involved in Lolly's murder or mates with one of those Serbian okes? Some of me is tempted to phone the Hawks in case there is a reward.

After a skinny latte and a *pasteis de nata*, I follow his VW Scirocco (sure, this guy's straight?) to see his spot. Opens up a bit of a gap going up Kloof Nek despite my right Converse-tackied foot being wedged to the floor. I hope he's leaving that cabbie behind.

We pull up in the driveway of this awesome spot with a huge deck, pool and a view basically from PE to Robben Island.

Ladies, form an orderly queue. This is gonna be the Jasonator's address. He shows me around. He has everything that opens and shuts, a model Spitfire that cannot be much smaller than the real thing (built himself – took off work for two months to complete) hanging from a skylight, glass-fronted Heineken fridges in about four rooms and music in the roof.

Disappointing? Not.

He has the odd glass floorboard with coloured lights that shine up. Maybe to attract his gerbils before they go up his botty. But it is kinda funky.

Then the only small drawback.

He is more anal than David Furnish about his dogs, Ferris and Gary Cooper. And they are uglier than Nikki Lauda, Rafael Nadal and Blade Nzimande put together.

To my mind, another giveaway. He probably spreads Nutella or biltong paté all over himself and these pygmy monsters lick it off his privates. I am nauseous.

There seems to be a few family snaps on the one mantelpiece – you know on the piste in Verbier, a yacht somewhere and the mandatory arm-in-arm with Richard Branson (not in the hot tub). But he may have cut those out a magazine to pretend he's straight.

He forgot the one with the Dalai Lama. Or Clinton.

I have to ask. Just for my own peace of mind, in case he's about to ask me for a swim or a shower. 'Who needs a costume when it's just the two of us?' or however it is 'they' start.

'Is there a Mrs Vlissedes?'

'Yes, but she's shopping.'

'Waterfront?'

He looks at me like I'm a Martian all the way from the Outer Hebrides. 'Dubai.'

Because he's married doesn't mean a thing. Just look at the guy from *Masterchef*.

Back to the business. The kid's (okay, point taken) bed is basically a Ferrari Testarossa with a duvet and there is a TV screen in there so big that Nu Metro would be jealous.

They have more decking than the *Titanic*. Indoor/outdoor entertainment area with electric concertina doors. Ladies, ladies, one at a time, please… well, actually not really… Ladies, two or three at a time will do fine.

'Where's the Jack?' I ask.

'Jack? Jack Daniel's? In the bar – help yourself to anything there.'

'Haha. No, where's the jacuzzi?'

'There isn't one.' Costa, with all his Carolina Herrera, *Mail & Guardian* and EQ can sense my disappointment. 'Sorry.'

To me it's a bit like the Queen building Buckingham Palace and then not putting on a turret. I mean, it's not like it's budget related. I hide my disappointment well because it's somewhat dwarfed by him handing me a Woolworths card.

'It's for essentials – get whatever you need to prevent scurvy. Ferris and Gary love the chicken fillets. Lemon and herb. And the droëwors. Tim Noakes approves.'

The maid 'walks' past. Rather, rolls past. He introduces me to her. Her name is, I kid you not, Abstinence. She should abstain from the Bar Ones and peanut butter. She makes the Michelin Man look like Roxy Louw.

'Don't worry about her money,' says Costa. As if I was. 'I have paid her in advance.' Oh good – that means we're not going to see her again after he has gone.

'Listen, I must shake a leg, have to be at the airport soon. Just make yourself at home. Thanks so much. SMS me your bank details and I will square this with you, I really appreciate it, bud. Really, have some mates round, do some shit. I am chilled. Give the Scirocco a spin once or twice, it cannot stand all the time. Just not the Q7.'

Q7???? Gulp. Control your heart rate, Jasie.

'It's my wife's and *I'm* not even allowed to touch it. Besides she hides the keys even from me. Women. You know.'

Yes, I know.

Tonight is the first night of my new life.

SMS from Phumeza:
   Phone me.

In your dreams – Bomb. #boundariesplease

THURSDAY 21 JULY 2011

Scirocco handles a dream. Went to Woolies at the Waterfront and topped up on some things – right through from some Norwegian salmon to some exotica like cherries and capers – not sure what they're for, but they'll look good on a countertop. I'm sure anybody in their right mind would regard a pair of Country Road boardies as an essential, so bag those too.

Too tired to walk Ferris and Gary Cooper. Besides one had shat in the garage so it's too late anyway. I will let them out tomorrow. Into the garden.

FRIDAY 22 JULY 2011

Not sure when exactly the oke is coming back. Dawesy mentioned end of the year. Hope Interpol don't take him off their most wanted list too soon.

Hayley's attorneys have been 'in touch' again. Which borders on the inconsiderate on one's first Friday in Cape Town in a long time. Talk about a downer. I mean the thing's just been born and we are already worried about her school uniform. Maybe she should go to a Waldorf or Montessori school where they just wear dungarees and hemp.

That setback aside.

Stevie and I cruise down in the Scirocco to Newport Deli for a latte and a perve. There is this really fat chick jogging at about 2km a year down Beach Road wrapped in lycra. Stevie laughs, and whilst I see his point, it is actually a bit childish.

'At least she is trying, Stevie.'

Across the road there are two much tidier ones jogging along the promenade.

'Jase, you know one thing I don't get, like not at all. It's like 24 degrees and they have their sweatshirts wrapped around their waists and they are running. You don't see okes running with sweatshirts around their waists.'

Afterwards to Caprice. I don't think there's one girl I don't try to invite back to my new thump dump. No-one wants to come back to 'my spot'. That's it, then – next Friday I am having a party.

SATURDAY 23 JULY 2011

> @dawesman: grass isn' t always greener, not even Norway is safe

I don' t want to get into Twitter titter with Dawesy so I mail him on a Sunday (changing world):

From: Jason Brydon
Date: 23 July 2011 at 03.16pm
To: Dawesy
CC: 'BADGE'; 'Slug'; RegH; Stevie
Subject: Dawesy! Again!

Okes

You okes saw Dawesy's tweet about this oke killing all those okes in Norway and trying to say that SA is as safe as anywhere else. And that you can get cleaned anywhere in the world.

But what he doesn't tweet is that in Norway you can eat sushi off a pavement in Oslo, leave your plasma on your stoep and nobody will take it, your (sizzling hot) daughter can sleep in the park and if you get flu they fly doctors in from Switzerland for free.

Try that in Hillbrow.

One swallow a summer doth not make.

JB

From: Stephen Fourie <steviewunda69@gmail.com
Date: 23 July 2011 at 03.24pm
To: Dawesy
CC: 'BADGE'; 'Slug'; RegH; Stevie
Subject: RE: Dawesy! Again!

Apparently the oke was worried about immigration and Norwegians becoming impure and polluted with other races and wanted to do something before it was too late. But Marian was not hurt.

From: Jason Brydon <Jasebrydon069@gmail.com>
Date: 23 July 2011 at 03.25pm
To: Dawesy
CC: 'BADGE'; 'Slug'; RegH; Stevie
Subject: RE: RE: Dawesy! Again!

You right – my old boy says you have to be black or asian or ideally a cross of that just to get into the UK these days. Marian??????

From: Stephen Fourie<steviewunda69@gmail.com
Date: 23 July 2011 at 07.40pm
To: Dawesy
CC: 'BADGE'; 'Slug'; RegH; Stevie
Subject: RE: RE: RE: Dawesy! Again!

Mariann Birkedal, Miss Norway and only the hottest chick in the world, Brydon. Less of the Transkei puff-puff and more focus. Check her out on celebopedia. Makes Minki look miff. With those lungs she could blow up a lead zeppelin.

Dawsey does not reply. Probably cos he knows he was talking complete and utter kak about Norway being as unsafe as SA.

SUNDAY 24 JULY 2011

What a silly place to hide the keys. In her panties drawer. Obviously when they're away I am going to have a rifle through them, like any other red-blooded male does. And bingo. Panties AND car keys.

The Q7 *owns* Chapman's Peak. Just Sunday drivers spoilt it a bit for me. Put surfboard on racks for an outing.

> **@jasonator069:** Made it in the Q7 from town to Hout Bay on a flashing petrol light. #lifeinthedangerzone

MONDAY 25 JULY 2011

To do list:
Start the diet.
Remove Q7 tweet in case Costa joins my other 49 followers – yip, up 6.
Get a job/career.
Go to Woolies – saw a nice Country Road plaid shirt in the *Sunday Times*.
Walk the dogs.

Two out of the five achieved is a start. Runs on the board.

Just one incident at the shops: I am googling Marian on my phone on the escalator and at the bottom of the escalator I don't see the chick in the wheelchair until too late. I must say, I get the fright of my life. One's natural reaction, when something shocks you, is to push the thing out of the way. Which I do. For a long time it looks like the chair would stay upright… that she could right it herself. It seems like an eternity it is on two wheels, not sure which way it would go, but looking like she would keep it upright. But I was to be disappointed. As was the crowd. Fuck, you would have thought I had disembowelled a puppy in the middle of Cavendish.

Obviously they all find for the one in the wheelchair.

TUESDAY 26 JULY 2011

It seems Peter de Villiers is trying to change his assistant coaches Dick Muir and Gary Gold with less than six weeks to go before the World Cup. Crazy stuff. Rex, referring to the Three Wise men's gifts, calls the trio Gold, Frankenstein and Muir.

Diet starts today. By the time spring starts I will be all cock 'n rib. Start the day well with some fruit and fat-free yoghurt (all Woolies), must just be slightly careful with fruit as it's high in sugar, but you feel so good after it. But then I meet Stevie and Muggs for a pizza at Col'Cacchio. Nothing goes quite so well with a pizza as a cold draught. Or four. But there is very little fat in beer. I order some salmon on my pizza and that is pure protein and very high in omega oils which are essential. But to be honest with myself, I put today down as a cheat day. It's actually not a bad thing to do – to get the cheat day out of the way for the week.

Somehow. Somehow Stevie found about Phumeza. She had posted something on Facebook. She apparently is going to out me as a 'player' on some website.

'What were you thinking, Jase? Low barriers to entry?'

'Do you have any idea what it was like living in that hole? Listen, if you happen to prefer sparkling water and have been in the Kalahari for six days without anything and someone offers you a glass of still, you're not going to say no are you?'

WEDNESDAY 27 JULY 2011

Muggsy has tweeted:

> **@muggsy:** As much as it's a waste, it kind of makes me sad that Amy Winehouse is trending way above the 92 who died in Norway who didn't have a choice

The thing is Amy entertained the world. Name one famous Norwegian. Other than, I guess, Mr Nobel after whom they named the prizes.

THURSDAY 28 JULY 2011

Our house party tomorrow night is all over Facebook. It's got like 92 likes and if half the people come and each bring a friend we are going to have like 100 (well, 92) people. Dawesy is a bit worried about the house, but Abstinence is coming in on Saturday morning, which I am paying for. Costa, in his haste to flee, did not leave *any* petty cash for operating expenses. I also don't want to mess things up here.

Of the 92 likes, 34 are female and a Facebook trawl reveals of those 22 are friends of mine or have low privacy settings so I can see 10 are single (nine excluding Mich and she doesn't count). It may not sound a lot, but I am the host. Do the math.

Plus one that is coming looks a lot like Her Royal Hotness Pippa Middleton.

SMS from Stevie:

What you doing for booze, boet?

BYOB?

Cheapskate

Easier said than done... then I remember Woolies stock wine and sparkling – do their cards have limits?

My tummy is in a knot when this comes in from Costa:

Enjoy the party – just make sure the boys are OK. Cheers C

Costa must give me my space or this is not going to work.

Oh shit, the dogs... they must be starving.

FRIDAY 29 JULY 2011

It's my pardy...

Not a bad tweet being retweeted:

Amy Winehouse, Kurt Cobain, Jimmi Hendrix, Ian Curtis, Jim Morrison, Janis Joplin all died at 27. Bieber turns 27 in 2021. Just be patient

I see the Beckhams have adopted a French bulldog called Scarlet to go with their existing one Coco. Maybe the dogs should be let out tonight?

The booze thing is causing me stress. Woolworths don't sell hard tack or beer – only like pseudo *spumante* and wines with the telltale W on them. Plus that card must be showing some signs of wear and tear no matter how much of what I spend goes to some school for AIDS whose textbooks didn't arrive.

Then I remember my mate Baxter, a.k.a. 3G. His name really is Baxter. Baxter Cruickshank. So he has two surnames for names. That's quite a Dutchman thing that – like Fourie du Preez or De Kock Steenkamp or Beyers Truter. It's not something we bluebloods go in for. Mind you there is Harrison Ford and Taylor Swift. Us *souties* are not scared of two Christian names like Ricky Bobby (still Will Ferrell's best work since *Old School*) and Gideon Sam, the oke who runs swimming South Africa from the shallow end.

Baxter is called 3G because he is fast, smooth, has serious bandwidth, little downtime and is far better than anything that has gone before. He gave himself the name and it stuck.

Baxter is in the booze trade on the wholesale side. Got some big brands in his portfolio. He throws those sick promo parties that I'm often not invited to. Things like a Grey Goose party at Tres Tigres Tristes – only Cape Town's hottest club, which means something like Three Tired Tigers or Three Sad Tigers – who gives a fuck? He is also the only oke I know with a pair of custom-made Earnest Sewn jeans. He's more hip than Shakira.

I call him. He answers.

'Hello, Baxter.'

'Howzit 3G, it's Jase.'

'Sorry, Jase?'

'Ja, Jason Brydon.'

'Brydon, oh ja… howzit brutha?'

Obviously didn't have my number saved. *Kont.*

But the upshot is he can bail me out. Has some cases of Grey Goose and some other stuff left over from a promo.

'Jason, you have a liquor licence, hey?'

WTF, I am not the Baron. 'Huh?'

'No, you have a liquor licence. I am telling you you do. Or I can't supply you. Come on, Jase, sharpen up, old cock. So you do have a liquor licence? Maybe you could fax me a copy – sometime before end of this year's fiscal.'

'Sure'.

'So, how many we catering for?'

I give him my calculation based on the Facebook stats.

'Fuck, bru, that's not a party, that's a conference call. You wanna get the numbers up? Leave it with 3G. Do you have bar ladies?'

'No. I could ask the maid and do some myself.'

'Fuck man, you not selling candyfloss.'

He is sending three of his promo chicks.

Mel – from Table View and is studying through Unisa. A comfortable 9.25, he says.

Whitney – Cape Spanish but you would have to be gayer than Liberace not to want to go there, he says.

Sasha-Lee – has a chest that Hooters in Tygervalley turned down because it made the rest of the staff look like surfboards, he says. Appropriately she comes from Big Bay.

'Errrr, how do I pay for all this, Threeg? EFT?' From which account I wonder.

'Look, the booze is left over promo stuff, it's off the books. It's floating somewhere in never-never land so you can just make me a little donation. The girls you must sort out yourself.'

WhatsApp Stevie who is online:
    Free Vodka, rest Cash bar. Three smouldering hot barladies. BOOM

By 8pm there are 11 people there, eight of whom are male friends and one of them is a neighbour with a goatee and a Vida in a dressing-gown, asking 'Who the fuck has a party in Cape Town in July?'

Black chicks are scary. Phumeza's put this on her Facebook status:
    Bring back the Immorality Act. It stopped us from experiencing very small, even minute, people like Jason Brydon

SATURDAY 30 JULY 2011

Aftermath:

I can only find Ferris. I have no idea where Gary Cooper is.

I have no idea who half those people were last night – all I know is that they were young. Two of them are still asleep in the Testarossa.

I had to go to bed early – I ate a piece of blitz. Showing off.

The floors are sticky. You walk, it sounds like you're walking on Velcro.

Who knows where the Spitfire is? That's lank childish – I will keep an eye on Gumtree.

There is not one surface not covered with half-empty bottles, mostly with cigarette stubs floating in them.

It seems Abstinence is abstaining from work too. Wakes me up with: 'Master, this is too much work for one person. No way. No. I am going home.'

Marvellous. At every robot they ask for jobs and when they get them they don't want them. I am going to tweet Steve Hofmeyr.

Oh, other than 3G's 'donation' (TBC) and finding someone to clean and fix the one curtain rail and replace the Weber top (missing), I have broken even. Ahoy!

The Boks lose 7-40 to the All Blacks. The World Cup is not going to go well. Right bus, wrong driver.

Oh, and *another* Royal Wedding. Zara Phillips (probably best of a bad bunch) to the England rugby captain. Zzzzz.

SUNDAY 31 JULY 2011

The pardi makes the Sunday *Argus*: POLICE TO INVESTIGATE UNDERAGE DRINKING AT CITY BOWL PARTY.

Fine, but rather worry about the elderly being strangled with their washing lines or single moms in their Corsas being hijacked than a few lighties enjoying a few Bacardi Breezers. Come off it.

WhatsApp Slug my legal advisor (last seen 11.47am).

> Hzit Slug. Shot 4 pulling thru fri nite. Did you see that thing in the Argus about my little soiree? Surely wot goes on on private property has nothing 2 do with the cops?

> Yip saw it. Would have been fine had you not charged them for booze. Gudluk.

That hardly helps my anxiety.

Stevie retweets a Francois Hougaard (was he here?) tweet:

> **RT @francoishougi:** What a pardy Friday – shout out to JB

Suddenly all seems worth it. Even if he looks like he got raped by a colour printer.

MONDAY 1 AUGUST 2011

Mega Monday: Make it Happen.

As in get a job. At some stage Woolies are going to decline Costa's card.

The only jobs in the paper seem to be those for telesales – those okes who call you from private numbers. That's not me.

Not a deal-breaker, but I don't particularly want an open-plan office.

Carbs eaten today: virtually nil.

Hayley SMSes the price of Pampers. Why would I buy her dog food? Take the brak back to the SPCA. Then I realise it's a type of nappy not pet food. Fuck!

Good tweet going round:

> **@WhiteGirlProblems:** cant remember what pizza tastes like # issues.

I hear you, babe.

TUESDAY 2 AUGUST 2011

Turbo Tuesday: Find Gary Cooper.
Also: Put Monster sticker on the back of my car (gathering dust and guinea fowl shit in the road).

That got Dawesy all worked up. But it's kinda obvious. The one oke (Dewani) looks like he is the F&B manager of the Holiday Inn Marine Parade and the other single-handedly disproves the Big Bang theory.

Surely GC has one of those microchips in him? You know what homos are like with their pets – they're like their own lighties.

I start by phoning the SPCA and all those lesbian feel-good animal-welfare places to see if anyone has handed Gary C in. No sign. Then I start with the vets in the City Bowl. I ask if anyone has handed in a French Bulldog, and if not, did they have Gary Cooper in their microchip system.

I get lucky. He is at a vet off Kloof Street. I screech down there in the Scirocco.

The nurse, who hands me GC, and is so fat she needs a bra for her back, says, 'Thank God, we were about to telephone Mr Vlissedes.'

Dodged a missile there, Jase. I buy him and Ferris a sackful of Woolies droëwors and treat myself to a whole chicken and a movie on demand from DStv on C-dog's account. *The King's Speech*. Complete snoreathon. Imagine making a film about someone trying to overcome a stutter. W-w-what were they thinking?

You win Oscars for that shit and making movies about kids battling cerebral palsy. Oscars, not fans.

WEDNESDAY 3 AUGUST 2011

Warrior Wednesday.

It's definitely the *Last Of The Mohicans* hairdo for me. The back of the head is strong, but the top is looking a bit… a bit, well, showing significant signs of deforestation.

We go to this try-hard cocktail lounge at the Waterfront. Is there anything worse than an ugly girl in a Stetson?

THURSDAY 4 AUGUST 2011

The wanker in the Mini – the only male driving a Mini in sub-Saharan Africa – thinks just because I was on my cellphone the accident is my fault. You shouldn't look at it like that. Does not mean because you are on a cellphone that it is automatically your fault. You must rather look at actually whose fault it is.

And it is *not* my fault. He should have made doubly sure that I was going to stop on the orange before trying to cross the traffic.

Look, by the time we actually hit, we were going very slowly so it's not a big dent to the Scirocco so I am not overly stressed and I don't think Interpol are going to give up their search for Costa for a while, so I will have time to find some panel beater who does 'after hours' work to papier-mâché the front right together again. The car can still be driven no worries.

It must have been this oke's period. This is how he starts:

'You were on your phone,' he screeches. Must be listening to too much Lead SA.

'No, I wasn't.'

'Buddy, I saw you.'

I may not be as tall as the dweeb in the ¾ length shorts (i.e. long shorts or short longs, depends how you look at them), but I am heavier and I had been to gym for a shoulder expression session so I was not scared. Not at all.

'Check my call history and see if I was on the phone,' and I offer him my 32gb iPhone 4.

'You were SMS-ing.'

'Wrong again, pal.' Truth.

I was in fact on WhatsApp, but I am not gonna tell the freak that, am I? Not at least till he has calmed down.

'Who's gonna pay for this?'

'Well, I suppose whose fault it was and it wasn't mine.'

He starts to resemble a beetroot. 'You went through on the red.'

'Orange.'

'It was red.'

'Orange.'

'Red.'

'When I arrived at the intersection it was orange. You should have waited before crossing.' Think I may try my luck: 'Maybe *you* were on *your* phone?'

'Listen here...'

'Don't "listen here" me.' The finger pointing starts. I think I draw first.

'You went through a red robot.'

A crowd is gathering. I try to smooth things over – 'Agree to disagree?' – and start beating a brave retreat.

As I drive off, I slide down the window of the Scirocco, 'Why you driving a chick's car anyway?' and speed off. Get back in your box, my son.

Honestly, some people just need a high-five – with a chair/brick.

FRIDAY 5 AUGUST 2011

Flat-out Friday. Bok Friday.

Tricky to wear a Bok jersey to work if you are 'between positions'. Let alone afford one.

The Old Boy phones to say that Dave from the golf club had flown BA to Durban from PE and there were a whole lot of Cosatus on the plane and they flew business class, even though the PE/DBN flight is only two par fives and a seven iron. And they slurped on the Liquifruits that were given out.

Stevie and I hit Long Street on the off chance we may find a lonely Danish backpacker or four. We were hacking a bit – you all know those nights when the drink is not going to do it for you; it won't take you to hyperspace or mumuland and you need a little *hulpstootjie*, so we chase a gram. We find some pitch-black campaigner in cowboy boots and a coat out of *Highlander,* but he turns out not to be a Nigerian, just a car guard who was once a dental technician in Rwanda.

Steve opines: 'He must have come down south because there was no market because there were no clients left up there, or maybe after spending the day trying to find a handful of sadza mixed with some gravel, dentistry is quite a long way down the Rwandan hierarchy of needs.'

'Or,' I chip in, 'the Hutsis chased him away.'

'Were those the bad guys?'

'Ja, they used to collect skulls like Obelix collected Roman helmets.'

We eventually find a dealer. His name is 'Gerald'. He wants R450 a gram. What's he smoking?

We go halvies.

SATURDAY 6 AUGUST 2011

Supercharged Saturday.

Peter de Villiers can relax. The Boks cannot lose today cos they have a bye.

Seems weird not to have any big rugger to organise the Saturday afternoon beering around. WTF. Who wants to watch the Currie Cup? It's not the same since we gave it away to Australia and watered it down like Oros.

We start at the Slug and Legless and then hit Orphanage, which is now *the* spot. I meet this chick called Megan, look she's not Miss World – her eyes are a bit close together – but she was still an 8 point something. Maybe a 7.5… We get on well. But to be fair to all the other competitors, with an iPhone 4 and Audi keys on the counter, I have a massive head start.

She's a web designer at some agency in that new part of Woodstock with a try-hard name like Bread. FFS. Those fucking types with their HTML and their Vespas. And the requisite Vida on the ground floor.

She is 25 and does some form of new-age fitness kak called Zumba (Zuma with a B as she puts it) which is sweeping the City Bowl and the dormitories of Vredehoek. I talk to her about this and work and the fucking weather and quantitative easing (not that either of us know what that is) and hedge funds (ditto). She is very friendly with me – but she is with everyone. You know – one of those irritating ones who laugh and put their hand on your upper arm, but you can't read anything into it because she does that with everyone. Or can you?

I lose her a bit when I tell her I know that Joost hasn't got MND. She looks at me like I've just chewed on a baby dove and swallowed it. Which I've never actually done, by the way.

But then I explain how he's just trying to get out of kak with Amor. I think she buys it.

So much so I think she may like me in a boy-girl way when she asks, 'So, Jason, are you married?'

I mean she wouldn't ask if she wasn't interested, would she? You don't go into Steers in Long Street and ask if they have burgers if you don't want one, do you?

'No.'

'Ever been married?'

'No.'

Please don't ask re kids. Please don't, please don't and thank fuck she doesn't. I think she thought she had covered that under the marriage questions. But, diary – and this sounds a bit blind – had she asked, I would have said no. If you think about it – and this may be largely a technical construction – Sapphire really belongs to Hayley. I mean we are not even in the same city. Sapphire, tweeple, and let's be honest here, was an accident. And Hayley chose to have her.

We hit a lull. Like over 30 seconds. I have to do something, play some form of shot, only I am not sure where this comes from.

'I saw action.'

'What? What type of action?'

'On the Border.'

'Border?'

'The Border. You know with Angola. We fought against the Cubans and the ANC.'

'You? Really.'

'Yip. I was in five firefights. Saw two of my best mates' heads blown off. One was from Plumstead High.' I should rather have said something like SACS. Or Reddam. I was just thinking don't say Bishops. Nobody would have believed a Bishops boy would have been unconnected or dof enough to find himself on the Border with an R4 in his hand.

'Really?'

'Yip.'

'That's awful.'

'Hey, I got through it,' hoping the conversation would change course quickly.

'But when was that? Surely before Mandela was released?'

'Just before.'

I had that pit in my stomach and could feel my tongue starting to dry out like Betty Ford. 'Want a Jägerbomb?'

She doesn't take up the offer, but hits back with, 'How old are you?'

Trying to bail myself out I add seven.

'37.'

'That makes you 16 when Mandela was released, so maybe 15 when you,' and she makes inverted commas with her fingers, 'saw action.'

There are three courses of action open to me in this little predicament. I split, I confess. Or I dig my way out.

As I am about to say that I left school early to fight for my country, I realise that I have to go. Now. I grab the key, dodge a doos with a handlebar moustache clutching some craft beer and exit. Fast. Don't even pay the car guard.

SUNDAY 7 AUGUST 2011

You have to look at supply and demand, revenue and costs. If I can't control or increase my top line I have to attack my costs. I am talking about Twitter, tweeps.

The realisation dawns that the only way I can get more followers than those I am following – which is basically the key to your Twitter status – is to reduce the number of people I'm following. Not easy but culled this morning are:
@KarlLagerfeld – not hard to cull the cock with the gloves.
@TableMountainCa – not sure why I ever followed a fucking cableway.
@JakeWhite_rugby – Jake Who?

@VanHaywood – may have been in *District 9* but she's so NOT hot.
@RobbieFleck – 900 followers and the doos hasn't made one tweet.

It's a start. @PumaUnity better watch out – who wants to know about street soccer in Dobsonville…

MONDAY 8 AUGUST 2011

> **@jasonator069:** So…. Malema wants our land, the poes. Says we stole it. How the fuck can we have stolen it – land is not a laptop – we have one of the most advanced estate agency and deeds office systems in the world. Like our banking. #ignoramus #racist #vegetable

Costa has a safe. Not a combination one. Wonder what's in there? The gun that shot Lolly? Thing is, would he take the key overseas?

TUESDAY 9 AUGUST 2011

Where do they find these blind okes to beg at robots? Unless, I can see socket I don't trust them. Only give to amputees – whole leg or arm.

WEDNESDAY 10 AUGUST 2011

Another missed call from Phumeza? What doesn't she understand? Doesn't she get the message? Must I tattoo it on her? In white probably – to stand out. I am not interested. I would like to give her

117

an explanation but I cannot do that to her. What must I say? 'If only you were white…' Nope, she deserves better.

Some lesbian was banging on on Cape Talk about various phobias. Arachnophobia is a fear of spiders. Homophobia is a fear of moffies. Or dislike of them. Whatever. But I would scream if I saw either one of them in my bath.

Meeting 3G at Vida for a coffee. We are discussing some business opportunities. He knows I am not chokkers at the moment in terms of my diary and was impressed that I had a party that made the papers and Francois Hougi tweeted about. Don't want to say much more about it than that right now.

My top two urinal brands are Vaal and Shanks. There.

THURSDAY 11 AUGUST 2011

There have been riots in London. It's caused our government to issue a Travel Warning. LOL – the irony of us warning people going there.

FRIDAY 12 AUGUST 2011

Things are progressing well with 3G. His work contract stops him from being involved in other businesses. 'Brutha, I couldn't even babysit my sister's lightie if she paid me. Not that I would – that thing's fucking hyperactive, boet.' So he needs me to set up this business. Not too much detail yet, but we are looking at playing in the high-end booze space.

118

Lesley's wedding next weekend. Haven't booked my flight yet. Rex has taken the view that he is not paying for me to attend that fiasco. On principle. I wouldn't mind going and sampling some of the Hogsback's famous magic mushrooms, but cashflow is, as they say, reality. Both for the flight and the shrooms.

I have combed every square inch – he must have taken the safe key to Greece, the fuck.

SATURDAY 13 AUGUST 2011

They are calling the London Riots the Blackberry Revolution – because that's how it's organised. No wonder it's such a stuff-up. If it was the Apple Revolution they may have a chance. Mind you, my iPhone's battery life is shorter than a goldfish's memory so the revolution may have petered out quickly.

Rex is in touch. He thinks it's funny that, for a change, the UK's natives are getting restless.

The evening promises so much. A few vodkas and Red Bull on the deck and down to &Union. I must say craft beers are getting to me. Not only do they cost like R10 a milliliter, but they are just so try-hard. With names like the Satan's Spawn Pale Ale and Nicklebockers' Foreskin. In some parts of town, if you order a Heineken people will check you skeef. Imagine if you ordered a bitterly cold Castle? They would be choking on their metrobeards.

Why does everything in this town have to be artisanal? To my mind an artisan is someone who works with his hands like the bricklayer or the oke in the Bantam bakkie who installs DStv. But it's been hijacked by the trendoids. Now we have to have artisanal pizzas, breads, beers, coffees, handjobs – everything is now artisanal. I saw a menu with artisinal chilli poppers. How else are they made? By robot? Like a Fiat?

The idiots in De Waterkant – you take some coffee beans, grind them in a *machine*, and then make the coffee in a *machine* and put a blackboard outside telling you to come inside and ask our barista for our famous artisanal coffees.

Anyway, we craft ourselves away. &Union. Parada. At House of Machines, where they won't sell a normal whisky and every barman has a handlebar moustache, I see Natalie – Mich's mate. I went to her 21st at Durbanville Golf Club.

After the mandatory kiss-into-a-hug and good-to-see-you-you-too and so-what-you-up-to-these-days, I think about her. After all, I am 1 km away from the Costa del Sol and in quite good form. I would say she was hovering in the high 6s, maybe even a 7 after another Bonecrusher.

She provides the gap: 'So, Jase, you looking well. Looking good.'

'You, too.' Whatever it takes.

'I haven't seen you since Mich's party.'

'No.'

'So, what do you think? Have I changed? Have I put on weight?'

'No, no. Not really. Only on your bum.'

120

SUNDAY 14 AUGUST 2011

After that epic fail, as 3G calls it, wetting himself with laughter, we hit some dives in Long Street. I'm hammered. When I park the Scirocco in one of those lanes off Long Street there's some friendly former vet from the DRC called Jean-Claude to assure me everything is under control. When we leave Joburg (the bar, people, not the town – come on) and I get back to the Scirocco the window is broken and my gym bag gone. And iPhone charger. Jean-Claude is nowhere to be seen.

But as Stevie points out, it is 4.30am and Jean-Clause is allowed to knock off sometime. That's the upside again. A 4.30-er. *Lanklaas.*

> **@jasonator069:** car broken into near Long Street at 4.50am. Price to pay for a big night #whatssleep

I stop a police van in Long Street. Two coloured cops. I point to my car. I know there is After S Aftershock hock on my G-Star Raw T, but I am the client here.

All this one called April (wonder which month his granddad was born in) asks: 'What were you going to your car for?'

'To go home.'

'How?'

'By space shuttle. There's my car.'

'Have you had anything to drink?'

'Anything?' sniggers Steve in the background. *'Everything.'*
3G comes in with a useful, 'I don't think he had a Drambuie –

I think he forgot that. Well that and Cinzano, but I think everything else got ticked off.'

'Shut the fuck up, you two.'

Sergeant April is unfazed. 'Up to you.'

SMS from Costa:
Which car? Mine?

MONDAY 15 AUGUST 2011

> **@jasonator069:** Remember the poor old scone. Obliterated by the muffin

> **@dawesman @jasonator069:** Both are dead. They are carbs

This whole Prof Noakes diet thing won't take off. It hasn't worked for me and I have been eating mostly protein, lots of good fat and laid off the beer. I am just going to go for balance.

To top it off I left the Scirocco in the drive because I was too mothered to negotiate the garage. And of course it rained. In the broken window. Those carpets are soaked. Such is crime.

TUESDAY 16 AUGUST 2011

In a funny way on the day that they are declared bankrupt and I get a call from Card Division, I can see the similarities with Greece and me. We both used to be popular, both have some areas that are revolting, neither have a great dental hygiene value set, both have decayed a bit all over, both are better in summer, both have a history, both struggle with South African chicks, neither are great in the GDP field, both have some body hair issues and both are broke.

I'm still on Rex's insurance – not the Scirocco, but I'm going to claim on household items. Case reported at Caledon Square police station (the constable could write) and case number secured. Mom wanted to know if they caught 'the buggers', but I had to tell her I wasn't reporting the crime for investigation, just for insurance purposes.

'You mean they didn't take fingerprints?'

'No, Mom. There is no point.'

'Oh, you mean they were wearing gloves?'

'No Mom, they don't bother.'

'Oh.'

She thinks more. 'DNA? Did they get any?'

That, I suppose, my friends, is one of the problems of DStv.

She's been watching the one with the guy from *Cheers*. Ted Danson. He was much better in that, apparently.

Items officially stolen:
• iPad 2 64GB plus cellular
• iPhone 5 64GB
• iPod nano 16GB

- Asics Gel Kinsei trainers R2,400
- Adidas Commander Cross Trainers R1,100 (the bomb)
- Miscellaneous gym equipment not claimed for (try and show them I am not pulling the piss)
- Tag watch would be pushing it so chipped in with a Suunto T6 heart rate watch
- Diesel belt
- North Face wind cheater – the new one

And you know what? I really don't mind if they give me the cash or make me buy the items – both options I would regard as essential to my quest to become more Monaco than Greece.

WEDNESDAY 17 AUGUST 2011

> **@jasonator069:** Morning Mother City. Lets hope for a crime free day

> **@dawesman @jasonator069:** huh? Because his car got broken into in Long Street at 4am he is now another 'stat'. Poor thing.

You know, I am not even going to respond.

> **@jasonator069 @dawesman @jasonator069:** errrr daws it was actually 4.30/45 when I got out the club and yip I felt violated.

> **@dawesman @jasonator069 @dawesman @jasonator069:** The car belonging to the guys house he is housesitting got violated. However in Denmark...

Zzzzzz.

Two planes crash into a mountain near Tzaneen. Both pilots are white.

THURSDAY 18 AUGUST 2011

Joost's diagnosis is confirmed. I am happy to have been wrong. But not happy that I was, if you get my drift.

> **@jasonator069:** Thoughts and prayers with @9Joost. Be strong my brutha #legend

Watch his followers tweetiply now. Keep an eye on it.

Meet with Stevie and 3G at Origin to discuss the new business. We're calling it Newco for now. What we're thinking is supplying booze and bar staff to top-end functions. I know it's been done before, but our USBs are:
• 3G's booze trade contacts and 'shortcuts'.
• My F&B experience.
• Focus on top-end functions – nothing in the suburbs, china.
• Top-end booze brands. 3G, for example, has just got the 'afterhours' agency for SSP (Soviet Space Programme) vodka – about twice the price of Absolut and twice as nice. That agency is going to be put into Newco because of 3G's ridiculous (and probably illegal) restraints of trade. No wonder our growth rate is lower than Mali's.
• Mel, Whitney and Sasha-Lee (the Storm in the Double-D cup). And he says there is plenty more where they came from. Apparently there is one called Kim, who used to be Afrikaans, who is world-class. She would be a 10 were it not for having slightly inflated

calves. And Max (girl) who also has ToDs (Tits of Death). I have seen these chicks in action. They could sell a rusty Volkswagen beetle to Kenny Kunene for 350K.
- We are (going to be, sometime) fully BEE empowered.
- 24-hour response time.
- Ice sculptures – my idea – brilliant.
- We are going to have an app (iOS and Android).

FRIDAY 19 AUGUST 2011

From: Julian Groenewald <JulianG@perfectrisk.co.za>
Date: 19 August 2011 at 6.11am
To: 'Jason Brydon' <Jasebrydon069@gmail.com>
Subject: Your claim 16 August 2011

Dear Mr Brydon

Perfect Risk Assessors (PRA) have been appointed by your father's insurers to assess your claim that you put in on Tuesday 16 August.

I am sorry to hear about your loss.

To process this claim I think it's best that we meet as soon as is convenient for yourself. We will need the boxes for the iPhone, iPad and iPod to process the claim as smoothly as we can or any photographs that you may have of them or the clothing items claimed for.

Please advise as to your availability.

Regards
Julian

Shit, man.

How can you trust someone who is firing off emails at 6.11am? He should be sleeping or at gym.

Things have changed in the 'next Knysna'. Rex had a 'misunderstanding with the local constabulary' as to what the legal limit is. So he is on foot literally and on the back foot domestically – and Val has seized the gap. We are all going to Lesley's wedding tomorrow. The whole Swiss Family Vegetable. I asked what sort of freak gets married while the Boks are playing the All Blacks? Dad says that was rhetorical. My mom's friend, Daphne, from the tourism bureau, has emailed an SA Express ticket to Slumtown. Like at 6am to be in East London. 7.30am when the fogeys will pick me up. #dreadingit

Voicemail from Jeff: 'You might want to know your daughter's seen the doctor. Twice. She has a chest infection. Actually, a spineless invertebrate like you probably doesn't want to know. But why don't you surprise us, Jason? And take responsibility. You said you'd put her onto your medical aid, so I will be giving them your details.'

Jeez, Jeff, that's tautology or whatever it's called. When you use repetitive, unnecessary words – of course, by definition every invertebrate is spineless. Where did you go to school, tjom?

I am going to get absolutely roostered tonight.

SATURDAY 20 AUGUST 2011

The mouldy smell in the Scirocco almost made me hurl. But then again I was in far-from-showroom condition myself.

I am much more *au fait* with battling hangovers on aircraft after OR Tambo-gate last year. Still I maybe over-clubbed it slightly last night. We played ToD (Tray of Death). You order a tray of half-SSP shots and half-water shots and from then on its very Russian Roulette. I didn't get too many blanks. I think 3G must have stitched me up because I came a distant fourth.

If you were to ask me what I regard as the lowest form of misery, I would have to say it's the 30 seconds before you kotch. Seems like hours. The sweat, the angst, the bile, the humiliation… it's a cocktail of desperation.

Happens just after take-off. I don't think we were even over the Hottentots Holland yet. But I am elegant in execution. It sounds just like a long cough with (quite a big) greenie. Neat and tidy in the paper bag. And therein lies part of the rub, and why Mrs Dlamini next to me didn't have quite the flight to Slumtown she had anticipated judging by the four-piece yellow number (hat included) that made her look like a bumblebee with an air valve blown up its nought.

Anyway, not her fault. She was probably an MP.

But W(why not what)TF do they make vomit bags out of paper? Vomit may have carrots in it, but it always, always has a strong liquid component. Now the cabin in those SA Express propeller-driven numbers is smaller than on a radio-control helicopter. So I am sitting with my full bag and looking to dispose of it.

I know if I get up the (not insubstantial) air hostess will have a baby. So I clutch my parcel, curled in the crash position as the plane climbs – unnecessarily high, I think – does the oke not realise he's not flying a 747. All he has to do is clear the Helderberg and head up the coast. I just want the seatbelt lights to go off before this paper bag saturates.

Seatbelt light wins. Up I pop like Kenny Kunene at an auction and I carry my bag of artisanal organic produce to the toilet, but some *charra* has beaten me to it. So I stand there smiling, pretending its not urgent, well aware of the dripping and the odour. I am more aware of it than 3C who is glaring at me. So is 8B.

When the charra *eventually* comes out (what was he doing?), I bolt in and bolt myself in. Fuck. I am greeted with a brutal sign telling me not to dispose of paper items down the toilet. WTF. This is a combination of paper and corporeal produce. I am not in a position to split the atom or invent time travel.

The parcel bomb goes down the bog. Sorry Hermanus.

Rex won't park the Camry at Ben Schoeman – as he calls the airport – cos he won't give Acsa Baba and the 40 thieves another cent he doesn't have to. He circles. I slip into the back seat.

'You had better buckle up, son. I know it's the back seat, but this is the Eastern Cape. We don't have fender benders here, son, we go big.'

Mom passes the flask and a cheese-and-marmite sandwich on Duens.

'Thanks Ma.' Great hangover cure. 'Are there any egg ones?'

There are. Dad points out that I would pay over R60 for that at the 24-hour shop, 'and they won't taste anything like your mother's'.

With a stark warning to keep an eye out for cattle and kids pushing wire cars, we head off on the R63 towards Alice. That, says Rex, is the home of the University of Fort Hare, 'that seat of learning where lots of their leaders came from. Even Mugabe. I think it's from this land that he got his agricultural policy.'

Shakes his head.

'Look at the erosion. Fort Hare has some white lecturers. But they are so liberal and open-minded that they don't live in Alice. They retreat up the hill to Hogsback before their cars are stoned for not passing the whole mob's exams, to go and smoke pot on the hill.'

Here we go. The wedding is not talked about. We are staying at the Hogsback Inn. Dad, for obvious reasons, refuses to stay at a place called The Faeries. 'It's probably booked out,' he snorted. Says if we stayed there we would have to sleep with the lights on. Like in '76.

I must say it's beautiful. All lush and green. Their vendors don't sell black bags and phone chargers, they sell clay pigs.

The less said about the wedding the better. But it's Fruit and Veg City. From the behind, when they were standing by the water/moss feature/tree stump that served as an altar for the 'priestess' (in traditional dress, but Belgian) they looked like Victor and Bakkies. After a few off-seasons.

Some bulky lesbians in the front row were snivelling away – happiness or sadness or jealousy or cos the cat died – who gives a fuck? Two people (sex indeterminate) were in dungarees and Rex was sucking on another form of flask, a hip one, which he called 'The Father's Friend'. Everybody clapped after we had passed a ring round on some length of satin and the couple had kissed. Mercifully, for my parents, soft lips, no tongue and circa 2-3 seconds.

Luckily the ceremony is over and the vegan buffet inedible unless you're bovine (majority of guests), so Rex and I flee to the Inn for the Hogburgers, Amstels and a great Bok victory. We did think it cruel that we could be so close to PE where the Test was, yet so, so far.

SUNDAY 21 AUGUST 2011

Kim Kardashian has also got married. I would rather have been at her wedding.

The Scirocco, when I drive it back from the airport, smells like a bioculture. And the house? It smells disgusting. Those two dogs have shat everywhere. Really. Not even housetrained. I had no clue what I was taking on when Dawesy asked me.

MONDAY 22 AUGUST 2011

A whole day's brainstorm at the Costa Plenti about Newco with Stevie and 3G. They both took a day's leave. Well, Stevie took a sickie even though he's been warned about sickies on a Friday or Monday, but he was clever. He went to the office first, said he was feeling awful and ducked. I've been tasked with drawing up the business plan.

It's go go go. The business is going to be called @IGLOO. We're going to supply booze and full bar set-ups and staff to private functions and corporate events. Our bar staff are going to be called Icemen and Icemaidens, although if a guy wants to work there he basically has to be the face of Hugo Boss. We are going just on premium bands. Obviously with what we can't get off the grey market (3G), we are going premium, from Ultra – we're meeting them Wednesday.

So Patron (Jose who?), SSP (or Grey Goose vodka wise), Johnnie Walker Black, Monkey Shoulder (whisky – trendy bottle), gin wise – Tanqueray or Hendrick's. No SAB beers. You get the drift. We are top-end, chinas, no 21sts at Mowbray Golf Club.

3G says, as a guide we ask them about their music. If it's any '80s, folk, grunge, metal, any fucking Green Day or Foo Fighters or shit like that, we're out. If it's deep house, progressive kitchen, funky garage, acid jazz, heavy chillout or any combination of these words, we're in!

I nod like I know, almost say something about Beggars and Choosers, but we can't lose momentum now.

We are going to freelance the Icemaidens, but with 3G's girls from the mansion we are well sorted there. Nobody worse than a Miss Bayside Mall 2009. No tax to pay there.

We are going to find someone to make ice bars and statues that you can take shots off. Stevie knows a Muslim guy in Salt River who works in ice who I have to go and see.

Igloo: ice, cool, trendy. It's happening.

We have booked our Twitter handle. @igloo. Stevie has had to send some papers and shit to Pretoria to register us. We have a shelf company for now. We are Magictrade123 trading as @Igloo. Nature of business: 'complete liquor solutions'.

Payoff line: '@igloo – you don't get cooler.'

We have our first function. It's a jammy, but it's 3G's brother's company's (some ad agency called Sydney Stringfellow's – even though the prick doesn't exist) first birthday. On the roof of their building in Loop Street.

We're each going to be 30% shareholders and we're going to have another 10% kept aside for a BEE partner. This causes some debate. Stevie is the most vociferous. 'Like who?'

3G says we have to. 'We can't go around and say we are fully BEE empowered when our names are Brydon, Fourie and Cruickshank.'

'Cruickshank could be coollie'.

'Shut the fuck up, Stevie.'

'We have to *be* BEE.'

'Very funny, Jase. What about her?' 3G points to Abstinence who, in her sea-rolling gait, is bearing north-northwest to the washing line.

'Can't really have someone called Abstinence in the booze trade.'

'But she will have an Af - sorry – a traditional name, too.'

Even I know that would take fronting a bit far. Besides she has recently ironed right across the logo on my Ben Sherman Tee (R999) so now it looks like I spilt custard on it whilst cutting myself shaving.

Stevie has (another) brainwave: 'Can't we find a Chinese rather?'

3G's impressed. 'Ja, they count now.'

It's minuted – kinda – that Stevie will ask at Mr Wong's who does Chinese food and sushi where he is a regular. Or as they pronounce it, legular. We remind Stevie not to bring a Jap because they don't count. Under apartheid they were white. Says 3G, 'That or go to the R5 store and ask there if they have one.'

Meeting closes at 3.30pm for a Weber (no lid so direct cooking). Abstinence has the cheek to ask for a lift to the station, but I point out it's all downhill.

TUESDAY 23 AUGUST 2011

Day one as MD @igloo.

> **@igloo:** looking forward to setting up the @sydneystringfellows first birthday jol this week. Gonna be a cracker. MD @jasonator hands on #leadership #goodtimes #alwaysbelieveinmagic

Mail from Stevie off his hotmail as per @igloo policy.

From: Steve Fourie <steviewunda@hotmail.com>
Date: 23 August 2011 at 11.12am
To: 'Jason Brydon' <Jasebrydon069@gmail.com>
'3G' <Baxboy7@gmail.com>
Subject: Setup

Howzit Icemen

OK, I have run some numbers. To get us through the first 6 months, and basically the first 'season', we are going to need 300K. That is to cover the basic Jase was after and the basic office and marketing expenses we agreed on. The bar staff will be pretty much cost of sale, including Sasha-Lee's chest, as will the ice.

But we need 300K start-up at least. Until I have chatted to Mr Wong, that's 100K each. By month end? You both have the new account details.

Later
Steve

Glitch.

So they basically want me to pay my own salary? That's bullshit.

From: 'Jason Brydon' <Jasebrydon069@gmail.com>
Date: 23 August 2011 at 11.16am
To: Steve Fourie <steviewunda@hotmail.com>
'3G' <Baxboy7@gmail.com>
Subject: RE: Setup

Shot Steve, that all makes sense. Just a quick one? Which month end? August?

Cheers & regards

Jason Brydon
Managing Director
@Igloo
Liquor solutions
www.@igloo.com
fb; t:@igloo

3G replies to point out that we don't have a website yet. That's on my to do list, together with the app and sourcing the ice oke.

End of August. That's this time next week? It's not like Rex has a lazy 100K hanging around.

Gulp.

WEDNESDAY 24 AUGUST 2011

As @Igloo rises, Tripoli falls.

We must be careful what we wish for. We all wanted Saddam out and now you can't buy an aubergine in a Baghdad market without a car bomb killing 38. #justsaying.

THURSDAY 25 AUGUST 2011

Muggsy posted on my timeline:

> ABSA the Aquila rhino, the first one back in the Western Cape since they were poached out 250 years ago, has died overnight from his injuries.

Not ideal. But then again you couldn't go from Cape Town to Newlands without a mountain lion coming through the roof of your hansom cab and devouring a few of your slaves. Before they got poached. #sameshitdifferentday.

I SMS Costa:

> Howzit Costa. Listen all is good here. Dogs alive and well and tired from their daily walks up Signal Hill. You chose a good winter to miss. It hasn't stopped raining here. Must be better off in Greece. But that's why I am writing. The roof is leaking. Like a lot. I have had a guy in and he says it's rotting and lots of it may need replacing. But it's going to cost like a 100K. Seems like a fortune, but not sure what choice we have. What should I do? Wait for you to get back or should I get someone in for a quote? Cheers Jason

Worth a shout. All he has to do is eft the 100K for 'repairs'. Hooks in the water.

FRIDAY 26 AUGUST 2011

Beyoncé's pregnant.

Not only that, but we have found premises. @igloo is going to sublet from some chick friend of Muggsy in Prestwich Street. Quite a trendy set-up – next to a casting agency – ahoy – with lots of movie and media types around. One parking bay (for the MD J Brydon Esq), an office and a boardroom. Shared kitchen and ominously shared toilet. Her name is Benjy and she has some children's mobile content business called Buzz. Zzz. She has three kids from her boyfriend, but they're not married. She does Hot Bikram Yoga, eats quinoa (whatever that is) and smokes hydroponics with her boyfriend every night on their deck in Bantry Bay. Two of her staff are world-class (one, Emma, 27 is in my crosshairs) and there is only one toilet. The Jasonator could do some damage here. In more ways than one.

The Scirocco is now a lot like a greenhouse. Not long to harvest time.

So now I have a few days to find both a 100K and a Vespa.

SATURDAY 27 AUGUST 2011

Watch some Absa Currie Cup. And then go and get transmogrified with Muggsy, Dawesman and, believe it or not, Slug (Lettuce had let him out).

We end up at the Power and Glory in Kloof Street. At 12.50am Slug says he has to go.

'Chaps, if I don't and am not home by 1, Lettuce will have my balls.'

'You need to grow some.'

'Shut the fuck up Brydon. At least I have a female partner.'

'And a white one at that.' I almost lose it with Muggs for that chirp.

I train my guns back on Slug. 'Well, you'll have to grow some balls for her to have them.'

And with that he just turns his back and leaves. Doos. I would rather be a Trappist monk than be married to Lettuce anyway.

I start chatting to this chick called Shelley. She is impressed that I am a CEO. I couldn't really see her chassis, but I got the impression that you didn't need the biggest drawbridge to cross her moat. But I had to put the yards in and get through the foothills to get her back to the Costa del Sol.

She smoked. I didn't care. It's funny when you first try to hook up you say you don't mind, but later it becomes an issue. But hey, I wasn't trying to get this thing round to my gran's house for some Yorkshire pud, I was just trying to get her up the road in the next hour or so.

I have to ask what she does and I hear words like liability, risk, assessments, actuarial – and my ADD kicks in. Why couldn't she just be a firewoman or something? I ask her what her favourite restaurant is and she says 'a little Mexican place in Shanghai'.

What the hell is that? A little Mexican place in Shanghai?

She is interested to hear that I also love freediving, but thank god the music is loud – to me aKING are the future great SA band – much better than those boring trendy try-hards Goldfish.

I am having to work for my runs here. I thought this was going to be a doddle. Having done all the groundwork she picks up her Kenneth Kors bag and says she has to go.

'Jeez, that's a pity.' But that is not a problem for the Jasonator. 'Just wait a sec, I just have to go to the loo, give me one minute.'

I had come in the Golf after Scirocco-gate. I bolt outside. Put the keys in the ignition. Hold the knob down and flee back inside.

'Hey, Shell, I'm going to duck, too.'

'Cool.'

We leave and I pretend to fumble for my car keys. 'Shit my keys.'

'Did you leave them inside?'

'Nope.'

'Should I go and check? Or maybe your friends have them?'

I make a theatrical shrug. I peer through the window.

'Oh fuck. Shit shit shit… I locked them in the car.' And there they are dangling on my baby Leatherman key ring with my Virgin Active card.

She peers in too. She's actually quite tight.

'Do you have spares?'

'Yip. At home.' I leave out the 'in Port Alfred' bit.

'Maybe one of your friends can give you a lift home?'

'Oh no, they've been drinking.'

'So what now? Can you get a cab?'

'I live just up the road.'

'OK, well I can run you up quickly.'

'Really, ag don't worry.'

'No, I really don't mind.'

A masterclass if you ask me. Well that bit was. I get her up and get her in. I must say the rest not so much so. Of course she was impressed with my spot (Costa's family snaps are now well settled in the broom cupboard), but let's just say I didn't keep my best till last and that maybe I underwhelmed. Which is to say, I may have opened fire before I actually engaged the enemy...

I take a picture of her asleep, but you can't see any of her 'private' areas.

> **@jasonbrydon:** Just another Saturday night./pic.twitter.
> com/lzhehduj71

WhatsApp from Stevie:
> Brydon wtf you doing. You not Robbie Williams. This is a small town.

It forces me to accept: I have had lots of sex in my life, but I haven't made a lot of love.

SUNDAY 28 AUGUST 2011

Manchester United 8 – Arsenal 2.

I kid you not.

MONDAY 29 AUGUST 2011

Oscar Pistorius has qualified for the 400m normal people world champs despite coming last in his semi. Boing boing boing.

Reply from Costa:
> My mate Nikos is in construction and will pop round to have a look tomorrow. Thanks a lot C.

My to-do list is now looking messy:
- Locksmith to get Golf back (the morning session with Shell made it worth it). Can also maybe help me find safe key that 'I have lost'
- Find the ice statue man for Friday night
- Make holes in roof to explain leak
- Do @igloo website and develop app (iOS and Android)
- Find 100K
- Get a Vespa
- Get the dogs their Vondis food (last three points all related)
- Drop 2kg by Friday.
- Floss. This week. And smell it.

I never thought it would come to this. Here I am on Costa's roof with a crowbar, loosening tiles and a hosepipe. I am not good with heights, but I can't take a chance. You know what these Mediterranean types are like. If he rumbles me on my ruse I could also be found floating face down in the docks near Quay Four (try their hake and calamari platter – great value at R79.90).

A locksmith comes – connection of Badger's. His name is Faizel from Mitchells Plain. Says he is originally from District Six. My father says he is sick of District Six being described as colourful and vibrant until the Group Areas Act tore that marvellous community apart and sent them to live on the sandy, wind-torn flats amongst Cecil Rhodes's Port Jackson bushes. To quote Rex, 'District Six was so "colourful and vibrant" it was the only place in the Cape where the police had to go in in pairs. That's how safe it was.'

Faizel is a good ou, gets my car open in under a second – quite worrying actually. If he were less honest it could have been on bricks in the Bo Kaap in under a minute. I then ask him if he can open the safe at the house. He asks if I am the registered owner. I offer to double his rate. He still says no.

Just my luck that I would choose the only honest one.

Not the start to the week I had in mind. And D day for the 100K and my Vespa looming and @igloo's first function on Friday. Tough in the rarefied air on the top of the Layer Cake, son.

TUESDAY 30 AUGUST 2011

Stevie has found us a part-time accountant, Gary. He is about 62kg and looks like he gyms at the World of Birds.

3G and I dial Stevie who is in Joburg on business after we meet Gary. Even though he wants us to keep all our slips, he seems OK.

As Stevie points out to 3G, 'He is a proper CA.'

'What you mean, is he also from Cape Town?'

Stevie and I piss ourselves at 3G's dofness. What Gary has come up with is that the 100K we each put in (theoretically), goes into loan accounts. I am to be paid my salary pro rata today for the work done so far since my appointment as MD this time last week. Gary will load on our banking system and 3G will do the release. Apparently I cannot pay myself. We're doing things properly at @igloo.

WEDNESDAY 31 AUGUST 2011

The Youth League call Helen Zille a witch. I can kind of see where they are coming from.

From: Jason Brydon' <Jasebrydon069@gmail.com>
Date: 23 August 2011 at 11.18am
To: 'Stevie' <steviewunda@hotmail.com>
'3G' <Baxboy7@gmail.com>
Subject: Funding

Icemen

We are T-2 days. Well T-3 working days till lift off @ Sydney Stringfellows.

The booze is sorted. The bar staff are sorted. We have two barmen, Ross and Jed, both part-time models who I got from the casting agency next door. They can help the chicks with some of the grunt work and will appeal to both females and poofs.

143

The ice at this stage is an issue, but I am going to see that guy in Salt River after my 10.30. Our plan is to have an ice bar with a Perspex top, as discussed.

Banks will drop the glasses Friday at 2pm. I will be there to receive them if I can just push my 1pm forward to 12.30.

So all good.

Oh, ja, two more small things. Firstly my 100K. It is in a fixed deposit at HSBC, Guernsey. It's going to take 60 days to get out. Hope that's not a problem for you guys.

Secondly should I go ahead and get the company Vespa? I think it would be cool, we could share it and can be branded @igloo.

Cheers & regards

Jason Brydon
Managing Director
@Igloo
Liquor solutions
www.@igloo.com
find us on fb; t:@igloo

The phone rings immediately. No Vespa. And I will have a negative loan account of a 100K and they will have positives of a 100K each. Seems harsh – it's like a 200k swing, but what can I do about it?

I have bought myself a couple of months and I still get paid.

Back of the net, my son.

THURSDAY 1 SEPTEMBER 2011

Spring is Sprung
da grass is riz
I wunda where
Da birdies is.

> **@igloo:** what do you call an eskimo's igloo without a toilet?
> Answer: An Ig

Stevie completely overreacts. Doesn't think a tweet like that helps our brand the day before launch and is now, apparently, wondering if I should have access to our Twitter account. Doesn't understand that humour marketing is about the best you get. Must be his period.

FRIDAY 2 SEPTEMBER 2011

Not only is it Bok Friday and one week to go till Rugby World Cup 2011, it's lift off!!!!

> **@igloo:** catch the icemen and maidens in action tonight as @igloo goes live at @sydneystringfellows pardi tonaaait. Pull in.

3G hits the @igloo WhatsApp group (Stevie, me, Gary and him):
J, take down the last two words. You don't really have a right to tell people to pull in.

Fair point. I am just so used to hosting my own shindigs.

I play a binder. There is a set construction company called Pole Position in Block B near our offices. Run, oddly, by some Polish oke

145

naturally called Lech with a ponytail and more earrings than George Michael has ever had, and drives a motorbike with a side car. Maybe he has never got over what happened in 1939. Not my problem.

But I see him at the Vida at Beluga. He can give us a light set tonight to light up the ice. For zero. Zip. Nada. When he has more time he can actually build us mini sets for what he terms a piece of the action.

From what I can hear between his veird (sic) accent and a mouthful of *chourico misto* is: 'My business is so fucking seasonal. Vun (sic) month I am partying like Prince Harry, ze next day I am load shedding my own flat.'

He is 'vanting somesing' that can get him in on the whole year action and is prepared to join up with @igloo for a slice of the equity pie. Maybe he can have Mr Wong's because I am not diluting. Not yet.

I WhatsApp this with the others and they think it's a great idea. We arrange a lunch at some Italian spot down the road for Monday run by some Israeli homos.

I must say I am very very very nervous. So much so that I forget to feed Ferris and Gary Cooper.

SATURDAY 3 SEPTEMBER 2011

Feedback?

WE HAVE A BUSINESS!!

Pluses:

- We sold out. Maybe this does not only belong in the plus column.
- We made a killing on the Soviet Space Programme (SSP) vodka which 3G 'got' for free. Every cocktail was vodka, virtually every shot. At R40 a pop. Hewlett and Adrian, the two (gay) joint Sydney Stringfellow CEOs were so wasted, flying higher than a SAM7, that they would have signed off on anything.
- It was freezing on the roof and the ice did not help, but it made the girls, well, very pert. Which went down a treat. Sasha-Lee certainly could have helped in a fire drill.
- They still drank despite the coke.
- Lech's lights made it very funky.
- Banks will live with the breakages.
- I kept it together despite all my vices being on one roof. I think it was M's words to Sean Connery in *Goldfinger* 'and don't mess it up, Bond' that were whirring in my cranium. Not to say I did not have a little shot or two, a *slangetjie* or put some gob in the mouth of a junior copywriter. I wasn't going to do coke, but you know the saying about gift horses. OK, maybe not in front of (or off) clients.
- We have two more verbal bookings already. So we can't have fucked up too badly.

Work-ons:
- The Ice Bar, oddly for Cape Town, arrived from Salt River a tad early. I must be the first oke ever to call a supplier in Salt River and ask why is your delivery so fucking early. It had already subsided a bit by the time the guests arrived.
- Selling out, I guess. One doos with lamb-chop sideburns and one of those silly flatcaps and a rose tattooed on his neck seemed a bit worked up about it. I told him to fuck off to Bronx, but luckily barmen Ross and Jed intervened.
- In future maybe let's make sure the lighting extension cords are not underneath the bar. Look, the bang and all that certainly shook things up and I reckon some okes thought it part of the show. Lech

was cool about it, but pointed out that water and electricity don't mix. My point about hydroelectricity was lost a bit.

I must say I got a bit of a skrik at the start. We have our own work gear for bar staff that Stevie organised. They're so tight-fitting they make a wetsuit look like bell-bottoms. The one barman, Jed, is a bit reluctant and says, 'Well, if you want me to wear this, you're going to have to hold onto this.'

He reaches and pulls something out from his back. I realise it's a gun. He starts dismantling and giving me parts to hold.

'Can you hang on to it, Jase?'

'Sure. But what the fuck's it for?'

'Don't you watch the news?'

SUNDAY 4 SEPTEMBER 2011

I know we have to get the website up and running as soon as we can. Our business is essentially soft launched and we need to make it hard very quickly. I swallow some pride and phone that Megan chick from that night at Orphanage who works for Bread, that hippy web design outfit. She answers.

'Howzit, Megan, it's Jason Brydon. Not sure if you remember me?'

'Course I do, you the guy from the Border.' Lot of emphasis on the word "Border". Too much emphasis.

'Ja, whatever, listen here, I was wondering…'

Oh my god, I realise then she probably thinks I am calling to ask her out. Or maybe not because then I would have WhatsApped her rather. But I throw in quickly that it's a work call.

She points out that it's a Sunday. I respond by telling her that this is why @igloo is carving up.

'@igloo?'

'You mean you haven't heard about us?' I feign incredulity.

We are going to meet tomorrow at the Old Biscuit Mill. She can't meet today. She is in Greyton. Greyton. WTF is there to do in Greyton? Pottery? Trim the brambles? Walk the terrapin? Massive red flag that, JB.

MONDAY 5 SEPTEMBER 2011

Megan is actually not bad in the cold light of day. She is wearing a pair of skinny Diesels.

She asks whether I have any pics for the site.

'How can I have any pics if the business has just started?'

'What about the other night?'

'Oh, ja.' Truth be told, I hadn't thought of that. We go onto the Sydney Stringfellows Instagram. I must say the ice with some mauve and purple shit and some of twin peaks (Sasha-Lee) in her @igloo outfit did look good. I tell Megan I will get some from the agency.

We're talking not much detail, not much text. Lots of hot flash up front. Basically a 'contact us'. Not even a real 'about us'. Just some bullets on what we do and provide. Flash with pics of our brands and from the agency jol, which we will add to, and some of the icemen and maidens' portfolio shots. That's it. Not even a pic of me in a T-shirt and an Armani jacket that revolves around with me looking like The Thinker.

'So,' she asks, 'when do you want it by?'

'I wanna try be live tomorrow.'

She splutters into her red espresso. 'Tomorrow? You know that's impossible.'

'I'm a tomorrow kinda guy. That's how I've done what I've done.'

It wraps up. She's going to get the domain www.@igloo.com, .co.za and .net reserved and send through a quote plus timeline by close of play. I am to source the photos.

We have 11 apps in common between us.

After that I go to Virgin Wembley. For a distressing arms session. Guns Guns Guns. By the time I finish, each bicep is the size of an RDP house.

A Peanut Butter Bomb from Kauai and I am off to the office – where I get an SMS with the remarkably bad news that Nikos is coming round tomorrow to fix the (at this stage flawless) tiles.

TUESDAY 6 SEPTEMBER 2011

I had to get up early to attack some roof tiles with a crowbar and a hosepipe, to ensure water damage. Nikos needs something to fix so I duly oblige. Quite fun actually.

Nikos is bemused. He thinks that the damage to the roof looks like it was done deliberately. I try to look surprised, like when Bafana lose.

I deal with it well. 'It must have been street kids.'

I think, only think, Nikos believes me. He has a necklace like Mr T from the A-Team and is so smooth you could ice skate on him. Says he has 'grilled more birds than a Weber'.

Don't forget, pal – you're just a handyman whose dad probably sells airtime and Chappies at a café.

Mara, the *Idols* judge, admits to drinking on the show. I would too if I had to listen to that mob and sit next to Gareth Cliff. I see she went for vodka which of course, aroma wise, is the way to go in those pressure situations. My dad says it got him through every wedding he went to. Including his own. That and Fisherman's Friend.

To add to those indicators of whites hitting hard times (but not so bad, really):

You use one of those Translux buses to go to another town.
You are an English-speaking caravanner.
You still go into the branch to bank.

WEDNESDAY 7 SEPTEMBER 2011

@igloo doing party for the outgoing Dutch Consul on Friday night at the Castle. Kerr-ching. Stevie landed it because he is having this on/off scene with this chick Floortje (really) who works in the visa department, but he says snores. But it's a win-win-win. @igloo gets the business, he gets a three-year Schengen for nothing (without having to prove his parents paid their TV licence) and a night or two holed up in the Radisson with Floortje, and she gets some Wunda loving. Paid for by the Koninkrijk der Nederlanden.

We're making an ice model of a tulip over a scale approximation of Table Mountain. Basically R21K just there for some frozen water. BOOM.

I am well aware of the tragedy of a work event on the opening of RWC, but given it's in New Zealand we will be well done and dusted by the time we have to start getting ready.

I have to do my SuperBru.

Rex is in touch to tell me about some right-wingers who have been caught trying to plot to blow up the ANC conference in a place called Mangaung. Never heard of it, but Dad says it is just outside Bloem. 'Right idea, just wrong execution,' is Rex's take on it.

THURSDAY 8 SEPTEMBER 2011

I honestly think we have a chance at this World Cup. I buy my Bok replica. I must say it's a bit sad the Springbok is so small, but I guess we should be grateful we still have it at all. Now that I am a bit cashflow positive, it's an essential purchase. I must say I got excited when the chick at the office said your cards have arrived, thinking it was my company credit card and petrol card that Gary had organised. But it was just my business cards.

I say just my business card, but there it stands: JASON BRYDON, MANAGING DIRECTOR. I turboscan a copy and mail to all and post on my timeline.

We have three functions booked next week and it's not even season. Come on, Bokke!

FRIDAY 9 SEPTEMBER 2011

Slight backfire if you like.

Jeff, Hayley's dad, calls. Luckily I have saved all his numbers so don't answer. But talk about a downer.

'Hello Jason. It's Jeff Jenkins here, Hayley's dad. I wonder if you could give me a call back. I think you have my number. I am sure you are dying to know how your daughter – remember her? – is getting on? And how her mom is coping? I can shed some light on this for you.'

No, Jeff Jenkins, it's okay. But then he comes to the crux.

'I hear your circumstances have changed, Jason. For the better. Great news. And that old cashflow model that we used to calculate your maintenance payments is now redundant. So maybe we can have a chat about this. No need to go legal, sport, I am sure you will do the right thing. Actually… come to think of it, I'm not so sure.'

Slug, help, Slug. But on Monday. There's an opening ceremony, All Black game and Dutch Consul-General's farewell to get through first.

SATURDAY 10 SEPTEMBER 2011

I think I'm probably the first guy since Simon van der Stel to have slept in that room. And on that chair. But I think everything – including the Heinekens, setting up the business and being the face of it, the moss in the Scirocco, Haute Cabrière Chardonnay Pinot Noir, spading Sasha-Lee, all the stress, WhatsApping Megan (about the site!), Jeff (Hayley's dad) – all caught up with me. All I know is that Van der Stel must have woken up with a very sore back every day before he found himself a Hottentot maid or two.

I take Megan to dinner at the Mount Nelson. I mean you don't take a trout rod to land a tuna off Cape Point, do you? In that vein, it's my new G-Star Radars and Boss long-sleeve (both bought this morning). A little congratulatory gift to Jase from Jase. Nothing quite like dropping 6K at the Waterfront and feeling good about it.

I think taking her is a legit company expense as we're going to be talking about the app and the site so I must keep the slip for Gary the human dungbeatle. Mind you, we are the client; maybe she is meant to pay. I really couldn't care.

It doesn't start well. We have a cocktail or two (called Liquid Cocaine – if only that existed) in the Planet Bar and, in fact, it's full of awkwardness. Like the poor black maid at the whites' wedding and where she must sit. I think I went a bit hard at those funny crunchy snacks, but as soon as the excellent, gooseberry-laden Groote Post Chardonnay kicks in, things pick up.

Afterwards, the Audi gets brought round to the front of the hotel and the doors opened for us.

Good evening. Good evening.

SUNDAY 11 SEPTEMBER 2011

9/11.

Megs and I watch the Wales game. I think about inviting some of the okes round as a few Heinies and the Bok game would be a great way of getting rid of the Sunday blues. But then again Megan was showing as much sign of leaving as a perlemoen. I think it's just a tad too early for full integration. Besides, I am her client so it may be awkward for her.

Of course, I have to be trendy and act that I'm not *Bok befok*. And that I have just a passing interest in the rugby. I have to play it calm.

'We may as well watch – there's nothing else on.'

Thank God it's a Sunday morning, I figure, so I can flick through a whole lot of church shit on Rhema and Gospel channels to get my point across.

'Wait, stop there,' she says as I flip past channel 120. 'Look – *The Graham Norton Show*, let's see who is on.' I try to blast past. 'Wait, Jase, go back. Thanks. Info it, please. I wonder who he's got on. He's just so sharp. Oh, look, Stephen Fry, Maggie Smith and Chris Martin. Wow.'

'It's a repeat, Megan.'

'But I haven't seen it.'

It's almost kick-off, and you don't want to miss the Welsh anthem.
'I have.'

Okay and with that I get to 201 to the rugger. There are lots of SA
fans there and no discernible drop in the anthem between the old
bit and the new bit. That should shut Dawesy up. I know that he
can't argue with the fact that the differential is dropping with each
passing year.

Of course, he WhatsApps me to point out that a fair amount of those
fans actually live in New Zealand. Whatever. I am more worried as
to how we will get on without Bakkies.

I flick on to Graham Norton a couple of times during injuries,
kicks and half-time to look balanced. It seems to work. Thank God
the game is close so I could justify my increasing interest and the
upturned pot plant. But then again, that we only beat Wales, with a
population of 12, by one point is not acceptable. How on earth did
Saru keep Peter de Villiers when he would be out of his depth in a
saucer of milk?

The 'Divvy Moet Vokof' WhatsApp group (administrator S Fourie)
goes off. I say:
> Why not swap him with the bus driver? He probably knows more
> about rugby?

Of course Dawesy argues, but I just point out that Kiwis really know
their rugby.

Megan and I make a fillet on the Weber. Direct heat. Top still missing. She likes my dogs. But thinks it's odd they don't like me.

To show even more balance I post on FB that we had a really nice meal at the Mount Nelson. And that the waiter, Elias, was great.

Stevie asks if he was South African?

Cynical bastard.

MONDAY 12 SEPTEMBER 2011

Crime stats are released. Lowest since 1994. Riiiggght, I think as I watch the micro culture expand in the Scirocco. Poor Volkswagen sports car – another statistic of crime-ridden SA.

It isn't plain sailing with Megan. She is of that school of thought that every time a man licks one of your nipples, Jesus sets fire to a school bus.

Plus her folks are getting a tattoo. Can there be anything weirder? #justasking

TUESDAY 13 SEPTEMBER 2011

Everybody is upset because at the World Cup the England vice-captain, who has the same nose as Gerrie Coetzee, has been caught hanging out with some busty blonde (go on, charge me then!). It seems the problem is he's married to the Queen's granddaughter

Zara Phillips. I think she is the best of a distinctly ordinary bunch, but I am sure Tindall is just maintaining an age-old royal tradition. You're telling me Prince Phillip has only been up HRH in the past 80 years?

They are also in kak for drinking too much, letting off fire extinguishers and tossing a dwarf. The papers have labelled them an embarrassment. I think it's just good touring.

WEDNESDAY 14 SEPTEMBER 2011

Every dog has his day…

It is Rex's court day about that (third) little misunderstanding with Port Alfred's finest. Rex has to take his punishment like a man. The 'entirely unintelligible, illogical, biased and racist' Magistrate Kgomo has ruled that he may only drive to run errands from 10-12am for the next two years.

Rex represented himself. Mistake. Mom says he ran a spirited defence. He pointed out that when they were broken into and the Wharfedale VCR player was stolen, he phoned the Port Alfred police but they had no transport available so he had to drive to the police station to fetch the constable to come to our place.

'It was OK for me drive after a few Scotches then, was it?'

Kgomo was not impressed by this, Mom says: 'So Mr Brydon, are you admitting to yet another case of driving under the influence?'

He had the old boy there.

'So basically I can never go to PE then?'

'Mr Brydon, you can get there in two hours.'

But is he allowed to get permission to vary these hours should he leave the magisterial district?

'I am thinking of leaving it permanently after this miscarriage of justice. It's a cause I wish to live for, but am also prepared to die for.'

'Yes, Mr Mandela, now you are discharged.'

He was granted leave to appeal, but he's not sure whether to take it up. He is going to ask old retired, and entirely pickled, advocate Ralph Schneider SC at the club whether he could do it. The only club out of his range in this regime may be the yacht club, as that hill apparently is a swine to walk back up.

It seems that the reason Megan's folks are having the tattoo 'M4life' done on their wrists is that Megan had some rare form of cancer that she has beaten. They had made a pact that if she beat it, they'd get the matching tattoos.

I google:
Is cancer also an STD?
Can you catch cancer from other people?
Victor Matfield twitter
SA's best cell contract
Oakley 2012 range, when out?

It seems that I am in the clear then.

That's quite enough parental issues for one day.

THURSDAY 15 SEPTEMBER 2011

I watch Tonga v Canada. I need to get into this World Cup.

I am shattered… that's three functions in five days.

Megan has even had to ask Bread to develop a booking enquiry form on the site, which goes live tomorrow. We are virtually booked out for December. We have expanded our bar staff with the rule being nothing under a nine.

It's been agreed that we start looking for an assistant for JB Inc. I am in danger of burnout. And my bench one rep max is dropping under 80kg for the first time since I was 21.

Is Megan now officially my betty? Not sure, but I do know that she is shweet.

In tonight's *Argus*, there's a panoramic picture from behind of a (fat) white lady walking on the Sea Point Promenade on a spring evening holding hands with a little black kid as a whole lot of seagulls take off as the sun sets. It's beautiful. The caption reads 'A lady and her son at sunset watch a flock of seagulls in a Sea Point sunset'. That's one thing you got wrong, pal. Whatever the kid is, he's not her son.

Unless it was PJ Powers.

FRIDAY 16 SEPTEMBER 2011

I arrive at a party we are doing for a wealthy pom in Fresnaye. There are a few of my old schoolmates who are all in banking and hedge funds and shit. At least now that I am also a CEO I'm not too skaam. Barry Burmeister is here. Haven't seen him since that fight at the Green Man. He works for Barclays. Not Absa, but Barclays.

'Fuck, Brydon,' he says as he grabs me around the neck. 'Tonight your liver is mine.'

'I am working, bru.'

'Not any more you're not, I am paying you.'

Later I'm talking to a few mates. Eppy from school is there, a chinless wonder who runs a fund called Scarecrow Capital – maybe cos he looks like one – and drives an Aston Martin. Our 'web designer' is there so that she can see what @igloo is like in action now that I have resigned myself that Twin Peaks is out of my grasp – deliberate pun.

We're all in a group with some freaks chatting and I say, 'So Eppy, what you up to?'

Megan pipes up with 'I thought your name was Alistair. Why does he call you Eppy?'

I bolt in with 'Because his surname is Epiminsky.'

Eppy develops, at the wrong time, a personality. 'No it's not, it's because I had an epileptic fit at sports day.'

Barry: 'That's right, in the long jump pit.'

'Oh ja, and he swallowed half of it.' I couldn't contain myself. Neither could Barry.

'Wasn't his only one. There was one at cadets.'

'And in Maths.' Barry is wetting himself.

Eppy leaves. Twelve years on and still running.

Megan leaves. Chicks.

But having monstered myself at the @igloo function I can report that decanting is a safe practice and key to more profits.

SATURDAY 17 SEPTEMBER 2011

A very good day. Other than the radio silence from our web designer.

I WhatsApp at 10.10am:
> Megan, sorry I teased Eppy last night but you don't know what a spaz he is.

I can see that her last seen is 10.20am so I know that she has seen it. Oh well, if she wants to be childish I haven't got the time. It's Boks v Samoa. True to form, one of them tries to decapitate Jean and another punches Brussouw and gets sent off. #justice.

But that's not the main thing. The *Weekend Argus* has a feature in which I, errrr, feature: 20 YOUNG CAPETONIANS TO WATCH. Stevie, 3G and Gaz the Other Spaz keep me on a short leash, and yet:

Jason Brydon, 29 – (I know, I know) – is the driving force behind @igloo, the premium bar service company that's setting the trendy parties of the Mother City alight with their exotic mix of top brands, gorgeous bar staff and amazing ice bars and funky-lit ice structures. In the short space of a month they have made serious waves and if you haven't got @igloo for your New Year party you're simply not in. Brydon has also made a bit of a name for himself with his ability to mingle with his clients.

Well, last line aside, it's brilliant.

Scan and post. Twitter (both accounts); FB (both accounts) instagram. Let's get VIRAL!!!

SUNDAY 18 SEPTEMBER 2011

Buy the *Sunday Times*, but there's no back page any more. So I turn to the sport: after yesterday's win against Samoa, Bok coach/bus driver De Villiers has asked us to keep our (the fans') feet on the ground as we prepare for our likely quarterfinal against the Wallabies.

Don't worry, china, with you as coach, our feet are firmly on the ground. Feet on the ground? In fact they are somewhere in the underground parking. FFS, we only beat that motley crew of tribesmen 13-5. Our feet are, in fact, in Middle Earth, Snor.

We have to beat Namibia first, tjomma. In fact unless we get a real, white coach one day we will lose to Japan or the Cayman Islands.

MONDAY 19 SEPTEMBER 2011

Of course Dawesy has embarrassed us all by rushing off to a vigil outside parliament against the Protection of Information Act. Does he not realise that he's not doing any good, that the old white liberal has the relevance of a pair of garters on a desert island? The only thing that worries the powers-that-be is when a horde of their own turn up with pangas and knobkerries – not a whole lot of mountain bikes, plaid skirts, goatees and wire-framed glasses.

Anyway, each to their own, I always say.

The shareholders (3G, Stevie and I – Lech v Mr Wong still under review and the Pole is still chilled, as the production season hasn't got going yet) meet for a brainstorm. Over lunch. A long lunch. At Baia. Unquestionably the best langoustine in Cape Town washed down by the finest Hamilton Russell Chardonnay the company can buy. Stevie hires our waitress and is basically in like Errol Flynn at a 1920s party.

A significant point of the earlier (aka sober) discussion was our social media strategy. Facebook is so tired. We want to maximise Twitter. We want to drive up our numbers.

I point out that we need a big tweet or two.

'What's that?' 3G wants to know. 'What's a big tweet?'

I am inhaling a langoustine. Stevie helps out. 'It's a tweet that goes big, that just gets retweeted and retweeted. Any ideas, Jase?'

'Well,' my hands in the finger bowl, 'the obvious one is that Mandela is dead.'

3G wants to know what it has to do with our business. I see his point. Stevie is more measured. 'Well, we know that, he died not long after the World Cup – I think in September/October. They're just keeping him on ice somewhere cos they know once he goes *officially*, that's it. They will all be coming over our walls and not just for our washing, and even the ANC knows that's the end of the economy and there will be no Chivas or Breitlings for anyone. Honestly, Mandela's blood is on Sepp Blatter's hands. Even in death, Tata unites this country.'

I assume my MD role. 'That is an option, but maybe it's not very PC.' My side portion of the Patagonian baby squid arrives. Nice and tender. I send both my business card and compliments to the chef.

3G agrees a big tweet is basically free ad spend. And it works because we are almost running at capacity, but what we want to do is build a brand and just own the space. 'China, name someone else who is doing it. It's like chopping wood in the Amazon. It's ours to take. There are fucking floppies in the Amazon who have never seen a boat or a car, boet. Well, these okes haven't seen anything like @igloo. And we're coming. We're coming fucking hard. With our bulldozers and forklifts and chainsaws the size of small Karoo towns. It's happening. Get used to it or fuck off back to the jungle.'

Honestly it was like something out of *Braveheart*.

The big tweet. I suggest something like KFC is poisoning white people and they have an asbestos-laced chicken for white customers. Stevie thinks it may run and that it may be true because he feels like Pik Botha the morning after a State Dinner after he has a Streetwise5. 3G again raises the thing about relevance to @igloo.

'But,' I point out over a soupcon of Mississippi crab (landed last night), 'it will get our name out there.'

'And in the high court.'

I think my thing that I saw on Facebook about Caltex putting something in your car's engine when you fill up so it breaks down after a kilometre and they hijack you may have the same issues.

'What about, "just seen Colin Farrell... in Beach Road".'

'Next thing some douche googles and finds out he's filming in Miami and then we look sillier than Jonty Rhodes' hair.'

Fair enough. We agree to work on the big tweet and order mains.

TUESDAY 20 SEPTEMBER 2011

Mr and Mrs Matthew Booth are on *Top Billing* again. I can't cope.

I have to start thinking of finding my own place. What if Costa gets sick of the revolting Greeks and comes back to *Citta del Capo* (Greek for Cape Town). Obviously there are some issues around the Scirocco (fixable) and the Spitfire (slightly trickier as he took a sabbatical to build it. I mean I couldn't exactly walk into Toys R Us and order another). The Weber lid? Small fry. Don't bother one of Cape Town's 'Bright Young Things' with Weber lids.

I start looking for somewhere to rent. Why is any effing rental house on the Atlantic Seaboard in Cape Town 'a villa' – if you want to buy it, then it's a house. But if you want to rent it, it's a fucking villa.

No longer am I going to refer to this abode as Costa's house. Henceforth it shall be referred to as my villa. I know I sound like that long-haired drummer from Queen, but why not?

WEDNESDAY 21 SEPTEMBER 2011

From: Megan Baker <mabaker@bread.net>
Date: 21 September 2011 at 07.37am
To: Jason Brydon <MD@igloo.com>
Subject: the App

Hi Jason

I have attached a dummy of the app. It is 90% functional so you can play around with it and see if you like it.

As you can see, as per your request, in the Staffing Solutions section, we have gone 'big' on Sasha-Lee. I trust that will be to your satisfaction!

Please let me know as I need to book it into final phase dev as we are busy doing the new 5FM app.

Regards

Megan

Colder than a dead coelacanth. All because of a nickname we gave some freak at school? Really?

Muggs thinks it's because I didn't go after her. I can't work it out. She storms out, yet I am in trouble for not stopping her. She wanted to leave and because I didn't fling myself on the bonnet of her Mini and clutch onto the windscreen wipers as she screeched along Kloof Road, I am toast. Sorry, don't get it.

Luckily I didn't tell her that my favourite Paralympic event, the one worth setting an alarm for (like I did in Beijing) is the T20 – that's track events with mental deficiencies. It's the one where they almost forget what they're there for, stop running, have tantrums, wave to the crowd between hurdles, stop and take off their spikes. Watch it in London 2012. Trust me.

From: 'Jason Brydon' <MD@igloo.com>
Date: 23 August 2011 at 11.16am
To: Megan <mabaker@bread.net>
Subject: RE: the App

Noted

Cheers & regards

Jason Brydon
Managing Director
@Igloo
Liquor solutions
www.@igloo.com
fb; t:@igloo
Download our app! Visit www.@igloo.com

I think some airtime from M is not a bad thing.

THURSDAY 22 SEPTEMBER 2011

International Rhino Day, again, I think, if there are any left.

Some game ranger chick was on Cape Talk (listen to it when 5FM goes all kwaito) complaining about the fact that some sort of feral cat was about to go extinct and nobody cared less.

Get a bracelet, sister. Get some awareness. Get a sexier cause than some cat.

Rhinos v streetkids – Dawesy is always banging on about it. That we are more worried about some dinosaur leftovers than human beings. I keep telling him – when he says what about the poor children sleeping on the street in their oversized jerseys and glue-filled milk cartons? – that in a few years' time there will be far more of them and no rhinos. Besides, try and sell a street-kid bracelet.

SA trounce Namibia. Given that the team is made up of 13 players, nine over 40 and that the rest work as dune guides, it isn't unexpected. I tweet Peter de Villiers to assure him that my feet remain firmly planted on the ground. Turns out it's a parody Twitter account.

I spend the afternoon being driven around by a fag in a jag called Greg Bax looking for a villa or a loft to hire. Reminds me a bit of Pieter-Dirk Uys but claims to be from Mauritius. I think he also has to wear male incontinence nappies. Not sure. But we don't find anything. I suggest working on email going forward and jump in Costa's outside shower the second I get home.

FRIDAY 23 SEPTEMBER 2011

I see Dave Peters, my old boss from 2Dye4 Paints, at the Engen by the Waterfront. Short-sleeved shirt and tie. He is the prick who told the whole of sales and admin that I was as 'useful as a turnip'. He's coming into the shop for an egg mayo, half of which will stay in his moustache for a day or two, as I walk out with my protein bar. The chat is awkward. He still calls me Brydon like he is my old headmaster when he was only Regional Sales Manager: Western Cape (yes, I know it stretched into the Eastern Cape, as far as Uitenhage). But I'm nobody's fool. I wait as he walks out the shop with his sarmie and Coke Zero towards his Jetta. I intercept and screech up – in the Q7 – and give him my card.

'This, this, Dave,' and I gesture around me and at the card, 'is largely thanks to you, tjom.' And speed off.

After all, at that one disciplinary hearing (my final written) he was racist. He referred to me as a 'tragic waste of white skin'. Burn motherfucker, burn!

On second thoughts, I stop. I wind the window back down. 'Send me your CV, pal.'

What a perfect start to a weekend.

We all meeting at Bascule Bar for a few Pepsis. And going to take it from there and see how far we get. Lots of talk of Mavericks. Shhh. And if you are in black Tods loafers, like *moi*, you can get pretty damn far.

The only flaw is that I know, like *know*, like I can feel it, is my weight. The truth is that this corporate lifestyle is causing some decay to the temple. I really could benefit from some portion control.

SATURDAY 24 SEPTEMBER 2011

It's 2.30am and I am in love. With Taťána. From Belarus. Spelt just like, and not dissimilar, to Taťána Kuchařová, the Czech Miss World 2006/7.

For those ignoramuses among you, Belarus means White Russia. So she looks nothing like anything out of *Borat*. She is blonde and she is amazing.

The capital of Belarus is Minsk. What a name for this Minx.

I need to rescue her from this human flea market. I know she likes me. She has talked to me most of the evening. It costs the GDP of Togo, but she doesn't have much choice. She is in semi-slavery, the owner has her passport and he makes them do chores and is, I can only assume, a very cruel man. Like Lukashenko, the Belarus president, who is known as the last dictator in Europe (if next to Poland is Europe). Well him and Berlusconi.

I google more about Belarus whilst she has to go upstairs for a 'pvivate' dance with some bonehead in chinos. 'Don't vorry, Jason, I von't be long,' she purrs as I do my damndest to prevent it to no avail, flashing, again, the @igloo platinum card. Apparently it's the rules. If I want her exclusive, that's another 4K and I think even Steve 'No Limits' Fourie would have an issue with that.

Belarus has 30 state banks and one private (go and see how that works, Juju, and why my Taťána has had to come to the bottom of Africa and have R100 notes stuffed in her G-string by okes with names like Marius and Hennie). Women hold more jobs than men and they still have the death penalty. You won't get a screwdriver up your rectum in your driveway in a botched hijacking there. The tennis star Victoria Azarenka is from there. She is as hot as Anna Kournikova, but she can play tennis.

The 'after hours' is expensive, says Stevie. He reckons you're supposed to negotiate directly with the 'dancer'.

'Not in my experience, china. These okes are all over them,' pointing at the heavy set dweebs in black.

I have her number. Her White Knight is ready to rescue her.

I look at Stevie and we both wonder how this little tab is going to get past Gary. Monday's problem.

It's National Braai Day. It's not really called Braai Day – it's actually Youth Day. But everyone braais. I want to invite Taťána for a topless (in all respects) Weber.

It's kak with a public holiday on a Saturday as you don't get the Monday off. But the upside is @igloo has their first Sunday night booking.

SUNDAY 25 SEPTEMBER 2011

'The number you have dialled does not exist. Please redial carefully or consult directory enquiries.' Those are the clanging chimes of doom, the ominous words that greet me as I dial T's number on her day off.

I must have written it down wrong. Or those bastards have seized her phone.

I shall have to go back. Or maybe I'll phone *Carte Blanche*.

We do a function for France Cortes, the darling estate agent of the Atlantic Seaboard. His name is France, his personalised number plate on his Jag is FRANCE C (pronounced Francie), he has an old Rolls and wears white slacks, but is straight. Hard to believe, but true.

172

We sting him for 35K to do a full-size ice model of his pride and joy, his 1972 Rolls-Royce Silver Shadow, and Shafiek and his boys in Salt River pull out all the stops. But he has a proper diva tantrum.

'It looks like a Hillman Vogue. Or a Soviet-era Riva.'

I take umbrage. 'It's based on the model you gave us, Mr Cortes.'

'So where's the fucking Spirit of Ecstasy?'

'We just supply alcohol, Mr Cortes, however if our client…'

'Sprit of Ecstasy is that Flying Lady on the front of the car, Jason. Your name is Jason, isn't it?'

'It must have melted.'

'Melted. Why the fuck am I paying for an ice model that has melted?' He is puce, almost deep purple with rage.

Really, I am going to have Shafiek's Middle Eastern balls for this. In a jam jar.

'I think if you cooled down a bit it may slow the melting process… haha.' That doesn't seem to help so I keep trying. 'Just a little ice-breaker.'

He is still venting. 'Besides there is nowhere to sit in it.'

I am gatvol. You asked for a fucking model – not to drive the fucking thing.

We knock the price down to 20K and Lech saves the day a bit by lighting the exterior a deep maroon.

Two hundred people at his villa in Fresnaye and you look *down* on FW's house. We graft hard that night. The new icemen Todd and Liam are awesome. 3G and Stevie have kept the stock of ice maidens world-class, led always by the unflappable, top-heavy Sasha-Lee. As we wash away with hot water what's left of the Silver Shadow, I ask her if she would like to go for a drink. I am pretty hammered at this stage. But given that I have landed a 150K 50th in Clifton in October (always a tough month), I feel I can kick back a bit.

She looks at me like I landed a toy UFO in her spritzer. 'What for, Jase?'

'What do people normally go for drinks for? Cos they're hungry?'

'Jason, I have a boyfriend. Mark. He kiteboards.'

Rather that than 'he kickboxes'.

'I didn't mean it boy/girl, Sash.'

'Well, if it's work you wanted to discuss, we can do that now.'

'Oh jeez. I meant just as mates.'

'No such thing with someone like you, Jason.'

Oh FFS. This chick must learn to respect my position or she is outta here, no matter how pert they, are how much they 'sit up', no matter how much clients love her. In fact I think its time @igloo brought her, not 'them', down to size a bit.

MONDAY 26 SEPTEMBER 2011

A mixed bag to start the week.

Firstly, Abstinence, who seems good at abstaining from some things (work, ironing, the gym) and not so good at abstaining from other things (white bread, the fridge, 440 winks), has shrunk my brand-spanking new Ted Baker pullover (Stuttafords Canal Walk R1 599).

I SMS Costa, who is probably busy throwing stones at Greek riot police.

> Costa, I cant go on with Abstinence any longer, its me or her boet.

> Jason she has been with us 20 years. I was very concerned to hear about my car window and my plane. Sort it out, buddy.

Firstly I am not your buddy. Secondly, it's a *toy* plane. Thirdly, you may have had her for 20 years, but I can't do another 20 minutes.

But the great news is we're doing Schalk Burger's party at the end of October. Lekker, Schalla. It seems 3G's mate Rod knows Schalla's missus and told her what we do. I don't want to bother him now during the World Cup, but I save his number. I must say I scroll down my contacts on my phone a few times – seeing the name Schalk Burger in the Jasonator's iPhone is shweet.

I love Schalliano.

I have arrived.

So much so that I think I've shot up so fast I have to skip the Vespa step. A while ago it was cool. But what MD of a growing, iconic brand buzzes around on a Vespa like the *Men's Health* art director?

TUESDAY 27 SEPTEMBER 2011

It's 50 years since *Dr No* came out. If it was released now it would be a film about Sasha-Lee. It seems they may move filming the new Bond movie, *Skyfall*, from India to Cape Town because the Indians won't give them permission to shoot on their railways. We still have railways, I think. There's the one that goes past Muizenberg to Simonstown. Or is it because of terrorism concerns? I wasn't really listening properly. But ever since Pagad got packed off to Pollsmoor, we don't have any of those issues.

They say that brown fat is much more attractive than white fat. So I head out in the Q7 to Table View, where nobody will know me, to a sunbed. Proper name: solarium.

The receptionist's name is Liezel. I tell her it's my first time. 'On a sunbed,' I hasten to add, but the humour is lost on her. I guess that's why she is here and not at Deloittes or working on SALT (SA Large Telescope project). 'Of course, it wouldn't be my first time…' but it's like bowling to Geoff Boycott. She just dead bats everything.

Thing is, it's not quite a sunbed. You stand in some silver tube with hundreds of lights. You feel like you could lift off at any second.

'I haven't done this before.' I don't want to mention the word fat cos I'm sucking in and if I do mention it she'll look at my burgeoning midriff. 'I just prefer brown skin to white – oh jeez, not like that, well, I didn't mean like that – of course I would, but you know what I mean – I'm very open-minded…' It's useless. Liezel, you see, is coloured.

Into the booth, Brydon. I hope she doesn't fry me and I come out looking like that old thing from *Something About Mary*, or the Peking Duck. Or, worse, orange like Roger Moore.

Drinks do at the Museum. A cool 22K profit for a Tuesday in September.

Jed looks at me as we set up (just lights, no ice because of health and safety blah di blah di blah). 'Christ, Jason, you been on the Med today?' Winks at Sash. 'Or have you been in the Tan Can?'

Do another crunch, you vacuous fuck.

Dead man walking. Dead man walking.

WEDNESDAY 28 SEPTEMBER 2011

> **@jasonator069**: If they trying to sell you clothes why do they make the lights in the trying on rooms so bright and the mirrors make you look so fat and short? You don't want to buy anything. #justasking

> **@dawesman @jasonator069**: blaming the mirrors JB?

THURSDAY 29 SEPTEMBER 2011

I spoke to Slug, now our paid-for (less 40% – mates' rates) official legal advisor. He agrees that Sasha-Lee doesn't really have a case against me. There is *no* evidence that I ever said she's not the only piece of silicone in town. And I never ever groped her behind the flamingo ice statue. It's just my word against hers.

And I never said anything about going to Tiger Wheel and Tyre. And if I did it was about me needing to have the tyres on my Golf checked and the alignment done – it was nothing to do with replacing her like she alleges. So she can CCMA away all she wants. #admin

FRIDAY 30 SEPTEMBER 2011

Hey hey, it's Friday.

Megan and I are WhatsApping again, but not naaiing yet. Still, it's progress. I ask her to add the line 'your best POP UP bar experience' on the site.

@igloo now has over 2000 followers. I am desperate that at some stage we trend. My gravestone must read one day: 'Here lies Jason Brydon, 1980 to 2030 (I am checking out at 50 – not going to steal other okes' oxygen and rates and taxes), HE TRENDED.'

I haven't been onto the Book for a while. Couple of reasons. Can't say I am too wild about this new timeline thing. RIP The Wall. Then everyone seems stuck in that 500-1,000 friends barrier. I even friend-requested Sash's boyfriend Mark – he is keeping me hanging, the doos – but I can't get through that 1K mark. It's got irritating features that piss people off. I don't want to know, even though *I* do it, that Muggsy was at OR Tambo airport. Who gives a continental?

Too many chicks are posting cats and babies (too many okes as well) and babies have become more prominent as we slide down from 30. Why does every fucking oke who has a lightie have to make them their screensaver. What's wrong with a massive wave at Mavericks? Or Scarlett Johannson in a bikini on a beach in Montenegro?

The newsfeed is a hotch potch. I have a beheading in Libya, the Port Alfred Open, Remember Kurt Cobain, The Sharks team to play WP, Natalie 'Bulbis' update, in no particular order in my news feed. Plus Mich posted something on my timeline about some pets fundraiser called a Wiggle Waggle or something silly. So I took it off and now she's all miffed.

Then it's also risky. I was doing some research on Jasmine, this new ice maiden, for work purposes. I didn't want to friend her obviously – that would be weird – but my mistake I 'liked' her selfie at the Locnville concert. Now she can see I liked it. She can see I have been there.

Fuck. Zuckerberg is busy porking it.

Massive function for @landroversa on Table Mountain Road this evening. Building an iced Defender. And nobody can complain if it's not in shape because I will tell them it's a fucking Land Rover.

I ask the brand manager, after a few Pepsis, if a white male has ever bought an Evoque. She seems offended.

SATURDAY 1 OCTOBER 2011

Rocktober. That's what it used to be. Now people are being encouraged to take the month 'off'. In other words don't booze. That's hardly good for our business. Nor 1 For The Road, our safely home partners run by thirsty Joff Senekal, a nice piece of scum from the Bluff. I suggest to Joff that we should lobby other players in the booze space, from the bottle stores, the wholesalers, everybody, to stop this kak. It's not good for business.

Besides, sugar is the new tobacco. *Not* alcohol.

Richard Burton died from a brain haemorrhage, Oliver Reed from a heart attack. And when Pik and Koos Kombuis go, I guarantee that it won't be from cirrhosis of the liver, so everybody just chill.

I get a new keyboard for my new iMac. There is a sticker on it, a massive big yellow one with 'Warning' big and bold on it.

WARNING! KEYBOARD USE MAY BE ASSOCIATED WITH PHYSICAL INJURIES. IF YOU EXPERIENCE DISCOMFORT OR PAIN STOP USING THE KEYBOARD AND CONSULT YOUR PHYSICIAN. PLEASE SEE PACKAGE INSERT FOR ADDITIONAL INFORMATION.

Really?

Sharks lose to WP. It's kak to be in CT when that happens.

SUNDAY 2 OCTOBER 2011

Chill at home with a Vida, two croissants and the papers. Then a Prostituto (from Col'Cacchio, not Heaven's Angels Agency!) and some sushi from Minato. Four Coke Zeros and a Woolies chicken. Some to the dogs, including the bones. It's not like I'm going to be inconsolable if Gary Cooper goes on a drumstick.

The searches/websites I visit today are:
www.news24.com/rugbyworldcup
www.breitling.com
google/sportsillustratedswimwear

www.lubetube.com
www.Rugby365.com
www.iwc.com
www.redtube.com
www.audi.co.za/newcarsales
Investec Private banking/login
www.mavericks.co.za/meetthedancers

Compare this to last year, as extracted from my warning letter from Dave Peters before the first disciplinary:

• Facebook
• Vodacom SMS interface
• Twitter
• Career Junction – good idea, by the way. This, I encourage
• Gumtree – cars section
• Google – Ted Baker shirts online ordering
• Autotrader
• Enjoyenergy.com – apparently this is a 'performance related site'
• 24hours of freedom.com – ditto
• Rugby365

And you can see how much I have grown in less than a year.

Gumtree? Autotrader? Wow. When days were dark and friends were few…

Speaking of the Dark Ages. Phumeza… Phumeza? Really, Jason. Really? Mind you, in some ways, it's a reflection on just how small the stock pool is in a small town. Brings out the worst in you. Still, she is a nice girl. Just never thought that I would be the type of guy to catch 'Jungle Fever'.

MONDAY 3 OCTOBER 2011

We won't give the Dalai Lama a visa because China has Zuma's testes in a vice. Some illiterate spokesman was on the radio to say that we didn't refuse his application – he actually withdrew it. But 'his people' say that he withdrew it because it was going to be rejected. Go figure. It's a bit like al-Qaeda saying they didn't kill those okes who jumped out of the Twin Towers to avoid burning to death.

Way I see it: doesn't matter that he withdrew it. It's like in cricket. If you're batting and nick it behind and the bowler appeals and you walk before the ump gives you out, you are still out. Doesn't mean because the umpire didn't actually raise his finger that you're not out.

I must say I don't see the Dolly Lama as much of a threat. It certainly seems to have upset Milnerton's most famous resident and the darling of the white liberal set, the Arch, our most adorable house native. My dad says we've all forgotten a few years ago when he was regarded as the devil incarnate, but now that he tells Zuma to behave himself, and says the ANC are like the apartheid government, we all love him.

94.5kg. I cancel Megan tonight. She can't see me like this. And it would be odd if I kept my new Gant Oxford on wouldn't it?

TUESDAY 4 OCTOBER 2011

Another *Idols* winner. Zzzz.

We have brainstorm at Haiku over the Groote Post Chardonnay. How we can grow @igloo, given that we are basically red-lining as it is going into season?

The following was what we loosely agreed, before the sake shots.

INTERNALLY:
That I am brilliant at what I do, but that (a) I am swamped and (b) detail/admin is not my forte. And, frankly, not what I'm paid for.

That I will employ a (much-needed) PA, although I see in Stevie's notes she is called an Office Administrator. *Action: SF.* (Surely I should employ my own PA to ensure fit?)

That we look to have an ops manager who can run some parties. Steve thinks it should be a male. But there is a case for Sasha-Lee. *Action: SF.*

That we look at containing some of our fluid costs, such as T&E. Travel and Entertainment. Gary, inappropriately, described it as something last seen in the dot com boom. We explain that we are growing a brand, not just a balance sheet. Well, as regards T&E, given that nobody has been further than Somerset West, this is more entertainment-based. Nobody orders dessert. In my case literal and figurative belt-tightening. This meant missing out on their amazing banana crepes. *Action: SF.*

EXTERNALLY:
We want to roll out @igloo in other cities. To be honest more a defensive strategy than an offensive one. And we all know what the best form of defence is – ask the All Blacks, not the Springboks.

We think Joburg may be out of our league for now. For one, I hate it. No surf. Too close to Hayley and maybe, just maybe, a bit big for us. I don't want Mark Batchelor coming down the complex path with a 5-iron.

PE? No – not trendy enough – there are five times the amount of Vidas in Mauritius and Ghana than in PE. To them Mad Dogs clothing is it, so that's out.

The answer: Durban – my town of birth. The Jasonator is going home. They try hard there, but just cannot get enough cutting-edge stuff. There is a good party scene, but very little clue. *Action: JB.*

Then it's off to &Union to get ratted.

WEDNESDAY 5 OCTOBER 2011

A BLACK DAY ACROSS THE GLOBE. And not only because the Jasonator is man down (with acid reflux, after following through on a fart).

An icon, Steve Jobs, has died (of AIDS).

What about iPhones 6 through 8? I'm sure before he died he must have finished the 5 and was probably half way through the 6, but after that?

> **@jasonator069:** sad day. so I suppose if one looks on the brightside, maybe the next ipad will have a USB port. #hereshoping #shotsteve

More insensitivity charges from some of my more sensitive followers (now 210). So bounce back with:

> **@jasonator069:** The man had 1 080 parody twitter accounts, Obama only 600. #respect.#shotsteve #RIPSteve

THURSDAY 6 OCTOBER 2011

Hangover gone. 18 hour-er.

I look at the minutes that Stevie did from our 'breakaway'.

It is agreed that we will be rolling out in London. Part of our marketing strategy is to brand a few black cabs and paint them so they look like they're made of ice. You're allowed to do that because Boris Johnson, Lord Mayor of London, mild genius and prominent philanderer, says it's OK to adorn the black cab.

We then thought about using Jordan (aka Katie Price), as the face (and chest) of @igloo-uk and to be our celebrity as maiden Jordan, or asking Kevin Pietersen if we can use his wife. Stevie's boet played Natal B with him till quotas forced him to go to England and *is sure* we can organise her.

Kate Moss, with all of us consenting, is not regarded as someone who could be a brand ambassador for @igloo-uk. You would be better off sticking a skeg on her, waxing her and popping her on the roof of the A3 and taking her down to Jeffrey's.

I notice the London plans, which include the directors attending Chelsea-Man U at Stamford Bridge and Robbie Williams live at the London Palladium, are not minuted. Johnny Clegg is also playing at the Hammersmith Odeon, but I wouldn't go to the nearest Woolworths Food to watch him, let alone the Odeon. Must say, he is a fit fuck.

These plans were hatched at Orphanage. But officially dehatched in the morning. To me this is a bit like trying to put a baby chick back into an egg once it's hatched. The idea is out there and with a CEO like JB at the helm, it's game on brother...

FRIDAY 7 OCTOBER 2011

We're doing an adidas function tonight. Would rather be doing Puma, but hey, their rand is the same size as Puma's.

Book my Durban trip. I know it's small things, but it is a real treat not having to log onto Mango, Kulula, 1time (a.k.a. Last Time) or Velvet Sky or whatever, compare prices and taxes, fly at funny times with trainee (black/woman) pilots. I go straight onto SAA and book it. Boom boom.

I choose SAA over BA. Not because of the air 'hostesses' on SAA, that's for sure – they sometimes get stuck in the aisle. But because I want to support the national carrier because the better it does the less rates and taxes I will have to pay to bail it out and pay their CEO.

I'm in a good mood and for some reason feeling a little bit sheepish about having never walked Ferris and Gary Cooper since Costa left. At the moment his villa is the only villa I have, so maybe a tweeted pic of me with the dogs in a park would really boost Greco-South African relations.

I load the runts into the boot of the Q7 and cruise down to De Waal Park where the Parlotones are playing on Sunday night – as a much needed alternative to the hummus-heavy hell that is undrinker-friendly Kirtsenbosch. Never been back since I fell into those lesbians' tzatziki and kotched in Lady Anne Barnard's bath.

I know you're meant to scoop, but I forgot to bring anything for these pooh factories. So I don't know where to look when Ferris Bueller starts offloading a steaming pile near the pond. I walk the other way as fast as my shot knees will carry me, dragging Gary Cooper backwards.

Some trendy type with a tweed jacket, shorts and smart black shoes without socks, but with a basset, Twisp and Starbucks travel mug pipes up, 'Hey, bru, isn't that your dog?'

'No,' which we all know is technically 1,000% true.

'Bru, I saw you arrive with them, bru.'

'Just looking after them for someone else, bru.'

'Who, bru?'

I don't know why I say this, it is just a first-to-mind thing.

'Arno Carstens, bru.'

'Bru, I know Arno, bru, lives over there, bru, when he's not being big in Belgium, bru, and those aren't his dogs, bru.'

#awkies

Trendy bru isn't shutting the fuck up. 'You know what to do, bru. Bag it, bru.'

Ferris is just adding a twirl to his heap and waddling off.

'Ja, sure, bru.' Again, a slip between brain and lip. 'Course, bru, nice meeting you.' Trendy guy looks at me like I have just pulled down his mom's pants. I disengage and head to Ferris' produce. I pretend to fumble in my Pringle (R3,999) windcheater for the non-existent bag. I kneel down. I sense trendy doos and one or two others watching. But I can't look around because then I'll look as guilty as Glenn Agliotti. Literally all that I have is my Harrington's Dry Cleaning slip for my Fabiani blazer and a Funny Money page of jokes that cost me 50c at the Waterfront robots.

Situation.

Anyway, after I've washed my hands, I'm chilling, WhatsApping Megan, when this absolute belter with a cocker spaniel walks past. 9.25/10 – and that's daytime in a park in flat trainers. Imagine her at night, dolled up and me with a few Fanta Grapes in me. That could be off the scale.

Downside (as there always is): she has a kid (whom she is speaking Afrikaans to) with her. Somewhere in the 4-8 range, not any older. He is wearing a green Naartjie anorak, if that makes any sense. But that's not the problem. The problem is his ears are at right angles to his head. He is like a fucking wind farm. I just want to take his mom and… well, eventually… shake her and tell her to get them pinned back. Please. Or he is going to get called 'Driekoppen' at school.

The kid stops to admire (sic) Ferris and Gary Cooper, who I think from the way they are walking must have shin splints. I suppose they haven't been out for a few months so their muscles (still to be found) must be getting used to it.

Mom wafts past with a broad smile (9.4) and a long linger of, I think, (if JB still has the touch) Acqua di Parma.

Hope springs… maybe she is just little Bakkies's aunt, or mom's friend, or au pair, but it's only in pornos that you get an au pair built like that – the rest are all part of the Mus species (mouse family).

But Erasmus (his first name – I know I know – but it's easy to get past when his guardian would give Cam Diaz an inferiority complex) confirms that the torso purchasing on some very long legs is in fact 'ma'.

'*Waar is jy op skool, seun?*' I ask him. He struggles with my accent (international), but tells me he attends Jan van Riebeeck. I'm surprised some toyi-toyers haven't had a hernia and changed it to !Chief Khoi High.

'*Wat is jou hond se naam?*' The spaniel is now running rings around Gary Cooper and Ferris, thus keeping mom hovering, ideally circling JB before she is forced to swoop. I think to myself that if I grab Erasmus's winkie she will come in fast, but that may shorten the relationship.

I WhatsApp Stevie while the dogs play:

> Mayday! Chick in De Waal park so hot that I will overlook the kid. For first two years at least.

'Dozi.' That's the dog's name. Good one for a spaniel. I go for the intel.

Softly, 'Does your daddy also walk Dozi?'

Erasmus replies in English. 'He doesn't live with us any more.'

'Oh.'

'Ja. He lives now with his friend Emma. Who he works with.'

God, how hot must Emma be? Just imagine.

SATURDAY 8 OCTOBER 2011

My love of dogs, children and cocker spaniels, in particular, has got me Yvette's number. I can get over the name very quickly.

I am obviously aware now that it's 'client insensitive' to have worn my Le Coq Sportif V-neck to the adidas function. I tried to point out to their rank average marketing chick the differences between the brands:

You are a German Company; they are French.

They are small; you are massive.

They are only retro; you are both.

You sponsor the Stormers; they sponsor Yannick Noah (he gets more tricks).

They are super trendy; you guys are more Shaun Pollock.

I really did not mean it like that.

But I cannot think straight, nor about the two functions we have tonight.

> **@jasonator069:** It's the Boks Australia in a World Cup Quarter Final – does it get any bigger than that?

> **@muggsymalone @jasonator069:** yip, a semifinal.

Haha, Muggs, haha.

SUNDAY 9 OCTOBER 2011

FUCK Bryce Lawrence. FUCK Peter de Villiers.

Australia 11-9 SA.

Get on the plane.

We don't need *De La Rey De La Rey, Sal jy die boere kom lei*? We need Louis Luyt – someone go and fetch him from Ballito to find out what the fuck happened here and have that horse thief Bryce Lawrence raped. Ideally by Zulus.

I am watching at Slug's. Lettuce collecting the coffee cups has just said 'it's only a game'. It *would* be her to say it. And before we've even heard from John Smit yet.

We're still at Slug's. On the Windhoeks. Stevie is trying to find Peter de Villiers's street address in Paarl. Things are... picking up.

I don't agree with Dawesy – it's not something straight out of the Darwin Awards. You know the Darwin Awards. It's where a good ol' boy with a name like Frankie-Bob puts his lil' brother Jimmy-Bob in a barrel with the words Funky Bunch sprayed on the side on top of a 300-litre mix of benzine and Jack Daniel's and sparks it up so Jimmy-Bob can get a nice aerial view of Rushton, Mississippi. Or the Malawian gardener who tries to clean the goldfish pond with the electric lawnmower, a.k.a. Deep Fried Man. Stuff like that.

My case is different – I haven't hurt myself – well, not yet. Will I repeat it? Probably not. Good party trick? Category C. Was it funny at the time? Fuck, ja. Is it killer? Hopefully not!!

191

So, after things picked up, then things kind of lost shape a bit. Muggsy ate some of his wineglass. Not to be outdone, I swallowed my Mont Blanc cuff links (R3,500). A good 2cm of platinum.

Like Peter de Villiers, we need an (as painless as possible) exit strategy.

MONDAY 10 OCTOBER 2011

Update: the cuff links are still on board. And there are 76,000 people on the 'Hang/Hate Bryce Lawrence' page.

I suppose everything else pales into insignificance compared to these. Including Gary le Weed's tantrum about us not factoring in tax for our employees. I know it's how they got Capone, but not how JB Inc will come tumbling down.

TUESDAY 11 OCTOBER 2011

Now that Schalla knows when he's coming home – home already – we can go firm on his party. I SMS him:

> Howzit Schalk, hard lines on the quarter. Its Jase Brydon from @igloo who doing the booze, ice and icemen and maidens for your party on the 22nd. Cant wait. Fuck Bryce Lawrence. Can I give you a call sometime to discuss. Your Biggest fan. Stan (haha – Jason)

Burger, Schalk:

> Sure, partner.

Partner? There. Saved.

From: 'Jason Brydon' <MD@IGLOO.COM>
Date: 11 October 2011 at 11.23am
To: Steve Fourie <steviewunda@hotmail.com>
'3G' <Baxboy7@gmail.com>
Subject: Schalliano

Guys

Quick one.

I chatted to Schalk – really and am going round to his pozzie tomorrow for a recce. @igloo the P in PARTY is now Preparation (and no longer Poes as we decided at the Hermanus stratplan). A is no longer Arse. The whole thing, as I told Schalla is Prep Ammo Real Time and Ys). There may be scope at the next breakaway to tighten up on this a bit.

His party will be in Newlands, old school rock, Eighties and no house. Offered him an ice Springbok sculpture, but he said it's cool.

Point is it's in the Burbs and there is quite of bit of Green Day and aKING in the music which is against our mantra.

Views? But it is Schalla.

Let me know

Cheers & regards

P.S. Gary is getting on my tits a bit. He told me on the phone that if this SARS thing carries on then he is out. I said go and knit another jersey, granny. I think that put her back in her box.

Jason Brydon
Managing Director
@igloo
Liquor solutions
www.@igloo.com
fb; t:@igloo

It's unanimous – we are brand sensitive – we're doing Schalla's.

> **@jasonator069:** nice chatting to my homies Schalk and @MicheleBurger1 about Schalla's World Cup, lovelife and the pardi that @igloo r putting together on 22 Oct. Pull in! #legends

> **@jasonator069:** sorry tweeps, there should have been a space AND a comma between love and life in my last tweet. And this is an exclusive jol, only pull in if you have THE invite #feelkak #sorry #liveandlearn

I haven't the toolkit to deal with the traumas of a day like this. Nor the other issues in my life. Besides, I am probably the only person I know who has made it not to have a therapist. It's the essential accessory, to be dropped into conversations, just like saying, 'I have a place in Hermanus'. I am going to phone Discovery and see how much they are prepared to cover in dealing with my ADD, PTSD and whatever else they will find. I'm going to point out that it will be cheaper for them to fund me some time on a couch than treat me for 40 years after I get a stress-related stroke and drool, have one hand folded inwards and slide into incontinence.

#nobrainer

WEDNESDAY 12 OCTOBER 2011

BBM is down all over the world. Bahahahaha. #toldyou

THURSDAY 13 OCTOBER 2011

It seems from the trial of his murderers that AWB leader Eugene Terre'blanche pulled down his labourer's pants. I must say that the leader of the Fourth Reich loses some of his 'mystique' when he goes after Philemon's charcuterie.

> **@jasonator069**: A girl was kidnapped, raped and burnt yesterday whilst walking to school. And it does not make headlines #refelectionofoursociety

I don't know why my hashtags aren't taking off. I want one to trend. Hell, before I die *I* want to trend (verb). In fact before 2013 I want to trend.

> **@jasonator069**: Lets hear how @dawesman is gonna blame this one on the dehumanizing effects of apartheid. The chick was going to school #moveon #stuckrecord

War declared!!

Dawesy phones. It seems he does not think that this tragedy should be used for a socmedia spat. Whatever. Chicken.

FRIDAY 14 OCTOBER 2011

How this evening ends is not going to come across well, I don't think, but the logic was sound. Really.

Stevie and I were discussing portfolios and how important is to have a balanced portfolio that encompasses the whole spectrum of risk and return. Your portfolio is built around the banker, the stock that you can rely on, from which you build everything else up. She is by no means a looker, any tenth of a percentile over 4.5 is a bonus. She must be 100% reliable, her own relationship status an irrelevance – as long as you can sext her at 2am – and there is a good chance of hooking up, but at the very least there will be a spicy SMS or two and a plan made. We're talking guaranteed yield. And with a few hours' warning the only issues are whose place and what position we're starting in.

Then there are the medium stocks. Higher quality, not as certain, but higher return. Not worth over-investing in. They're expensive shares that don't yield that much. More class, better management, but somewhat harder to forecast – these chicks are 6 plus and issue profit warnings. You can't have a portfolio full of these as they are neither guarantees nor Miss Denmarks. But you need to hold these for some diversity, to hedge a bit.

Then of course there are the high-end stocks.

These are the 8 or 9s – the ones that you focus on to the detriment of the rest of your portfolio (and oft a stark reminder as to the importance of having a banker even if she is a 42 waist). High risk, high return. It should be from this stock pool that girlfriends are sourced – here they can meet parents. The Blue Chip stock. A banker doesn't meet anyone other than your digs mate if you (are poor enough to) have one.

OK that's the overview. Where do I stand? I don't hold any Blue Chip stock. Nothing on the radar. Erasmus downgrades the belter from De Waal Park.

Neither tragically do I have a banker. Which is pure, rank irresponsibility, I admit. What about those lonely nights at the villa?

Those nights that you don't want to go out, that you don't want to suip, but still play a bit of twister.

I'm thinking of whether I can convert Megan from the web agency into a banker. Not sure she's up for it, but if she would, that'd give me something to build my portfolio up front. The problem with Megan, which does not fit well into my portfolio concept, is that she has the potential to become girlfriend material. She has a personality. Some stocks do defy the market – that's the market for you. If it was all entirely predictable there would be no market.

Anyway tonight, as part of this banker conversion process and moving her towards high-end (6+!) banker stock, I whip her down to Haiku. Fuck me: R1,290 including the Rickety Bridge Wooded Chardonnay, but excluding the 18% tip to some leech called Clinton. 10% is too tight, 20 too generous, 15 too calculated. I could have gone 20%. Anyway Megan and I hit Jackal & Hide a bit in Kloof Street and then taxi it up to the villa. We are fairly wasted.

So it comes down to the crunch. She gets onto the bed and sort of lies seductively like some purring sex kitten from the Playboy Mansion. I think. Well, assume.

I dim the lights. (Less out of romance and more out of concealing the 9-11kg of La Dolce Vita.) I slip off my Ted Baker brogues, Ed Hardy tee, G-Stars and Calvin Klein briefs. I'm naked. Then I hit on a plan. I slip down the passage and grab my CamelBak, the cycling hydration pack last used in the 2009 Argus. I chuck in about a litre of H2O, slip it on and head back to the bedroom.

She sees me, and bolts up like a cat that's put its tail in the toaster. Not because she has seen *me*, but because of what I'm wearing.

'Jason, what on earth is that?'

'It's my CamelBak.'

'I can see that. But why is it on your back?'

'Jeez. Megan can't you work it out. I know what's going to happen now, you know what's going to happen now. We've had a fair bit to drink and I don't want to be busy with you and have to stop because I have the droogies.'

She leaves. Chicks.

SATURDAY 15 OCTOBER 2011

Roger Goode and Flash Republic playing at St Ives tonight. So I book a room for Megan and me at The Bay Hotel (only hosted Jennnifer Aniston, Sir Alex, the hermaphrodite singer from Jamiroquai, Dolph Lundgren, Rio Ferdinand, the oke from *24* and now of course the Group CEO of @igloo). Why? Because I can, that's why. With Megan? Yip, because not much point in doing it alone, as much as I back myself to snare something on the dance floor at St Ives. Of course The Bay, like every other place in town, has a private beach club (a.k.a. the pool and the bar, but you must call it a Beach Club these days). We get lathered on mojitos (on the room – tomorrow's problem) and head across to St Ives. There is something about Tamara Dey. If she would lose the red hair. Like structurally, face wise, you reckon she is a flat 4, but the package is probably an upper 7.

After they've played *Twister* – 'I don't even know your name!' – repeat chorus 700 times – she is chilling at the bar with a caipirinha. I walk up to her.

I know what a caipirinha can do to a 90kg muscular male, let alone a 50kg waif of a singer.

So and so is not watching.

'Well done. That was awesome. Can I get you another one of those?'

Straightforward, simple, pleasant. No need for any more of those devastating 'weren't you also in a Bond movie?' lines that the Jasonator is revered for the world over. Of course delivered with a smile exposing my newly whitened teeth and an impish sense of humour. Another trademark.

She smiles.

Of course.

'Don't I know you?'

Told you. The igloo, the igloo, the igloo is on fire.

I give her an enigmatic, skew-lipped 'maybe'.

'You're the guy that weed on me at the Deadmau5 concert last year.'

Oh fuck. And that wasn't even a question. Was it her? I didn't recognise her then at all. Maybe she can actually look ordinary. It's a bit of an exaggeration to say I weed on her. Well, I didn't wee purposefully on her although I concede some Jurine may have hit her. Tamara Dey, of Flash Republic fame and the darling of the SA dance scene.

Marvellous, as Clint Eastwood would say. Marvellous.

What had happened was that Mich dragged me to watch this anaemic little Canadian DJ rat who goes by the name of Deadmau5. He would have been very Deadmouse were it up to me. It was at the Good Hope Centre and was packed with all those dooses flying on MDMA. I had quite a few draughts at the Dias Tavern to get myself up to speed. And some shooters. I was squeezed in so tight I could hardly move. Which in some ways was not a bad thing because it meant I didn't have to dance, but also meant you couldn't get to the toilet. So I took a chance and whipped the old J-schlong out there and then, figuring they were all tripping and watching deadrat…

Anyway, that's the background to Tamaragate. Not sure how Mich got home – never asked.

So that was that. Didn't really see the situation with Tamara as recoverable so exited stage right back to 3G and them.

That's my interaction with SA's self-styled Queen of Kwaito. She may have performed with Arno Carstens at the Elle Macpherson Intimates launch and opened for Groove Armada on their South African tour, but she also got hit by a J-Bomb.

Of course she leaves with 'And of course, I don't even know your name'.

I really feel like bliksemming Craig Massiv tonight. He is anything but. Chop.

SUNDAY 16 OCTOBER 2011

I really don't think this is my fault and possibly something that should be taken up with the manufacturers. I mean if they warn you not to drive a forklift after drinking this should be a warning, too.

I am hung and jaded so have two Beroccas and the full English (buffet – recommend it – Jeremy Irons did, too). The Beroccas are lifesavers and Megan and I head to the pool.

I go for a head-clearing dip after lying and watching the plebs trying to park and walk for the privilege of lying on Camps Bay beach, with its icy cold thundering water, crowds, litter and granadilla lollies that run down your fingers and get caked in sand. And you can't actually swim, if you wanted to, when you realise your body is kak.

I dive into The Bay pool. Obviously I am dehydrating after such a big night and treat myself to a little wee through my Hurley (who still does Billabong?) boardshorts, not realising that the Beroccas have turned the urine to a lumo orange, worse than Stoke City's away strip. Some Germans gasp and point. A Swiss moffie laughs. Megan heads back to the room.

So I'm just saying the manufacturers should put a little warning tag on their product stating it could light up the Wanderers. It's just considerate.

Well that's two urine stories in two days and that's quite enough, diary. Even if another happens, I am keeping shtum.

MONDAY 17 OCTOBER 2011

I think there is a stark warning in yesterday's *Sunday Times* for all of us and a reason why I'm switching to the 5:2 diet – stuff Noakes.

It's two days a week of limiting myself to less than 700kj and then the rest of the week you can eat what you want. And apparently weight falls off like a jellyfish on horseback. And it's much more palatable (five for the pun, Brydon) than a one-day-a-week cheat day.

The point being that this oke, Albert Buitenhuis, a chef from Pretoria (and that may be the problem), sick and tired no doubt of having his daughter stolen, tried to immigrate to New Zealand, but was bounced for being too fat. Even though he had dropped 30kg since he had been there. Apparently he would put a fair bit of strain on the New Zealand healthcare system. To be fair to those self-satisfied Kiwis and their nanny state, he would put a fair bit of strain on a front-end loader.

But the warning is there for all of us. When they start coming over our walls with cutlasses, AKs and bloodcurdling screams and we wanna take the gap to another Sanzar country, we had better be in shape.

I order the new Vibram barefoot running shoe online (R1,799) – for serious distance. #borntorun

TUESDAY 18 OCTOBER 2011

Meant to be going to Durban today to look at rolling out @igloo there, but bumped it back to Thursday. Was a schoolboy error to think of going early in the week. One, because what do you do on a

Monday or Tuesday night? It's not Ibiza or NYC. And two, because we can stay on and catch the Sharks/Bulls at the Sharktank.

CVs are pouring (pun) in for the new positions we've advertised. I worked through an agency. Some siff thing called Melissa made me take out the line where I asked that they send a photo of themselves. Says you can't do that any more.

From: 'Jason Brydon' <MD@igloo.com>
Date: 11 October 2011 at 12.08pm
To: MelissaD@getyourgunrecruiting.co.za
Subject: RE: Your Ads

Melissa,

Quick one: I am the client. We are building a brand here, not an NGO. We can't have – to quote Paul Simon – 'a roly poly bat-faced girl' representing @igloo.

Cheers & regards
Jason Brydon
Managing Director
@Igloo
Liquor GIANTS
www.@igloo.com
fb; t:@igloo

It's hard to forget that I have been on the other side of the job-application fence. Not nice. Thanks Virgin Active.

WEDNESDAY 19 OCTOBER 2011

I am deep enough to know that I am shallow.

THURSDAY 20 OCTOBER 2011

Touchdown in Durban, home of the invincible (sort of, this season) Sharks. My first touchdown at King Shaka International. #originalname.

But honestly WTF were they thinking? Sure, it's got a Kauai, a Woolies and a Mugg, so it's world-class, but it's almost in Richards Bay. Were they trying to service both places?

Dad says it's cos it's closer to Zuma's traditional homestead.

Pretty messy unless you have someone to fetch you. Or, according to Rex, 'until Mad Mike Sutcliffe, the traditional-dress-wearing Durban City Manager, piss poor apologist, urban decayer, and the housewhite of the ANC, builds the Durtrain. © Rex Brydon.'

Rex has an unusual fascination with airports. Claims to have flown a lot in his day when he was in 'banking'. I suspect this statement contains some grey areas. I remember him going to a conference in Joburg, and going to Durbs a couple of times, once to Aunt Cheryl's (overdue) wedding. Well, if being a branch manager at Trust Bank is being 'in banking', then he is right. That was before Nedbank apparently 'poached' or 'headhunted' him, only to retrench him later because of affirmative action. Never mind the half jack of J&B that was in the second drawer down and the fact that he had never successfully managed to boot up his computer.

'That technology, that was the end of me. I banked the old fashioned way, man-to-man, handshakes, look a man in the eyes, build a relationship, ask him how the kids are. I refused to bank with a user name and password.'

I get into a taxi without a meter driven by a charra called Sydney Naidoo. He says the afs call him Sid Vicious because he doesn't take their shit. And if I had been in in one of their cabs, they would have ripped me off.

But he is helpful: 'While we at it, boss, can I hook you up with some of Durban's finest?' I'm not sure if he is talking about punda or poison, but I decline in case he is an undercover Hawk.

Charras are not bad people, just thieves… after all, *Ali Baba And The 40 Thieves*…

Is that also banned because of Schabir Shaik? Like Tintin (colonialist) and Noddy (racist and homophobic – just like Mugabe)?

We breeze from Richards Bay south past Ballito, home to Louis Luyt, and into Umhlanga. Thank God we're staying there cos that was 350 Durbs dollars – imagine what the Marine Parade would have been? Probably a grand!

I had booked Holiday Inn Marine Parade because it sounded nice and was near the Elangeni where the Stormers stay (if it's good enough for Schalla…) and where, Dad says, the typists of Smith Street used to queue up to 'do' Julio Iglesias in the '70s. But Stevie almost had triplets when he heard that I had us in at the Marine Parade (he is flying in later from Joburg where he had to go do some Nashua boreathon). He is far more in tune with Mad Mike's New Durban.

'Fuck, boet, nooit, boet. Not the Marine Parade, boet – there you step outside the hotel, they steal your fillings. Onetime. We only stay on the Rocks, china.'

Oh, ja, and Gaddafi got his pipes cleaned today. Goodie.

FRIDAY 21 OCTOBER 2011

Lots to report.

LiLo (Lindsay Lohan) as part of her community service is working in a morgue, but was late for work.

> **@jasonator069:** Massacre my chest at @virginactive Classic Kings Park, so badly I feel sorry for it – I want to donate it some money #chestfest

Durban girls compared to Cape Town? Pah! It's like stepping on snails up here, boys.

Our meeting falls through – not to worry – we get a good feel for the place – and we DOMINATE at Cottonfields in Umhlanga. I was in my brand-new Ben Sherman pink shirt and True Religion skinnies and marinated in Armani Code. Girls, girls, form an orderly queue.

SATURDAY 22 OCTOBER 2011

More hung than Jessie James. So I didn't come right unfortunately, but I wasn't after guppies or barbell, I was after yellowfin – and

KZN is fresh out, it seems. Vomit in my mouth probably didn't help much.

Sharks win their semi against the Cheetahs. *We are black, we are white, we are fucking dynamite!*

Too sick to drink before the game – one Debonairs Hawaiian, two Steers burgers, three Cokes and one Cream Soda, chocolate milkshake and two Energades, packet of Doritos and King Pie Cornish. And six Essentiale.

First Amstel afterwards tastes like human faeces with fish hooks, but I focus, power through and a couple of 'quilas later, I'm at Tiger Tiger.

SUNDAY 23 OCTOBER 2011

South African referee Craig Joubert helps New Zealand to the World Cup. Sexy Rexy thinks this as a good thing as, to quote, 'The French are just downright rude.'

It seems that mom and dad went on a camping holiday to Europe not long after they were married (*not* their honeymoon – that was Eight Bells near Mossel Bay where dad tried to hit a guy who he said moved a ball when he wasn't looking with a cue in the billiards room and ended up with six stitches). They were in Paris and he asked the way to the nearest Metro and (a) the guy could not understand him and made no effort to speak English, (b) the next lady he asked sent them to a further Metro with their backpacks, and (c) they *both* stepped in dog pooh on *two separate* occasions.

Why do we think we can get away with farts on planes?

MONDAY 24 OCTOBER 2011

Now that we've started 'finessing' a few things our margins are even better. Are you telling me some photographer's assistant is going to tell the difference between Tanqueray and Gilbey's, JW Blue and J&B or Grey Goose and Count Pushkin after four drinks? Answer: no!

So are we diluting? No.

Are we short-pouring the odd tot? Maybe.

Are we decanting? Yip. Look, the bloke asks for a vodka and he still gets one. That his company is prepared to pay R30 a tot is not his or our problem, is it?

Look it's not ideal to be in the garage with a funnel and pouring Gilbey's into a Tanqueray bottle, but two things:
• Discretion – the less that below-director-level know, the better;
• I always will be a hands-on CEO. Sleeves are there to get rolled up. #rememberstevejobsexample

TUESDAY 25 OCTOBER 2011

I have had some time now to reflect on this whole Megan thing. Sure, I misjudged it with the CamelBak. I accept it's not something out of the 'Seductor's Handbook'. But what Megan fails to understand is that being a banker is about, inter alia, rampant pragmatism. It is *not* meant to be something out of Mills & Boon.

Minister of Finance Pravin Gordhan says we must tighten our belts. Mine's two notches out but still very very tight.

WEDNESDAY 26 OCTOBER 2011

A cancer patient in Mpumulanga is raped by a male nurse. Everything in that is just wrong. Raping a cancer patient? Having cancer not bad enough? Male nurse? It's all just wrong.

The good thing now, with the success of @igloo, is that I can afford my own medical aid and, therefore, my own therapy. I think it's important to start some sentences, especially in female company, with 'my therapist says…' It just screams depth. First session today.

We're going to 'work on' Rex: his failure to watch the game that I scored that try against Kearsney; his treatment of my mother; and how Leslie turned out *skeef*. Oh, and my failure to commit to a woman and the destruction and shattered hearts that I leave vanquished, wailing in my trail.

I decided on a male one. Just to remove that element and save a female one the torment of realising her feelings for a patient, sorry, client, could end up compromising her career.

As it turns out I think my therapist, Jon-David (what – couldn't his ballies make up their minds?) may be battling those feelings-for-a-client issues anyway. He went to the German School so that's a sign. Jon-David? The one is the name of Jesus' number two (John the Baptist) and one is the name of the King of the Jews (David), and he went to the German school. Go figure.

Issues with therapy:
- Jon-David doesn't so much as offer me a glass of water let alone a Nespresso which he makes himself.
- After about 20 minutes my narcolepsy kicks in.
- He never tells me what to do. Just asks questions.

• Never talks about himself when I ask him shit.
• I always need a lie-down afterwards.
• I think going every week means it might come round too quickly. Maybe I must think of going monthly. Still can say 'I am in therapy'.

Starting the pre-Movember growth so we hit it with something more than what looks like some leftover Marcel's strawberry frozen yoghurt on my top lip.

THURSDAY 27 OCTOBER 2011

Costa wants me to take Ferris and Gary Cooper to visit their siblings – two other French Bulldogs – obviously – called William and Harry at some poof's place in Franschhoek.

I do feel a bit swak in that I've not exactly suffocated them with love and droëwors (especially since Costa cancelled the Woolies card). But I cannot abide Franschhoek. Its twee-ness, its pseudo Frenchness, its Poms in Panama hats playing boule. They celebrate Bastille Day, FFS, when nobody there even knows what happened on Bastille Day. It's French cos of the Huguenots who had names like Du Toit and Du Plessis but who 300 years later are just common or garden Dutchmen who think the French *'trek aan snaaks en ruik snaaks'*.

I am not going. I am getting my own spot anyway – I cannot do another week with the Cape Sloth, a.k.a. Abstinence. Plus I think the more distance and time I can build up between Costa and me is probably for the better. I am reasonably confident he will come after me about the Spitfire, unless I stage a break-in.

FRIDAY 28 OCTOBER 2011

Day before Schalla's party.

I do a venue check. Just part of the @igloo way. Schalk's Hummer is there so I'm hopeful, but he is out. Not at practice because Province are not in the Currie Cup final – bahaha!

We're doing an ice flying springbok, lit up in green and gold. Surprise for Schalla otherwise he may feel obliged to include the King Protea.

In other news Julius Malema stages a march and then fucks off to Mauritius. George Michael doesn't try to top himself or drive his Range Rover into Selfridges, but declares himself overweight. Just shows how anti-retrovirals can work, Manto.

I shouldn't have done it but couldn't help myself. I went onto Hayley's Facebook page. Mistake. I saw exactly what I didn't want to see. I was so brutalised by her post that I had to take two, yes, TWO, Stillnox to get to sleep. There it was.

> 'Thinking of taking my beautiful daughter Sapphire to Cape Town to visit her daddy, if we can find him.'

Stunning. Sms Jon-David and tell him I need an emergency session.

SATURDAY 29 OCTOBER 2011

A few petrols in me, I ask Schalla, my *tjom*, what colour his hair really is.

'This colour, partner.'

'So not highlights?'

He grabs me playfully (I hope/think) round the neck with his forearm, rubs my declining hair and says, 'Better red than dead.' #backfire

I don't think he's mad about the 'YsBok' as we called the sculpture, even though you could take Jäger shots through its tail. I think it's because its horns melted quickly and it started to look a lot more like a cocker spaniel.

Sick party though – who *wasn't* there? Duane Vermeulen was, Jean de Villiers was, Bryan Habana was. And Roxy Louw was – but, diary, frankly she no longer tops up the Jasonator's oil and water.

Sash was at her best – party was in Newlands and her nipples were in Claremont.

Schalk tipped me. Generous, but maybe he did not see our relationship as equals? #awkies

I pass out in his garage in his BM.

SUNDAY 30 OCTOBER 2011

You know the Brits invented concentration camps (in the Boer War) and the Afrikaners invented Affirmative Action – go figure...

My grandpa Ted, Rex's dad, was a major in the UDF. Not the mob who marched on Whites Only beaches, but the old Union Defence

Force. His unit was the Transvaal Scottish (sic). He was up north chasing the only decent jerry – Rommel – all over North Africa. Ted was English-speaking and when the Nationalists took over Ted was marched out the army and became the groundsman – sorry, Estate Manager – at St Johns. I think things must have really gone backwards there because nowadays it appears you need a 4x4 to get across the school grounds.

MONDAY 31 OCTOBER 2011

It appears the only thing that lasts shorter than an iPhone's battery life is a Kim Kardashian marriage.

From: Gary Baumgarten
Date: 31 October 2011 at 07.57am
To: Jason Brydon <MD@igloo.com>
CC: 'Stevie' <steviewunda@hotmail.com>
'3G' <Baxboy7@gmail.com>
Subject: Loan Account

Hi Jason

Just a heads-up your 100k funding is due tomorrow as per the partners' agreement. Obviously it is, as I explained on the phone before you went through another tunnel, vital for @igloo's cash flow in the short-term. Can you just send me your proof of payment so that I can get it in the system ASAP?

KR
GB

KR GB? WTF! Kind Regards... But then again 'GB's' email etiquette is low down on my list of worries. I think there's more chance of Ronald Reagan becoming US President again than there is of me coming up with 100K by tomorrow.

Sure, proof of payment. That's not a problem. Some (much underrated) Tippex and a scanner and that's easy enough, and that may buy me a couple of days, whilst we try figure out 'what the fuck Absa have done now'. But at some stage the money is going to have to appear in OUR account. The old JB might have gapped it, but not any more. Now I stand firm. Now I make plans. Now I front up. I have made – no, am making – something of myself and am *not* going to cock it up now.

From: Jason Brydon <MD@igloo.com>
Date: 31 October 2011 at 07.57am
To: Gary Baumgarten <Gb@GBINC.net>
CC: 'Stevie' <steviewunda@hotmail.com>
'3G' <Baxboy7@gmail.com>
Subject: Loan Account

Hi Gary

Sure, no problemo. Just waiting for it to come in from HSBC. Must just check with Guernsey.

Ciao

Jase

TUESDAY 1 MOVEMBER 2011

It was all a misunderstanding, but also a tragic reflection on the political correctness that is destroying our country. Steve Hofmeyr must feel like he is fighting a one-man battle against these forces of anality and PC-ness. And today I see it first hand.

I am thrown out of the Wynberg Girls' swimming gala. By some lesbian in a tracksuit and under a perm. Whether she had a whistle around her neck, escapes me. But by the time the 'debate' started, she was joined by some other concerned members of staff and apparently even more concerned parents.

The Scirocco was in much better shape. I had taken it down to the valet at the Waterfront which was poes expensive but better than having some clueless Af attack it with a bucket of drain water and a shammy. I have put some StaSoft in the back so it smells a bit more of lavender and less like a damp peed-in wetsuit that's been sealed in a greenhouse. Am going to mail Costa the invoice for the valet to try claim that back. I will sponsor the StaSoft.

Anyway, so I was driving past the school after gym – went to train in Constantia to see if I could see one of the Spencer sisters, but they were obviously on an off week. When I was walking out I couldn't open my shake so pulled at the top with my teeth and a few hundred mils of finest Evox protein ended up all over my vest. So when I got to the Scirocco I took it off as I was going straight back to the villa. Out, out damned suburbs…

Ja, but I can see the gala going on and think I may as well have a look and see if there is a hot mommy or two. Seems like a vibe. Perversely, and appropriately, I realise that I cannot go in vestless. So I grab my 'for emergency' Outrage of London duffel coat (1,200 GBP in 2008, as worn by Paddington Bear in tan) out the boot. It's black, it's mean and smart, but also warm. So for those days you are cold, or it rains unexpectedly or you just need to smarten up a tad, you haul it out the boot and Bob's your (straight) uncle.

I slip into the crowd on a bench and am watching these fine athletes parade their skills when some interfering cow next to me says, intently, 'You are too young to have a daughter swimming.'

I work it out. 'Now, mathematically, I may have. This is the high school, right?'

'Yes,' the lady who probably drives a people-carrier glares.

'So the youngest here would be 13, right?'

'Ja.'

'So, if I had her when I was 17…' I don't think this concept helps my cause. 'No, of course, I am not a parent.'

She keeps coming at me, her hair in a bun. 'So do you have a little sister swimming?'

This time I do the maths subtly. 'Nope.'

'So why're you here?' Her glaze is penetrating, so much so that I know, absolutely *know*, she is boring into the fact that my outfit is less than ideal. Expensive, *sí señor*, but less than ideal. Gym shorts, duffel coat and no shirt underneath.

'I am very interested in sports.'

Her husband, some defensive cunt in a pullover, leans across. 'This is not the Olympics, pal.'

'School sports.' I shrug, like, of course, what's your point, buddy?

The people-carrier-driver is back on her high horse. 'This is the Wynberg Girls' gala, hardly the sharp end of school sport. Did you watch the boys' one last week then?'

Why the fuck would I do that? I'm not bent. But I'm too wise to say that.

'No.'

That's when they call Mrs MacIntosh. The one in a tracksuit. She also demands to know why I'm there. I'm not as lucid in my argument as I could be as she has a cold sore bigger than Lesotho that is impossible not to look at. It's like when an average-looking chick shows off her cleavage and you say to yourself 'Don't look, for Pete's sake, just don't look' and the more you say that the more you do. And as Mrs MacIntosh was letting me have it, that cold sore was locking me in. And it would be so much more pleasant to be locked in by a cleavage than by a smouldering, blistering lunar landscape of a cold sore on a 75kg, 3ft9 PT teacher. If it's still called PT or PE, that is – probably called something like Human Movement Mechanics or some shit. When I was at school, admittedly Model C, we still had standards. (Model C is the one where we let a few, only a few, in.) We had standards literally and figuratively. Not like today where you basically have to be clinically brain dead, in fact medically in a vegetative state, not to get a matric. And if you smoke at short break, you have to make sure it's in a designated smoking area. Most schools have metal detectors now. Fact.

So when 'Mrs Mac', as her entourage call her, manages to prove that I do not know the name of one competitor or anything about the events, my interest in school sport is shown to be flaky. I am 'withdrawn' from the event. Well, asked to leave.

At this stage Mrs MacIntosh has raised a posse of hissing, snarling suburbanites. Some prickess shouts from the back: 'You should be ashamed of yourself!'

'Fuck off back to church,' is all I can come up with.

Fuck them. Honestly, fuck them. And Gary Bumgarden. And anybody who lives south, north and east of Buitenkant Street.

Just for watching a swimming gala?

Less said about the erection the better.

WEDNESDAY 2 NOVEMBER 2011

I shave the rest of my face and, voila, almost a moustache. I see Steve at gym and he laughs. 'Just had a carrot juice, sport?'

Things seem to have gone a bit egg-flied with Mr Wong. It seems he wants to have a say in the business, but he can barely speak English, just keeps saying @igloo is 'velly good'.

This is good for me as it takes the minds off my fellow dilectors and Gally the dog turd off my loan account 'position'.

We meet with Wong at our offices. You could blindfold the oke with dental floss. We have to become more BBBEEE or whatever it's called – they just keep adding Bs and Es – after some of our corporates have asked if we have BEE partners. And corporates are over 65% of our business. The market of parties run by wealthy hermaphrodites in De Waterkant and Constantia is probably 15%. The other 5% is random shit.

Here's the exchange that prompts the meeting with Wong. It's a WhatsApp conversation with Mike from Puma.

> Jason, you know we want to use you guys from the launch. But we need to know you are properly empowered. Its all about being unashamedly ethical Puma.

It's Puma Cement, not the clothes, so I am not too worried. But I reply.

> Mike, its funny you guys ask this. Schalk didn't.

Get back in your box, Mike from Puma, back in your box. You heard me, SCHALK BURGER didn't even ask, you did… Tragic little little man.

When Wong arrives we get off on the wrong head when I bow. Like I had seen on *Shogun* on the MGM channel on DStv. Wong now wants his son involved. The directors repair to Vida to come up with a plan. We know we're going to lose business if we don't make a BBBBEEEEE plan. Tragic? Yes. Good for the economy? Definitely not. Reality? Yip. Just like farm invasions.

3G declares over his Frappuccino that we have to find someone.

Stevie is in agreement. 'But I am not sure Wong was right. Haha. Wong was right. Ha. He was too light. Haha. Light? Right?'

3G says it would be better to get something more ethnic anyway.

I pipe up that especially if Little Wong, Wong junior, is to get involved.

Stevie: 'I think if we were in the chop suey business, or the rhino trade, the Wongs could add something. But not like this, it's not what we do.'

He then mentions that his dealer, a Nigerian (funny that) called Alfonse, may work. Alfonse didn't make his money peddling coke. Well, Skip Intelligence, as Steve calls it, because he says Alfonse dilutes it with washing powder. The fact that he had a runny nose in winter and soap suds came out his nose may have been a bit of a giveaway. It's what we called Stevie's 'cycle'.

3G sees the good in this: 'Shows that Alfonse is sharp, business-wise.'

'Maybe too sharp,' I point out. 'Plus shouldn't we keep the pleasure side of life away from the business side?'

'We never thought we would hear that coming out *your* gob, Jase.'

'Plus, I think don't they have to be South African to count?'

Stevie says they don't and that he thinks Alfonse could add some real value. 'And he does count.'

'How do you know?'

'Well the Beast does – he counts when he plays for the Boks.'

And when he plays for my Sharks, I think. It's a valid point from Steve. Beast is from Zim. Like Alfonse, he has lips that could blow up a hot air balloon.

Alfonse made his money out of having online love affairs using various aliases, one of which was Johan Kroukamp, to milk fat ladies out their savings. It made him a mint until that Bongani of *Carte Blanche* tracked him down to a café in Yeoville. So he came down to Cape Town and got into 'pharmaceuticals'.

We agree to meet him. He is tame, wily and not going to give us any gears.

On the way home my tummy tightens (not physically unfortunately) when I hear on the news that there is panic in Greece over some referendum and shit. I hope that doesn't mean Costa Cutter is thinking of heading back. This could present a problem, due to the following:

• The left rear light of the Audi (and some surrounding metal work).
• The Spitfire. WTF. What sort of man has a toy plane anyway? #ridic
• Gary Cooper and Ferris. They could do with a de-flea and maybe put on 3kg each when he comes back. (Going to put Nutella and duck fat in their food. And maybe Big Korn Bites.)
• The marks on the passage wall. Who knows? But can be painted over, I'm sure.
• The Weber lid. Got to get one that does not look brand new.
• Two items of his wife's smalls. Nuff said.

THURSDAY 3 NOVEMBER 2011

Hugh Grant, the floppy twit, has made his Chinese next-door neighbour, Tinglan Hong, pregnant and bought her an R18-million house. Who says money can't buy you happiness? I could have told Hayley (and Jeff) to get stuffed and just made them a once-off EFT to disappear out of the Life and Times of Jason Brydon Inc.

Meet with Alfonse. He is switched on. He is cool. His Twitter handle is @ngr. Very clever. Calls himself nigger, but says the Ngr stands for Nigeria. He drives an Audi with windows so dark the Pope could be inside dressed in lumo and you wouldn't see him.

He is interested. He wants to go legit. Says the market is flooded and he is sick of getting chirps from trumped-up white 30-somethings about his quality, or delivering to the housewives on the hill.

I have valued the business at one-point-two. According to Gary that is a 'preposterous' P/E of 12. I am not sure what any of that means.

I am going to charge Alfonse 100K for a 10% share in @igloo. A discount of 20% if he EFTs today. Genius? *Moi?* Not really…

Dawesy's says it's fronting. So what, I say? Everybody's doing it.

I ask Jon-David at today's therapy session what I must do about Hayley.

His response: 'What do you want to do?'

He doesn't get it – I am asking YOU pal. *You* must tell *me*.

'Never see her again,' I reply.

222

'Is that what you really want, Jason?'

Jesus, man. Can't you just tell me what to do instead of asking questions? #hadenough.

P.S.
Q: How many psychologists does it take to change a lightbulb?
A: One, but the lightbulb has to want to change.

FRIDAY 4 NOVEMBER 2011

I appear in court.

I call my parents to tell them. My mom answers (normal), my dad is in the background (abnormal).

'I have to appear in court in Grahamstown and thought I would pop in on the way back to say hi.'

My mom is taken aback. But then again a fly flying in front of the fridge could break her stride these days. 'The Maintenance Court?'

'No, Ma.'

I can hear The Man They Couldn't Hang in the background say, 'Just a question of time.'

'Mom, it's the traffic thing that you so thoughtfully signed for.'

Dad's advice is that I must find a bribable one.

So. The original fine was R300. I have paid now:
- R1,870 (BA to PE, inc airport taxes).
- R1,150 (hired Audi – you need a solid machine on these roads in case you come upon a herd of Aberdeen Angus grazing on some of the grass coming up through the N2's tar).
- R500 contempt of court.
- R2,700 Opportunity Cost – what I reckon I earn a day at @igloo.
- R180 (sushi in PE).
- R150 (biltong bought at airport for folks).

About six-and-a-half K for a R300 fine. There is a lesson in this to us all, chinas. And it's this: if you get a fine, make sure you have no comatose member of family dumb enough to sign for the summons.

The notorious Facebook rapist appears in court – there but for the grace of god…

By 11pm I am into some psytrance at Jackal & Hide in Kloof Street. What a day. James Bond would be jealous.

SATURDAY 5 NOVEMBER 2011

Actually good to have a weekend off rugby. I need this break.

Megan and I seem to have made a bit of a comeback. Not sure how that happened. Think it was the Jägerbombs last night. We go out – starting at the up-itself craft-beer spot, The Power and the Glory, and pop these new MDMA pills called Mr Min. Free from our 10% shareholder. They had no effect. Zero. Until some goblins started nibbling at my earlobes. I was swatting them away like flies. Nobody else seemed to see them they were so pissed.

SUNDAY 6 NOVEMBER 2011

The downer is awful. Megan sticks around like a perlemoen that secretes superglue.

I get out of bed for four loose stools. I follow through into my boxers, once. I decide not to throw them away as they are Calvin Klein so they become a domestic (worker) issue.

By the time the dreaded chimes of doom start – the *Carte Blanche* theme song, the anthem for the doomed – I am ready to have a go at my wrists with a jaded, pre-owned butter knife. Or as it goes: 'Hi, good gvening, I'm Derek Watts and your weekend is now OVER.'

Megan fails to understand that it can't always be hours of lovemaking on white Egyptian cotton sheets with a fan whirring overhead. Sometimes a guy just wants to read. *Men's Health*. Harry Potter. Anything.

MONDAY 7 NOVEMBER 2011

I have fired Jon-David as my therapist. Truth is my ADD was kicking in after about 6 or 7 minutes. Surely I don't need to tell him why he is fired because, if anything, as a therapist he should work it out, work out what's going on in my mind.

I have replaced him with Jordan, my new Life Navigator, basically a shrink and personal trainer rolled into one. And she is a 34D. She may just have to help with this:

From: Gary Baumgarten
Date: 7 November 2011 at 11.02am
To: Jason Brydon <MD@igloo.com>
CC: 'Stevie' <steviewunda@hotmail.com> '3G' <Baxboy7@gmail.com>
Subject: New shareholder

Hi Jason

Thanks for your loan account payment of R100K which was received from the Freedom Peoples Bank of Abuja yesterday.

Well done on securing us our new shareholder. Could you advise as to when we can expect his payment for the shares and valuation of such?

Kr
GB

From: Jason Brydon <MD@igloo.com>
Date: 7 November 2011 at 11.58am
To: Gary Baumgarten <Gb@GBINC.net>
CC: 'Stevie' <steviewunda@hotmail.com> '3G' <Baxboy7@gmail.com>
Subject: Loan Account

Hi Gary

Shot. I valued it at 10 million which is a good price. I will advise in due course re the shareholder payment. He has to cash in some hedge funds which will take a few weeks.

Ciao

Jase

I see in the new Bond film, Moneypenny is black. Most characters come in black these days. And if that isn't enough, it turns out she is single and was bullied. It's like a box-ticking frenzy. Albert R Broccoli must be pleased he now lives in a cemetery.

On the step machine at Virgin Active today, there is nothing to look at so my mind wanders. If your girlfriend, hypothetically speaking, let's say in my case Megan, kisses another girl, is that cheating on you? It's a vexed issue so I WhatsApp a few of the lads hitting them with this riddle. It's 3-2 that it's not cheating – with my casting vote. Dawesy obviously says it is. Muggsy says if your chick is swapping spit with anyone from Enrique Iglesias to a cocker spaniel, it's cheating. I vote with Stevie and 3G that it's not cheating. In fact, it is to be encouraged.

My final ruling: it's not cheating if it's in front of you, and if it's not, it must be on video, copy of which must be forwarded to you.

On Wednesday night I am speaking at Reddam School to some assortment of precious brats. My topic: *Entrepreneurship in post 2010 SA – how to build a brand.*

Of course, I am chuffed, and it's probably overdue, but I can't help feeling someone is pulling the piss. I haven't used PowerPoint since I presented the 2Dye4 Washable White (which is also how I described Regional Sales Managers Dave 'the Poes' Peters) to the retail hardware industry in 2009 – before I got 'transferred' and bitten by an Alsatian at a panel beaters in Alberton.

I am going to go in my new Fabiani suit, black Boss formal shoes, open-necked Ralph Lauren (horse facing out, not the SA rip off, horse facing in). Ted Baker socks.

TUESDAY 8 NOVEMBER 2011

Stevie's tweet, not helpful:

> **@steviewunda:** anyone seen the size of Brydon lately? #ladolcevita.

I DM and tell him to piss right off.

I get on Costa's Russell Hobbs scale. THREE FIGURES. Oh my aching tit. Hundred up for JB Inc – that's fine if you're Jacques Kallis, but I have to face the reality that my temple needs a refit. I can't wear the Fabiani suit tomorrow night. I think I may have to go in traditional dress. They use that to hide their African beer tum-tums.

I try to convince myself that it's all the gym work – and we know how heavy muscle is – but I find myself sucking my tummy in every waking hour. The thing with breaking the 100kg mark, especially at my height, is that you lose confidence. And suddenly you're fishing for carp, not for yellowfin.

WEDNESDAY 9 NOVEMBER 2011

Honestly I haven't the time to do a PowerPoint for a bunch of pleased-with-themselves runts. Well, I start and I get the first slide.

@igloo – the logo with the pay-off line 'You just don't get cooler'. Then at the bottom: 'Reddam Entrepreneurship Talk November 2011'.

Next page: @igloo MD: Jason Brydon.

And it takes me about 20 minutes to get a 2009 picture of myself (91kg) that kind of shivers and shingles onto the screen. I also find a picture of Caroline Wozniacki that looks great, but not sure how to talk about it.

I must say that the quality of women tennis players has improved so much since I had to spend every July growing up, like we all did, watching Wimbledon. Steffi Graf used to win and probably would also have won the Durban July had she entered that. My word, women's tennis has changed a lot. If a piece of biltong like Martina Navratilova turned up at Wimbledon these days, the TV guys would send her home and tell her to come back when she looks less like an elongated mongoose and when she has some tits and maybe a boyfriend, ideally someone like the bassist from Alphaville. Even in the '80s you could get 'them' done, I mean even, ironically, if she sterilised two tennis balls and asked some East German quack to pop them in it would be better than the nothing she has/had. Basically we are saying, 'We don't care about your double-handed backhand or that you have redefined the woman's game, you are *not* doing the sport any good.' I mean, you don't get petite little St Anne's girls watching some 121kg Bulgarian half-chick squatting her way to bronze in the Olympics wanting to be like her. However, if Scarlett Johansson won a medal, there would be queues outside the SA Weightlifting Union's offices from here to Tzaneen (if it's still called that).

So that's where my PowerPoint hits the wall. I look on YouTube for a clip of some guy without a head winning a triathlon or something or that scene from *Chariots of Fire*, but end up getting 'distracted' on RedTube.

I phone Jordan, my life navigator and 8.25/10, and ask her advice. She tells me to be authentic and to 'own both the room and the presentation'. I ask her how.

She says, 'The How is the easy part – as long as we have the Why.'

We agree to debrief over a 6km jog-walk along the Promenade tomorrow. I ask her if part of her life-navigation service could be that she come along this evening to do some live coaching and then maybe we could go and grab a (lean) steak and salad and a few Johnnie Blacks.

But she has another client she is working with at an MMA fight. For some reason, I feel a bit jealous. I wonder how much exclusivity would cost.

We agree that spending three hours hacking through a PowerPoint presentation when I have a corporation to run is not a good ROI (Return on Investment), especially when I am *not* being paid for this talk. Why I said yes, I don't know. I ask Jordan if this was not my inner ego talking.

All she says is, 'Every ego is inner.'

This chick is sharp.

It's lurking in the back of my mind that this is all a set-up. That Stevie is going to appear from behind some pillar saying it's all a joke and 'who the fuck would want to listen to you, *Wortelbrein?*' But it's not – and in a way, the way it turns out, that is a pity.

I don't go for the suit, as it is a little 'snug' and I cannot bring myself to actually wear something ethnic. So I Google what Steve Jobs used to wear at his iPhone releases and he was often in a denim shirt. So I go in my new G-Star dark denim workshirt tucked into my new True Religions (R3,500!!!). So Steve Jobs meets James Dean meets Johnny Depp, if you get it.

Eight pm kick-off and it starts well. Some acne-ridden thing in a blazer welcomes me. There are probably about 40 in the audience – overwhelmingly white with the requisite genius charra and sponsored or adopted isiXhosa. About 12-13 are girls (the school is co-ed), but all, except one who was sitting towards the back, are all mid-table. I get a great intro from some twerp about how honoured they were to have the MD of @igloo here to address them.

I had been asked to send through an abbreviated CV which I did this morning:

- *Studied at UCT.* True, cos didn't say I graduated.
- *Trader at Lehman Bros in London.* True, I did work there, though I traded more in photocopier cartridges than securities (I worked for Trader Support Services).
- *Royal Bank of Scotland.* OK, it lasted 18 days. Not because I did anything wrong, but I was staying all the way down in Southfields which is basically somewhere below Dover and they were in the City so I was late a few days. But I just think my boss was threatened by South Africans in general and pissed off about us cleaning their pipes at the World Cup that he used the punctuality as pretext.
- *2Dye4 Paints – revolutionised the way paint is sold in SA.* In some ways, true. Maybe how paint is *not* sold, but that's semantics. Obviously leave out that I was known there as the Human Turnip.
- *adidas* – OK, I applied, and missed out due to affirmative action, but if it was on merit I would have got the job.
- *Took a year off. Hit 30, semi-retirement on the Wild Coast playing a bit in the hospitality space.* All true.

It sounded good, even if I say so myself.

'Right, howzit, guys. As you have heard I am Jason Brydon. *The* Jason Brydon, a.k.a. the Jasonator. Haha MD of @igloo global.

'Listen, I had prepared you fuckers – haha, learners, or whatever you're called now – a proper 64-page PowerPoint,' pointing at my brand new MacBook Air styling on the lectern. With my first slide (of two) on the screen. 'But I know it's probably the last thing you guys feel like after a long day of hanging out at the mall, playing Grand Theft Auto and doing roids or crack... haha.

'You don't want 40 minutes of me talking about Return on Investments or P/E ratio. P/E ratio [thanks Muggs] are Price Earnings Ranking.'

'Ratio,' pipes up some freak from the back.

'Correct – you are awake.' Good comeback, JB, still in control, lad.

'It was Richard Branson, who I know quite well, I wouldn't quite say he is a mate of mine, but I know him. You have all heard of him, no doubt. He said that one must have fun and "screw it, just do it". And that's how we roll at @igloo.

'Or as some bonehead put it: *"poes voort"*.' There are a few gasps. They are lapping it up.

'Look, like Richard, I believe in the youth. You guys, and girls, are the future. That's why I'm here, not charging – came for free.'

Same little prick comes up with, 'So did Raymond Ackerman.'

'Well, pal, he is retired now so doesn't have much else to do.' Elegant pause while I let that sink in.

'Richard once told me, "There is no greater thing you can do with your life and your work than follow your passions – in a way that serves the world and you."'

'Where did he tell you?' Same prick again.

'Online.'

Not my best. Luckily the teacher, some ponce with a goatee, pops up and asks Noah to stop interrupting. And to wait for questions.

'I don't think of work as work and play as play. It's all living.

'So, guys, I'm sure you have lots to ask me and it's better if I tell you what you want to hear rather than me second guess it and tell you a whole lot of shit, sorry, stuff, you're not interested in… so fire away…'

Noah is pissing himself. I think I hear him whisper, 'This guy…'

One of the Indians is up first. Predictable. With a voice like he has he should be yodelling at the Drakensberg Boys' Choir. He asks me quite a convoluted thing about turnover. I must say the only turnover I really remember is that one Francois Louw made against the All Blacks at Ellis Park. Turnover?

'Well, as we say in the business, turnover is vanity, cash-flow reality and balance sheet sanity. And relying just on turnover, insanity. Right, next?'

Where that came from, I don't know, but it is inspired and shuts Gandhi up.

Another one: 'Mr Brydon.' That's better. One with manners. And specs.

'Jason, please,' I say.

'How did you fund @igloo? Was it private equity? Or did you go to institutions? If so, what sort of debt did you choose? Mezzanine?'

'Yip.'

Some other twerp pops up like a cork.

'My dad remembers you from school and says you really struggled at school.'

'Well, maths wasn't my thing.' Broad, confident white smile (Cape Town Aesthetic dentistry R2,000).

Twerp keeps coming. 'Nope, says you struggled socially.'

Goatee doesn't say a word or intervene, just fiddles with his earring and stares at his Livestrong bracelet.

'Let me tell you, Richard Branson is dyslexic and didn't finish school and neither did Steve Jobs, so why don't you rather than sit here asking silly questions and worrying about your chorbs, get out there in the real world?'

Noah is back up again. 'Why're wearing a onesie?'

I look down.

When I get to the (not my) car, not long after, it says 8.18pm.

Fuck them.

THURSDAY 10 NOVEMBER 2011

I am acutely aware of the need to find my own place, but as I told that agent Bax, there is no point if it's not *Top Billing*-able.

The need is more pressing after this SMS from Costa:
I havent ruled out the possibility of criminal charges.

Over a model plane? Really? *Really?*

We have landed turnover of 2-bar already. Try and stop Jonah Lomu with a wet wipe.

Stevie thinks because of this – and to help me get over Costa's third stage of syphilis madness – we deserve a treat. He is taking me for a Thai massage (a.k.a. a rub) at some upmarket spot in Green Point. It's my first time and I'm not quite sure of the protocol. I mean it's definitely not one of those siff massage parlours, it's all 'above board', but it's also not the spa at the Twelve Apostles.

But I am tense, I am stressed. I've been nuking the candle at both ends building this business. And let's face it, and this is what Gary Baumgarten, the human gnome, fails to understand: I am the face of the business. I live eat sleep smoke snort it. I am it and it is me. Thus my personal life is work. I am the brand and the freak needs to understand this and stop going on about my credit-card expenses.

Anyway I'm looking forward to the massage. We arrive. Thais are too close to chinks for me and don't do anything for me. Not my department, but my one has the hands of an angel.

It's awkward at the start. 'Clothes off. Put that,' my little lotus flower tells me, pointing at a handkerchief of a towel.

Again, I am unsure of the protocol. Do I keep my Calvin Kleins on or not? I don't want to be presumptuous. In the end – to be on the safe side, and to avoid regrets – I slip them off, cover my privates with the hanky, and lie face down on the bed and listen to Richard Clayderman.

I don't bother with small talk. I don't care about her family in Hanoi or how long she's been in SA. For once I am not worrying about other people and I am putting JB first.

My word, it's nice. I fight it, but I nod off. I drool and, I suspect but can't prove it, I snore.

The other night whilst trying to check whether I snore (as I suspect that Megan has exaggerated) just before I nod off, I start the voice recorder on my iPad 2. Not pretty. Not pretty at all. Sounded like a Sappi sawmill.

I mention it to Dawesy and that I am thinking of going to one of these sleep clinics and maybe to get an op. He looks at me. 'It's not that, Jason. Have you ever seen a thin man sore?'

He is just bitter because Costa and I have our differences over the management of his property.

Anyway back to matters at hand (pun). After I come to, she starts moving down towards my glutes. She kneads them like pizza dough. It's rather nice. In fact it's very nice.

Now look here, I am not made of Alcolin Wood Glue. I start to get 'interested'. To my disappointment she finishes. But then again, in a bit of a physical roller coaster, she says, 'Would you like happy ending?'

Thought you'd never ask, darling. Don't care where you're from, couldn't care less if you are half Eskimo. 'Yes,' I stammer.

She leaves the room. I lie in eager, very eager, anticipation, while she no doubt goes to slip into something more comfortable.

She is gone a while. It's almost sore. After a very long time the door opens. Ling Ling or whatever her name is – like I care – comes back in. Dressed much the same.

'Finish yet?' She asks 'Happy ending, it finish yet?'

Some happy ending.

FRIDAY 11 NOVEMBER 2011

The only good news today, I guess, is that Julius Malema has got five years. For tax evasion. Rex says that's also how they got Capone.

There's no Rémy Martin or Hennessy in Pretoria Central.

Right, Sasha-Lee has resigned. Says when she comes into my office she feels like an object.

I don't respond as I possibly should have. 'Object*s*, you mean.'

That seems to be the straw that broke the camel's bra-strap. She wants to go somewhere where she is valued (she is) and where it's not about her assets. Well, sweetie, we didn't employ you because you got a B for Home Economics at school.

So she's gone.

Want to go and look in Constantia for some more ice-maiden stock. It's not called Silicone Valley for nothing.

Fuck, you so much as scratch a cyclist these days and they want you raped.

They say cyclists 'stay alive at 1.5'. But if you have to choose who is staying alive, well, that's going to be me, my china. I am not overtaking them so wide that I'm into the path of some Stuttafords Van Lines pantechnicon driven by some deranged Zimbabwean called Paddington. If it's between you and the doos with shaven legs on the Cannondale, the laws of both physics and preservation dictate only one winner.

So, in this case, I did not actually hit them. Yip, *them*. No I wasn't one of those guys who comes back from a club at 5am (which I often do) and ploughs into a bunch of Mamils (Middle Aged Men in Lycra) training for the Argus and then a few days later have to hand yourself in at the local cop shop. Nope. Not my style. But, yes it was *them*. Two *guys* on a tandem. WTF? I understand a couple being on a tandem, but two guys? That the one guy is prepared to just sit at the back and have no control over the steering – just peddling away staring at the other one's *gat*. Maybe it's a fetish? After all this is Cape Town. Everybody who gathers at the accident thinks I have knocked them off this bicycle made for two. But I don't touch them as I point out to the one called Hans who has a badly scraped elbow. Dieter is on the pavement looking for his Oakleys, mincing around like he put his tampon in skew.

When I saw them topple knowing I hadn't hit them, I wasn't going to stop, but the next light was red and the traffic stopped in front of me. And I guess it looks bad. You go past a pair of cyclists and next thing, they're on the pavement upside down.

'We know you don't hit us, but you were so close you blew us off,' says Hans.

Blew you off? Now I've heard it all. Go back to De Waterkant and blow each other off. No serious injuries. Nothing that TCP and some turps couldn't fix.

To settle my frayed nerves, I head off to the gym for a squatathon. As I'm getting out of the modified Scirocco, a freak pulls up next to me in a double cab. There is a sticker with a weightlifter on it saying DO SHRUGS NOT DRUGS. This behemoth gets out with a vest that would probably fit a Boeing. You obviously do both, bru. Vitamin S.

SATURDAY 12 NOVEMBER 2011

OK, it's escalating. Costa tries to call, but I now know the Greek country code now and that any 'Hellenic' calls ought not to be dealt with 'live'. Made that mistake before. I wait for voicemail, I listen, I can virtually smell his aftershave over the phone. It seems a sheriff tried to serve papers at his work last week for him, in October in the Scirocco, overtaking in the Huguenot Tunnel. I think that was me. Well, I know that was me. There was this truck doing about 12 and nothing was coming, but it sounds like overtaking in the tunnel is as taboo as tweeting 'Allah is overrated'.

Costa is talking of flying back. I am going to call Crime Stop and alert them. Maybe they can intercept him at ORT (Oscar Thambo Airport, for those of you who don't fly much).

239

We have a party tonight. A 50th in Hout Bay. 300 pax. On the phone the guy says he has had to warn the caterers that they have been having a terrible problem with the otters lately. He clearly doesn't live in a complex then… Apparently, like most other rich weirdos, he made his money in online gambling software.

There is an incident. Not ideal and not good for the brand, but not irreparable. It involves me getting seen with a funnel and apparently pouring some First Watch into a Johnnie Walker Platinum bottle in the back of the new @igloo VW caddy. A lot of what was seen was not true. The first thing that I would say is that to say I was replacing Johnnie Walker with First Watch is not accurate. There was a lot of Johnnie left in that bottle, I was just topping it up with the first whisky I grabbed. Bar staff, even those as highly skilled as ours, don't want lots of half-empty bottles lying around. We want premium brands, full and flying.

The nuances of this are lost on the host. The idiot who has a problem with the otters. Says what I was seen doing by his daughter (not bad at all) is illegal. Phone the cops, I say. It is certainly not illegal. I tell him he is the one operating on the wrong side of the law, probably doing some online casino based on Tristan de Cunha.

He says he's not going to pay us. He has only got 300 of Cape Town's biggest try-hards and over 150 Land Rover Discoveries on his property.

'OK, guys, pack up. We're outta here.'

'You can't do that, pal.' He almost has a finger in my reasonably well-defined chest.

'You said you weren't going to pay, so why should we stay?'

240

'I have 300 people here that need drinks and you were diluting drinks.'

'I wasn't diluting.'

'Amber saw you.' The not bad daughter is nodding.

'Technically, diluting is mixing something with water. Mixing whisky with whisky isn't diluting.'

'I would rather it was that than First Watch.'

'We offer that service, too,' I chirp. Funny I thought.

I assure him it was just a one-off, was really sorry, just done for convenience etcetera. 'Everything else is real.' Peace is brokered. We agree to stay on, he agrees to EFT the balance of what is owed. I knock off a good faith 5K discount. We shake hands.

As that happens, and the earringed DJ that looks like a cross between Huey Lewis and a chimp (and drives a Beetle) starts playing Men at Work's *Who Can It Be Now?*, this self-tanned, all-in-white couple stride round the corner looking for Rodge (our host).

'Rodge, taste this? Taste Fluffy's G&T. Just taste it. You're telling me this is Tanqueray? Taste it.'

Fuck. Time for the Jasonator to exit stage right. Or as the mayor of Hiroshima no doubt said when he saw the bomb go off, 'We will deal with the fallout tomorrow.'

I hope nobody orders our 'craft beer', a.k.a. Hansa.

SUNDAY 13 NOVEMBER 2011

I was having sex with Sasha-Lee's mom. She is rougher than Jack Parow. Stevie calls her Mrs Doubtfire, which is harsh. But I see the analogy. Sure, Sasha-Lee and that rack are like the Mercedes SLK Kompressor, 2011 model. Maybe 2010. Mom's not. Mom is one of those 450 SLKs that Bobby Ewing used to drive in Dallas. 1982 model. But that's not the point. Of course I would prefer the Kompressor, but I can't have that – and they're still both Mercedes Sports, you see.

What I can tell my diary is that I now can see where Sasha-Lee gets it/them from. Sure gravity comes into play a bit stronger given mom is somewhere north of 55, but the infrastructure whilst, like our railways, maybe crumbling a bit, is still sound.

She had come round to confront me about Sasha-Lee's controversial exit from the @igloo family/community. And, in particular, the post I put on our FB page about how we would miss 'them'. She starts off quite feisty, but after I manage to uncork one of Costa del Sol's Meerlust Rubicons or three, things literally start to loosen up a bit.

The only downside to this real-life fantasy and significant scalp to the Jasonator's burgeoning list is the fact that she runs her own business. It's a pet cremation solutions company. It's just not ideal to have a Renault panel van parked outside with FIDO's FAITH – DIGNIFIED PET EXITS festooned across its panels. Not at all. The neighbours must be a-twittering.

When I look at Ferris lying across the passage I am half tempted to say to her 'While you're here…' but decide against it.

MONDAY 14 NOVEMBER 2011

Cosmopolitan phone me. Some chick called Jenna, with a husky voice, who I manage to track down on the Book (FB) where she looks like an 8.2, so in real life that would be adjusted down to something in the early 7s or late 6s. But it's just important to know who you're speaking to, texting or mailing. Just so you know whether it's worth investing any time or effort into the comms – you know, thinking of funny one-liners and mulling over whether to end a WhatsApp with an 'x' or not. Not easy stuff and not worth worrying about if she is somewhere south of a 5/10.

She wants me to appear in their January mag.

'Oh,' I say, 'in your calendar? With Ryk Neethling?' As hard as I am gymming, even though this is an off-week, it seems, I will still not look good on the same line-up as South Africa's swimming Adonis and Francois Hougaard. Unless of course they are like Mr January and Mr February and I am, say, November and we have a black December – say a Bafana player.

It turns out it's not for the calendar. The feeling is one more of relief than disappointment, as I am failing in my *Men's Health* 'Knock it off and keep it off' diet. I am failing in both those categories.

No it's for a feature on some 'Hot young Bucks making bucks'. Couldn't have put it better myself.

She emails me a form to complete.
- Favourite food: foie gras (shows both class and a disrespect for lesbian animal lovers).
- Favourite drink: mojito (never tasted one – can remedy that later).
- Five people you would most like to have for dinner: Cameron

Diaz, Scarlett Johansson, Sienna Miller, Elle Macpherson. Oh and Mandela. And if he can't make it, then Barry Hilton, cousin.
- Motto: Screw it, just do it.
- If you had 24 hours left what would you do with your money: Buy Ecstasy.
- Who in Rock 'n Roll most epitomises you? Cross Keith Richards and the oke from The Doors
- What book are you reading? *Rich Dad, Pissed Dad!!!!*
- Pet Hates: Sasha Martinengo, craft beer, artisanal everything, not having a Vida nearby, cyclists, Joburg, Jonty Rhodes, ugly lesbians, okes not replacing their weights, Greeks, SARS, the Stormers, fat chicks in Stetsons, private numbers, SABC, *Carte Blanche* theme tune, golf, Dion Chang (who's trending now, you gay chink fuck?), the bouncers at Caprice, behind-the-neck shoulder presses, domestic cricket, Kwaito, Luke Watson, Zuma, people stopping too early at orange lights, minibus taxis, After Shock.
- What you would like as your epitaph: 'Heaven won't be big enough for him.'

She says that I'll have come into the studio for a pic.

I ask: 'Colour or black-and-white?'

Luckily it's not colour so that's another relief. No need to dust off the #betterredthandead campaign!

She says she is going to have to edit my pet hates a bit so I suggest she take the bit about that insufferable Dion Chang out. And maybe the thing about Stetsons in case it offends Leigh Bennie or PJ Powers.

TUESDAY 15 NOVEMBER 2011

How is this for a Facebook post:
> Whatever you do, whatever you do, never ever hire @igloo bar
> services unless you have money to literally piss away. They water
> down drinks, replace what they promise to serve with the cheaper
> stuff and the rat who runs it is rude and still passed out during my
> (the client) party and then blamed his narcolepsy.

Obviously I am straight onto Muggs in a WhatsApp:
> Muggs can we sue this guy please. NOW. And get him to remove
> the Facebook post and get an urgent Supreme Court interdict to
> stop him writing or saying shit about us. It's not true.

He writes back; this is the exchange:
> Which parts?

> ?????

> Which parts aren't true, Jason?

> Well we dont dilute. I want to sue for defamation

> For a successful case of defamation, which hardly ever win
> in SA, you would have to prove it was (a) untrue and (b) in the
> public interest.

Bingo I think. Got him there.
> Well so we can sue??

> So if he was to send his 'Grey Goose' off to a lab he won't find any
> H_2O?

Well not much

But he won't find much Grey Goose?

Technically not

Technically?

Well its vodka and labelled Grey Goose vodka so it is vodka

But, Jason, is it made by Grey Goose?

Technically not

Nothing technical about it. Is it made by GG or not?

Well they not directly involved

Jason.

I sense Muggs is getting a bit exasperated.

Agree to disagree?

That keeps him a bit quiet, but it's still awkward.

Muggs, surely the chop can't call me a rat publically? It's neither true, to use your test, nor in the public interest

Technically Jason, he may not be wrong.

Come of it Mugs. You can't call me a rat

Well, I think he will say it's a metaphor.

Fuck, whose side is he on? Given it's got 18 likes by the time I log off, I am not happy.

WEDNESDAY 16 NOVEMBER 2011

I tweet:

> Seems Peter de Villiers is on the shortlist for the new Bok job #don'ttheyeverlearn? #awkies

31 retweets. There.

THURSDAY 17 NOVEMBER 2011

I suppose it was inevitable, but without social media it could have been a lot worse off. It's the whole Sapphire thing.

> Since our attorneys haven't been able to, little Sapphire and I are heading down to Cape Town to see if we can find her father, one Jason Brydon of @igloo and Royal Port Alfred Golf Club fame to see if he can honour his maintenance commitments. #nameandshamethem

Awesome. Wonder if her ballie, DJ Jazzy Jeff, is coming down, too? But as I say without that post (and without the Instagram pic of Sapphire in a babygrow sitting in the snot green Kulula seat) I would not have known the Pissed Off Woman's league was coming to town.

247

And I am meant to be reviewing some new restaurant in the Old Biscuit Mill for my blog tonight.

I try and halt take-off:

> how's it Hayls. Hope all well. Just checking you got my EFT.
> Sorry it was late. Better late than never. Just like with Little Saph?
> Xxxxxxxxxxx

Let's see if that works. I mean I can pay it, but then I realise I don't have her bank details. But how can I ask for them when I have already said I have paid…?

FRIDAY 18 NOVEMBER 2011

Just a thought: imagine if horseflies were as nippy and mobile as their normal fly counterparts? Sometimes I almost feel sorry for them. They hurt you so hard, but you can catch the buggers and kill them. But imagine if they could evade like a normal fly and still sting. #justimagine

In some ways Hayley is a bit like a horsefly. Massive sting, but slow, sluggish and easy to deal with. Don't mean I would swat her or kill her. Course not. Not at all. Not really.

SATURDAY 19 NOVEMBER 2011

Rex has been on the phone. Well, I was on the phone to him. I got an SMS:

I wonder what Rex Trueform is up to now? My first reaction is that it's something to do with the fact that HRH Prince Charles is speaking at UCT this afternoon and they want a pic or souvenir.

But then again they've started getting to that age where you start thinking the worst – you know, mom's gone and broken a hip, called someone a muntu at the Spar, hasn't got long now, knocked the postie off his bike (again), etc etc.

But he is serious and businesslike when I get hold of him and he answers with the normal, gruff, 'Brydon.'

It seems he is Chairman of the Port Alfred When Mandela Goes (PAWMG) chapter. Self-appointed and self-founded, I guess. He says it's going to be big countrywide and Port Alfred is going to lead the way. The whole club is behind him.

'Jase you know all this nonsense about websites, tweeter (sic) and social media. Can you please set it up for us? We need to communicate to our members for when he goes. If he hasn't gone already. You know – assembly points, where they can collect rations, home guard units, what to do when they start attacking white nurses and all that.'

Seems all a bit alarmist to me. Course there will be kak and a few okes may lose their farms and there will be load shedding and maybe we stay home a few days, but that'll be it.

But, to be fair to Trueform, in '94 he wasn't one of those baked-bean stockpilers.

SUNDAY 20 NOVEMBER 2011

I must say I am a ball of anxiety by the time *Carters* play their 'Anthem for the Doomed'. It is far, very far, from ideal knowing that Hayley is in town and could strike any time. I just don't know when, how or with who. It's a bit like a scene from *Braveheart* or something out of Rorke's Drift – you know, you're in camp and you know they're out there and ready to strike.

Carters has something about this earthquake in Japan that has claimed 20,000 people. But Derek Watts has cocked it up. It's 15,000 dead so far and 5,000 missing. That's not the same as 20,000. Quite a few of those 5,000 may wash up alive or turn up at work at Honda tomorrow as if nothing was wrong. Let's wait and see exactly, Derek.

Plus how does Hayley know that I hadn't genuinely done the EFT? They have started to not only name drunken drivers in the papers, but also maintenance defaulters. Bracing myself for a wave of publicity.

I also think it's one thing being named for DUI – these things happen – but a maintenance defaulter? It's not going to help you land a firm, former Miss Matieland, is it?

MONDAY 21 NOVEMBER 2011

Rex Trueform is back on the blower. Things have gone well with 'the merger'. I wonder if he's going to claim that he's involved in some corporate deal via the financial heartbeat that is the Port Alfred CBD.

'What merger, Dad?'

'Between PAWMG and WMTO. Cliffy has brought WMTO to the table.'

'WMTO?' I expect to hear When Mandela's machine is Turned Off.

'Cliffy runs WMTO. When Malema Takes Over. They share similar ideals to us and the same plans and visions. In fact their solar power thinking is way ahead of ours. But we're going to keep the PAWMG name. How's our Facebook coming on? We need to splash the merger. Like yesterday. People need to know they don't have to panic.'

TUESDAY 22 NOVEMBER 2011

A.k.a. Black Tuesday. Something to do with some secrecy bill. Haven't really been following.

But I still think it's the right name for today, given the below:

From: Greg Dawes <greg@askarimedia.com>
Date: 22 November 2011 at 11.02am
To: Jason Brydon <MD@igloo.com>
Subject: FW: Jason Brydon

Hi Jason

This is bullshit mate. I did you a favour here now sort it out. Mind you it's probably more my fault than anyone else's. I mean if it walks like a duck, looks like a duck, talks like a duck, don't be surprised when it shits on your pool paving.

Unacceptable. See below

251

From: Costa Vlissedes <cv@appolloequity.com>
Date: 22 November 2011 at 10.04am
To: Greg Dawes <greg@askarimedia.com>
Subject: Jason Brydon

Hi Greg

Sorry, mate, but you have to help me out here. Honestly I am so angry with your mate Brydon that I am tempted to fly out a Cypriot to remove this little stain on society.

Mate, he's broken half the house, been unacceptably rude to the maid, smashed a car, driven my wife's, lost my replica Spitfire, starved the dogs, done cocaine on our wedding picture, vomited in the passage, had three parties and lost the Weber lid. That's just what I know about. Basically because he has told the world of social media.

He is a sociopath and given that you recommended this piece of human faeces to look after our spot, your intervention would be appreciated. I have my attorneys onto this, but he takes them as seriously as he probably does his retirement planning.

I am trying to get there asap but just flat out with the Andersen Oil deal. But I will and if you/the attorneys haven't got him out then, I will get this leech out.

Kr

Costa

I know that Hayley and Sapphire are in (the DA controlled) metro, but no news. I phone her toppie's house from a landline with the plan to bliksem it down should he answer. I hope he answers. It

252

will mean he is safely in KZN. But I get a big warm female African 'Ellooo'. It's the maid whose name is Miriam. Says 'master is in Cape Town with madam'. It feels a little like the noose is around me and the hangman is just making sure the knot is tight below my right ear.

I need a release. Stevie buys the schnarf (unfortunately Alfonse, our BEE partner, can't take credit card for his 'product') and out we go on a Tuesday to slaughter ourselves. Brandies and Coke. Old school. Going down like the proverbial homesick moles. Or Air Congo.

After some missioning we end up at Joburg in Long Street. There we drink like it's Friday night at a hostel at Western Deep Levels. I pocket dial Megan four times. #error

She phones back straight away (#desperate) and wants to know where I am. I tell her I am in Joburg. It's not a lie. She just has a sarky, 'Sounds like you're having fun.'

I order two more trebles and tell the barman, 'See the brandy, assume the Coke.' He says he is not allowed to sell trebles.

So I order a double and a single and in front of his ugly DRC mug pour the single into the double. And down it.

'Fuck all you can do about that, Serge.'

WEDNESDAY 23 NOVEMBER 2011

More hungover than Pik Botha at a bosberaad. Sky-high levels of nausea and anxiety. As much as I tell myself this is purely chemical, it doesn't change anything.

So I'm battling self-worth issues before I see a missed call from Hayley. Awesome. Can it get any worse?

The answer to that is yes, it can. She has left a voice message. It's not without a tremor I dial 121. Voicemail. Maybe she is saying something nice, trying to build bridges rather than chasms. Maybe she is dismounting from her very high horse?

Answer to this one is a resounding no. No. In a voice colder than an Eskimo's fridge: 'Jason, you know who this is. And you know why I am calling. And you know why you are not answering. Quite pathetic. You make no effort to see your own daughter. Well, I am coming past your trendy little office tomorrow to discuss your failure to pay maintenance as agreed. I will be at your office in Prestwich Street at 9.'

You might be, I won't.

People don't realise. I am viewed like I am Satan Personified but if I really was the Devil Incarnate I would go to a shebeen and pay R5,000 or R500 to have the problem removed. I can but it's not the right thing to do. I derive some credit for the fact that I haven't even got a quote to have it done. Shows that I am not Beelzebub.

We call them at @igloo 'bored meetings'. Just because they are not our style – it's not the @igloo way – but that human amoeba Gary Baumgarten has insisted on an emergency *board* meeting, as his email calls it. As far as I know, the little Yid fuck is not even a director. Going to double check.

Horrible thing this. I am waiting to go up to our floor. The lift comes and I step in and luckily I am alone. I push '4' and the doors close and as its starts to ascend I let one go. You know one of those where

I could actually smell last night's brandy, bolognaise and King Steers in it. Unfortunately the lift stops on '2' and a dizzy blonde, a junior Miss World I am sure, comes clattering into the lift on heels. Aware of the odour, I try and block her.

'It's actually going up,' and I virtually break my index finger I hit the Doors Close sign so hard. She smiles, and she's almost in the kill zone. 'So am I. I'm going up to four.'

And in she steps, into a lift that Saddam Hussein would have funded as a chemical weapon. Chat in lifts is always a complete hack. But nothing can beat the awkwardness of a lift fart. #awkies

That and then right into Gary's 'issues'. One of which is that of Alfonse's R100,000 equity payment, over which he is apparently 'confused'. The other is an Excel print out of my credit card statement that requires some explanation.

J Brydon @igloo Visa Credit Card week Monday 7 - Friday 11 November		
Supplier	amount	comment - GB
1 Yindees Tha restaurant	R1 000	Tip R250!!
2 Woolworths Foods, Green Point	R2112.00	
3 Engen	R770	petrol
4 Paul Smith, Bree Street	R1 250	assume more 'corporate' clothing
5 Nelsons Eye	R1 450	
6 Café Caprice - Camps Bay	R2 450	Tip R450
7 Jakes Steenberg	R700	Meal for 1 judging from slip
8 Woolworths Food, Sea Point	R221.89	
9 Kloof Street vet	R770	A vet?
10 iL Leone Italian - Green Point	R3 300	Tip R600
11 Kauai Virgin Active Point	R120	
12 Gant Waterfront	R1 900	
13 V&A parking	R20	
14 Joubert & Monty biltong V&A	R200	
15 Ster Kinekor V&A	R65	2.15pm show!
	R13 995	

I agree, on the surface, it does not look that flash. I can even sense some disquiet with Stevie. His, 'Jeez, Jason' is a bit of a giveaway.

Et Tu, Stevie, I think to myself. Kick a man in the balls when he is on the ropes. Besides I have more dirt on him. Like proper compost.

Gary is banging on about him completely understanding investing to grow the business and understanding corporate hospitality, but he has two concerns: one, some of the lines seem to be stretching corporate hospitality a bit and are hard to fathom and, two, the, as he puts it, 'sheer quantum'. He then starts picking out some examples.

'Like the vet bill?'

I concede this straight up. 'Sorry, okes, my bad, I used the wrong card by mistake. Sorry, man, course I will pay back.'

'Biltong?'

'Corporate wellness,' I point out, looking at Stevie to help bail me out here, but he is deadpan. 'I am off carbs and we need the MD healthy and focused.'

'Ster-Kinekor?'

'Corporate destresser.'

'Paul Smith for R1,250?'

'What's this, fucking Nuremberg?' I crack a laugh.

3G is looking bleaker than Afriforum. Baumgarten is like a demonic flyweight pummelling the ribs of a giant heavyweight who's on the ropes (JB),with his arms tied behind his back.

And so it goes. Despite the hangover, I feel like I need a drink.

THURSDAY 24 NOVEMBER 2011

20 years to the day that we lost Freddie. To AIDS. Or as the ANC call it Cerebral Malaria or a 'protracted illness'. Like Steve Tshwete. Mr Break It, as Rex called him.

'I can see clearly now, the rain has gone.' What I mean is I can see some daylight. Sure, there are some issues at a corporate level, but if you let work rule your life you are a 'sad little fuck', as Reg Hobson once called me. Don't think he was talking about work, but anyway.

There was some British politician who once said that of the 37 ways of avoiding trouble, running away remained the best. So I give the office a wide berth this morning.

As I subscribe to the Platinum level service, Jordan, my life navigator sends me a quote every day. Today's is an African proverb: 'The river may be wide, but it can be crossed'. And boy, is she right. As usual.

The daylight comes in the form of:

One. Trying to see if I can return to my office without having a cup of boiling water thrown at me or something engraved into the door of the Audi, I look at Hayley's Facebook page. Don't ask, but sometimes it just appears; He works in mysterious ways. She is at the airport about to fly back to Jozi. Probably flies cargo.

Just like his old man: Jason Brydon, The Man They Couldn't Hang. Ahoy!

Two. One 'bored' member, so far, has approved my London trip in January 'to see what they're doing there' in liquor solutions. Shot, Stevie. We're just sticking on class of travel.

Three. I am being proactive on the Costa thing. He is not on the Interpol wanted list on their site. But I've phoned Crime Stop to warn them that he may be coming back. Just in case he is wanted for anything or he has been finally connected to Lolly Jackson's murder.

A small little irritation, though. When I found Mrs Costa's Audi, it had the My Family stickers on the back. A dad and his Weber, a mom in gym clothes, some brats and of course the two dogs. I peeled off the mom and kids. So it was guy with Weber, a few gaps and then the dogs. I didn't want to scare away the single (not essential) ladies of the City Bowl, did I? Will have to replace those stickers in case the human greaseball slips through our porous borders.

Also, he can't come back now, not until I find Gary Cooper. Those fucking microchips they put in dogs are useless – don't make the mistake of thinking they're trackers cos they're not. You can only find the owners when the dog is already found. But they can't actually find the dog. They can plot a great white chowing a few Seychellian fishermen en route from here to Perth, but you can't find a French Bulldog (maximum speed 2km per annum) in Tamboerskloof.

Four. I have a date with this girl Jade – a date date. She is a friend of my new mate Gary and is basically in the middle nines. Gary, no relationship to Gary Baumgarten, the human cuttlefish, plays in the online mature adult space. House in Clifton, called Hotel Garifornia, that has its own escalator. We did a party for him and we just clicked. Drives a pimped-up camo Cayenne – *sick*. And two Harley somethings with tassels in the garage. And straight. He tees me up with his ex Jade, who was once a swimwear model. Really.

I bump into Muggs at the Vida. He is with (a still seething) Dawesy who is paying. It's a bit awkward.

'Howzit Muggs. How's it, bru?'

'Howzit Jase?'

'Ja, cool hey, your side?'

'Lekker, bru.'

'Lekker, bru.'

'So, man, what's up?'

'Ja, lekker, boet.'

'So what you up to?'

'Not much, bru.'

'What you up to this evening?'

'Got a date.'

Dawesy joins in. Muggs tells him about the date. His advice is: 'Whatever else you do, Brydon, don't be yourself.'

Honestly, I think I have outgrown them.

Two Mr Mins, two Jose Cuervo shots and a line or two of China Crisis and I am anything but myself.

With the 'products' kicking in, my new True Religions fitting snugly (I know), the company card now ATM-enabled (= thicker wallet), I slide into the leather of the Scirocco (roof down) and I ask myself:

'Jason, my boy, honestly, where did it all go right?'

Obviously I haven't told Megan about 'Le Date'. I don't think one
is obliged to tell a banker. And that's the thing with a banker – you
build an innings around that. You don't want to scare it off. There're
two types of banker: the one who knows she is a banker, is open-
minded and there is a mature understanding; then there are those
who do not know they're a banker, and would probably strip their
guavas if they knew. I think Megan falls into the latter category. She
probably is under the mistaken impression that she is my girlfriend.
In fact, not telling her about #Jadedate is just Jason being sensitive,
considerate and caring.

FRIDAY 25 NOVEMBER 2011

Amber's old man, that freak whose party we did in Hout Bay, has
gone on the Book with this post:

> Keep an eye out on Carte Blanche for an insert on the fraudsters
> @igloo, the 'bar solutions' company and their CEO, one Jason
> Brydon. They the pricks who diluted drinks at our party. They
> about to get their comeuppance.

Here are the stats:
He has 786 friends.
That post got 32 likes.
17 comments – not going to up my self-esteem to open them.

Mich SMSes me:

> Did you see that post Jason? Is it true? Are you finally going to be
> on TV? Bahahaha. Hope it's not true. Coffee soon? Mwah x

I have to block out this rubbish. Like any good CEO, if you're going to worry about the odd bit of bad publicity you are not going to provide shareholder value.

Literally, the highs and lows.

What's that saying again? Epic fail?

Two things really. I pick her up from her flat in Beach Road, which is a promising start. Better than meeting her there, which leaves too much room for escape. She is very tidy. Look fairly high mileage and showing some signs of damp coming through the paintwork, but tidy. Her voice is more irritating than Pommie Mbangwa's, but that's not why we're here. But as we hit the pavement, I step, with my suede Paul Smith loafers, into a steaming pile of dog turd. As much as I do my best with a branch and some of the *Sea Point Bulletin* that was floating around, it has been absorbed into Mr Smith's finest suede. There is not a tap anywhere in sight. There are no taps on streets any more in case someone steals the water and you have to enter into a payment plan with the City of Cape Town.

I get most off and she is very good with all the 'shame', 'people really should pick up after their dogs' and 'this evening can only get better', the last of which, tragically, is not true.

You couldn't smell it so much in the November air (powered by a Force 9 southeaster blowing anorexics and Toy Poms off the Promenade to Robben Island), but once we got in my car, my god. Sewage plant on wheels. She still tried to be polite with 'shame', 'doesn't matter', 'it will soon go away'. Again the last statement of which is patently untrue. Even with some of Bogota's Best up my schnoz, I can still smell it. As much as it is not my fault and as much as we're putting up a brave face, it is affecting the quality of the date.

We are going to Bungalow (the old La Med). A bit of atmosphere is lost by the fact that the southeaster is so strong it's repositioned Lion's Head and there is dark grey cloud rolling through. I leave the shoes and go in barefoot feeling like somebody out of Woodstock (the concert *and* the suburb). And very self-conscious.

I go to the toilet to 'regroup'. Far from ideal as I can feel the inaccurate sprayers and bounce-back urine on my bare feet. Obviously while I am gone she takes out her iPhone 5 and gets on Facebook.

When I get back she shows me a picture of Phumeza. 'Who's this Jason?' The coke helps the slick reply. 'Oh, that's my old maid.'

'Says she's in a relationship with you?'

Hell hath no fury like a woman scorned… There was no need for her to post this…

'What!!? I think she means employer/employee relationship.'

'Nope.'

I try my best after that but the damage is done. She says it's because I lied to her that she got a cab. I'm not so sure. I think she's just a racist and, as such, I want no part of it. Deleted her number in case the tequila kicked in and I lost my racism-repellent control system and tried to patch things up.

But I do SMS Phumeza. I thought it funny even if she didn't:
Hello Darkness my old friend.

Fuck, that car honked when I got in. I am not sure whether it was that or the Stroh Rum that made me puke on Kloof Nek.

MONDAY 28 NOVEMBER 2011

On what will be forever known as Black Monday, this one pops up in a PDF attachment. From Greenstein, Goldberg, Goldblatt and (the requisite) Modise Attorneys:

Dear Sir

The writer acts on behalf of Hayley Jenkins. We are instructed as follows:

You are the biological father of (*full name of child*) born on (*date of birth*). You have the clear legal obligation to maintain your child, which is enforceable in a Maintenance Court and in the criminal justice system. Your liability includes the costs incurred by our client whilst on maternity leave and pursuant to the birth. She has already provided you with copies of the medical accounts which you are required to pay forthwith.

Our client has calculated the costs of the child, which include an appropriate contribution towards accommodation and living expenses. The monthly costs in respect of the child amount to R10,000 per month, excluding medical costs.

Our client's financial resources are insufficient in order to sustain her personal maintenance expenses. In the circumstances, we submit that she is entitled to payment of the child's full maintenance expenses.

We are instructed that you have repeatedly made undertakings to pay maintenance. However you have failed and neglected to make any such payments. Our client has concluded that you have no intention of upholding your legal duty.

We are instructed to take appropriate legal action. Our client intends to institute an enquiry in the Maintenance Court in accordance with Act 99 of 1998. You will be served with a subpoena requiring you to attend Court and fully disclose all documentary proof of your assets, liabilities, income and expenditure.

We are instructed to demand, as we hereby do, that you forthwith make payment of the arrear cash maintenance in respect of the child being the sum of R50,000 for the last five months, and that you make payment of the sum of R10 000 by or before the first day of each and every month, without deduction or set-off. In the event that you fail to do so, our client will claim all such arrears in the Maintenance Court.

Our client will separately compile a spreadsheet of all medical costs incurred and will continue to do so on a monthly basis. You are required to forthwith make payment of all such sums as presented and vouched to you.

Our client is extremely disappointed at your disregard for your obligations and duties towards your child and your repeated failure in this regard. She will not grant you any leniency or indulgence in the future. In the event of any default by you in the future, she will take appropriate legal action in the civil and criminal Courts. In doing so she will claim the costs thereby incurred from you.

Yours faithfully
Alan J Goldstein

Adolf was misunderstood, I sometimes am forced into feeling.

And while we're at it, this email:

Dear Mr Brydon,

YOUR UNLAWFUL CONDUCT

We refer to the above and confirm that we act on behalf of Costa Vlissedes. He has instructed ourselves to address this missive to you, in respect of your ongoing housesitting and occupation of our client's premises whilst he is overseas (where he remains extant). He has become aware of certain events which are of grave concern to him.

We are instructed as follows:

1. At all material times you agreed to housesit our client's premises for a period whilst our client was overseas.
2. The express, alternatively tacit, alternatively implied, terms of the agreement were inter alia that:
   a. You would not make use of our client's luxury vehicle;
   b. You would not engage in any parties;
   c. You would remain in communication with our client and timeously respond to all and any messages and attempts to communicate;
   d. You would conduct yourself in a manner that was befitting the area in relation to noise, nuisance and the like vis-à-vis the neighbours, giving due consideration thereto;
   e. You would remain within the spending limit as agreed in respect of our client's Woolworths card;
   f. You would properly maintain the premises in a state of good condition and repair including, but not limited, to the crockery, glassware, ornaments and other paraphernalia.
3. Moreover, it was an express term of the agreement that you would be responsible for our client's dogs. You were to ensure that they were well looked after, fed and walked.
4. In breach of the aforementioned, you have conducted yourself in a reprehensible manner, to wit:
   a. You have utilised our client's vehicle without his prior consent;
   b. You have held 'parties' at our client's premises;
   c. You have caused certain movable items to be broken;
   d. You have abused and overspent on his Woolworths card;
   e. You have failed to communicate with our client and failed to return his messages;
   f. You have conducted yourself in an anti-social manner to an extent that our client has received a multitude of complaints and with the consequence of certain fines being imposed; and

g. You have neglected to look after our client's dogs in a manner in accordance with his requirements.

In the circumstances we are instructed to demand, as we hereby do, that you forthwith vacate our client's premises and deliver up the keys thereto to our offices. Should you not attend thereto by close of business on Friday 2 December 2011 then we hold instructions to immediately launch the appropriate court proceedings for your eviction and/or other ancillary relief. In such circumstances the legal costs incurred will be for your own account.

Our client is presently quantifying his damages and we shall in due course be directing a further letter of demand in this regard. Rest assured that our client insists that he will recover all and any losses incurred by him as a result of your unlawful conduct. Suffice to state that our client's rights remain reserved.

We trust that you will be guided accordingly

Yours faithfully
SSKTK Attorneys – Africa's finest

I google. They are: Shapiro, Shapiro, Khumalo, Taylor & Kerzner. Almost feel sorry for Mr Taylor with that lot.

Charming. Fucking charming.

TUESDAY 29 NOVEMBER 2011

Twenty-one people are killed in an accident on the N1. So obviously there's a taxi involved. But what else? I know they can fit a lot in, but there has to be another car or two involved to reach 21. I scan the names, but there are no whites involved. Yes, there is a Coetzee amongst the dead, but his name is Riccardo which means he is probably Cape Spanish. People don't realise that there are about five million whites in SA and about 50 million blacks. So proportionally that means if 21 whites were killed in an accident, that's the equivalent of 210 blacks!

I order the Diesel Larkees on Amazon. Yes, you can get them in SA, but if I was to use the company credit card at the Diesel shop Gary Bumgarden would have a triple bypass. However, if he sees Amazon on my credit card statement he's going to think I bought books and I will say they were business-management books and some kak from that frizzy-haired Malcolm Gladwell who couldn't benchpress a packet of sultanas.

It was a bit disturbing to see that customers who bought these also bought Calvin Klein low-rise mens briefs – fine – but also groin enlargers – not needed in the case of JB Inc.

WEDNESDAY 30 NOVEMBER 2011

OK, so we have got into a little bit of dilution. And when I say a little bit, I mean a little bit. You know, people order a double Jameson's and soda with ice? That ice melts, right? And what happens? The drink gets diluted, right? So what if we just start the process a little earlier, but dropping in 30ml of the DA-led city's tap water – the best metropolitan tap water in Africa?

Who the fuck's going to notice? We don't do it for beer or wine obviously, but anything that requires an ice cube or two is going to get a drop of H_2O. What I know about business is it's about the margins and every percent counts. So if in a 750ml bottle of

Platinum Blue you put in 150ml of water, that's 20% right there, china. And it's actually a public service because everybody from *Fairlady* to *Men's Health* tells you that you should drink some water with your booze. Well, at @igloo we provide that service free of charge, gratis. *Vir niks.* Lekker.

And Gary the garden gnome sees our bottom line look a bit more like it used to be in the old days. I point out we are growing revenue rather than his attacking our costs all the time. Every vegetable who knows anything about business knows you can't grow a business by cutting the cost lines (and the company credit cards). Doos.

THURSDAY 1 DECEMBER 2011

OK, that's New Year's Eve done. Some fucking Russian has booked us for a New Year jol on his fucking yacht which is so big it has to berth in the working harbour. Two pools, a helipad, a lift, a tennis court, floodlit, of course. I had hoped it was Roman Abramovich so I could tell him to keep André Villas Boas as manager so Manchester United can keep on cleaning their pipes inside out. But it's some other one who owns Vladivostok and Nevada or something.

How did we get the deal? You won't believe it, but thanks to Stevie's Mavericks 'connections'.

Apparently the one, Nadia, used to service the ships engineer when it cruised the Caspian Sea. And she had an 'after hours' arrangement with Stevie. Small world. Globalisation is rampant. You no longer need to read *Time* magazine to see what's going on out there.

Anyway it's worth 300K to @igloo. Ahoy.

THURSDAY 1 DECEMBER 2011

The party month. The shorts get smaller, the skirts shorter, the arms barer. And they flock into the Mother City. I reckon even a professional, top-10-ranked Namibian seal-pup culler will have a lower strike rate than Jason Brydon this December.

I am not sure if Megan is my girlfriend. On her FB, I am. But on my FB, I am still single. It's a WhatsApp exchange.

Jsn, y is ur status stil sgl on fb? Xx

Oh, haven't been on the book for ages

Didn't think that through as I had posted the pic of Stevie, 3G and me on Gary's boat off the Radisson on yesterday's sunset cruise, careful to avoid posting any of those belters that were on board.

But Megan is palpably not going to design a rocket to take us to Pluto.

B sure 2 wen u nxt on. C u @ mine 4 dnr. Tie grn ckn curry xx

Even if she is my girlfriend – and that *if* is bigger than the Eiffel Tower – to cheat on her would be very French. In France, every man is allowed to have a couple of mistresses in sunny apartments where he goes for long afternoons. Not sure who pays, though.

Anyway, of course December is our busiest month by far. But I am not going to hold back on any front. Do you think if Keith Richards looks back now at his life he would have gone to bed at 10 o'clock every night?

FRIDAY 2 DECEMBER 2011

Jackie Selebi has lost his appeal and is going to *tronk – finish 'n klaar.*

Obviously our first Christmas office party of the season and quite predictably that's Nashua, thanks to Stevie. He is being a bit of a chop about it.

'I thought you were meant to be the rainmaker, Brydon.'

Nasty and churlish.

'Steve, it's the company you work for, china. If you can't land that, then we may as well give up. It would be harder to land a lead sinker.'

'And Mr Ozorensky? New Year's Eve. Just the 300k. Jason?'

'I see the southeaster's up.'

To shut him up, I land the Xanontech Christmas party. They're new on the copier scene. Small, but 'disruptive', I warn Steve. 'Sleep on your backs at Nasha, china.'

Abstinence, in case you're wondering, is still full of it. She says she wants to go back to the Transkei for 'personal reasons'. She's a maid – what are personal reasons? If she was Kevin Cusack, Spacey or Pietersen one would understand personal reasons, but she is a domestic worker. Then she says she wants her holiday. But I can't really let her go now, not this month, not when I have so many functions and the washing and ironing is going to have to be at its sharpest.

She says she goes every year 'when Mr Costa goes to Knysna'.

'Well, Costa is not here now, is he? I am the baas now. Sorry, mamma.'

'Hayi, suga. Mr Costa wants you out the house, says I should phone Mr Shapiro the lawyer.'

I take the perlemoen position – I'm not moving. Who is she to tell me what to do? It's like a Cessna pilot giving Neil Armstrong tips.

I text my old maid Delicious. That's how low I am prepared to go. I am even prepared to fund her myself.

> Hi Delicious, hope all well. Not sure what you up to but assume your lotto money is running out if it hasn't already. Which days are you free? I am looking for someone for three mornings a week.
> 8-1, R100 a morning plus pie, tea/coffee (Ricoffy) taxi fare. Jase

Another *'hayi suga'* as a reply.

And they wonder why they're poor. I know I am not offering much, but that's R1,200 a month. Is it really not worth it? The fact that she thinks she's better off loitering around the township sums up exactly what is wrong with this country.

So we do the Xanontech do and lay it all on. The biggest mammaries we have. Some doos in a blue short-sleeved shirt with the Xanontech logo above the pocket gets up and makes a speech about what a year it's been and despite the economy teetering in recession they are up year on year… zzzz. He eventually gets handed a Jägerbomb by some blonde thing teetering on a pair of heels so high they make her bum look small, but at ground level, would be massive. He downs it, and another, grimaces and yells, 'Now let's get savage,' and the 'party' starts.

Or splutters along. Some are savages, some hacks and, to be honest, for the first time in this life well lived I almost feel sorry for a

Muslim. Watching this bunch of clowns throw as much of my 10 percent water product down their gullets as possible, I hope I am not like that when tipsy.

So far, unfortunately, nobody has taken their top off.

Then the thing in heels comes tottering to the bar, slips on the melting water from the ice-model Xanontech JX1300Y copier and breaks her fall by cleverly using her (somewhat buck) teeth on the bar counter. I am opposite her behind the bar and I just see blood and the odd piece of enamel. One thing about a Brydon is that he knows his timing. I grab the Scirocco keys. Stevie is going to have to, literally and figuratively, clean this one up.

The only grey area is that one of them asked for the sculpture to be on an absorbent mat to avoid slippage. Yes, I forgot, but technically it was never in the budget, nor quoted on, and @igloo is not the Mother Teresa Health & Welfare Foundation, are we?

But I have an advanced social barometer and I know when I can add value and when I can't. No problem is so bad it's not better solved in the morning. Adios. Phone off.

SATURDAY 3 DECEMBER 2011

Schalk getting married today. Surprisingly I am NFI.

The Verve sang that song 'and drugs don't work'. They were obviously buying the wrong shit because they do. How else would I have pulled Roxy at Jackal & Hide last night? Hmmm?

In my hungover, but pleased-with-myself, state, I watch the Sevens in Dubai. We are a very 'representative' team. That's because, Rex says, you can get away with smaller players in 7s. 'You can play a couple of street urchins, slippery as greased eels.'

England have a player playing for them called Christian Lewis-Pratt. And they wonder why everybody hates them? Nobody must feign surprise when in a few years he kidnaps and rapes a Boy Scout.

It's not ideal that on a hungover Kauai-strewn day like this Sir Alex arrives. I would much rather he came tomorrow as Meg and I are 'staying in' tonight. I am just not up for him today. Sir Alex of course is my new Boerboel cross Great Dane puppy – but already bigger than Costa's spastics.

I must admit, I ordered him in leaner times. When the Jasonator's strike rate was about 0.1 – approximately one pull in 10 nights out. Chris Gayle's is about 1.6 on and off the field. Having a puppy is basically followed by yelling, 'Ladies, ladies, calm down.'

Diary, if it's the last thing I do, I am going to make Gary Baumgarten lick my balls.

SUNDAY 4 DECEMBER 2011

Costa on Facebook has posted this:
> Leaving Greece next week. Can't wait to get back to prosperous SA, magical Cape Town and a good braai. Can't wait to get back to what's left of my home.

And what's left of Gary Cooper's ear, pal...

I do have some understanding given that Sir Alex has been particularly playful. A lot of people are saying I should walk him, but I feel it's just too soon.

Oh, the braai bit reminds me: must get a new Weber lid. The Spitfire? Shit happens. Will tell him it got shot down. Over the Channel.

Wonder when exactly next week that is. I need to put some tarmac between me and the Big Angry Greek Family.

And is next week the week starting tomorrow or week starting next Monday? What does next week mean on a Sunday? People?

MONDAY 5 DECEMBER 2011

I phone that hermaphrodite of a letting agent Greg Bax and tell him to recalibrate our target. The spot I want no longer has to be *Top Billing*-able, must be dog-friendly (I can't very well leave Sir Alex at the villa) and you must be able to see the sea and have a deck. And be fully furnished and available this week.

'You don't half ask a lot, do you?' he/she squeals.

I take the Audi to Dougy's Coachworks and beg them to repair the damage by Wednesday. They think it's unlikely. I tell some gangsta with a spray can and an attitude I will 'make it worth his while'. I don't worry about the Scirocco – I was allowed to use that. Actually it smells okay with the StaSoft. On the way to Dougy's, some warning message comes on about being overdue for the 50,000 service. Problem, but, to quote Jordan, my worth-every-cent life navigator, 'it's only a problem if YOU let it be a problem'. Spot on, girl.

There is a lesson in this and it's stark and clear: as much as you shouldn't text when drunk, don't order things (pets) online when lit.

As the day is about to slip away into cocktails I get a double mega whammy. Firstly, a call from a Joburg number. Not Hayley's so I answer. Its some native from *Carte Blanche*. OMG, they want us to do a party for them. OMG! Even *Carte Blanche* wants to use us. Trebles all round. I tweet it.

> **@igloo:** have arrived. Doing @carteblanche party. #unstoppableforce

Then it hits me. It could be a trap.

I get an email on my phone about a million words long from Costa's big fat lawyers. I scan it quickly as I am due at Caprice. Something about me failing to vacate the house. And 'urgent remedial steps'.

Tomorrow's problem.

TUESDAY 6 DECEMBER

We've turned over half a bar this month already. The one party in Bishopscourt was worth R160K by itself, chinas. Bishopscourt – a suburb with streets with names like Norwich, Chester, Gloucester and Upper Torquay. Don't send the Eurocentric police or the street-renaming coalition out there. In fact, they're not even 'streets' in Cape Town's leafiest suburb – they are 'drives'. But I do think renaming one of them Mao Tse Tsung Boulevard would be bloody funny and have them spluttering into their Pimms Number Ones. And while we're at it, we change Canterbury Drive to Avenida Joe Slovo.

Anyway, you're nobody in those parts if you don't have a guard hut with reflective glass at the gate (theoretically so you can't see how many guards are inside, but also suits the guard so you can't see he's fast asleep). If I lived in Bishopscourt, I would also have one.

You see in the morning all the service providers flood in, on foot, on bicycles, in spluttering old bakkies, the smarter ones with the white driver in shorts and Oakleys and the overalled mob on the back. All visitors.

They say one prick has his own robot on his property, but not sure that's true.

I can be accused of lots of things – partying too hard, risk taking, being a gym bunny, a clothes gay, a player, living too fast, some substance dependence, focusing too much on balance, slaying women's hearts, probably not a nominee for Father of the Year – but I cannot be accused of stupidity. I guess when I discovered dilution it must have been a bit like Cecil (really?) Rhodes. When he was starting Rhodesia and he saw the Victoria Falls that he couldn't cross, he didn't just say, 'Fuck it, let's turn around.' No, he said, 'Right that's my tourism sorted. Let's have a look at the rest of the economy.'

No we at @igloo are not stupid. We don't dilute straight up. If you come early on in the function, your Johnnie Walker Blue is going to be 100% Johnnie Walker Blue. Keep Walking (which by the way is going to be on my gravestone in Antibe or wherever I check out at 60). But later on, when the noise level of conversation is up several decibels and the first chops have started ordering the bottles with the red dots on, their caps come out. Those puppies are down 25-30%. And nobody notices. The whiskers and brandies have a little cold rooibos just for 'maintenance of colour integrity'. Very important.

And the money, to quote little known Jamaican reggae outfit, Eek A Mouse, 'it pour like rain'.

Somewhat brought back to earth by this SMS from Costa:
> Jason, did you really send this sms to Abstinence: 'Abstinence my True Religions are filthy. Where did you wash them? The fucking Ganges? I am docking R50 off tomorrow's pay and this SMS serves as your final written no matter what Jimmy the Greek says.' Really Jason? I am back next week to sort this and you out.

Probably just closing the 7/11.

As Kenny Rogers, one of Val Brydon's favourites, sings in *The Gambler*, 'You gotta know when to hold em, know when to fold em, know when to walk away, know when to run…'

And as the Nude Girls sing in *Blue Eyes*, 'Round about, round about, round about now.'

WEDNESDAY 7 DECEMBER 2011

At the robots in Buitengracht, a guy selling *Funny Money* wearing a Santa Claus hat, oversized yellow sunglasses (thanks Elton) and blowing one of those party whoopers, leans over my windscreen and blows it out. I am texting and shake my head. I edge suddenly forward so he has to step back quickly to evade and he almost hits a cyclist who shouts 'Watch out, bru'. Karma.

Then he reappears at my window, the saddest face ever blowing a whooper in and out. I turn to look and he is indicating to his stomach that he is hungry.

What the fuck? I already said no.

'Can't you see I am busy, bud?' And hold up my iPhone 4s.

Surely he must try other cars? I will the light to change. But, like Megan on Sundays, he (over)stays.

I lose it and wind down the window. 'Fuck off now, buddy, I already said no!'

'Boss, I haven't got a job.'

'Whose fault is that?'

'Boss, I need food. I have a family.'

Why's he picking on me, the poes?

'Go ask Zoomer.'

Green light, thank god, and gone, a little bit of rubber left on the tarmac for his Christmas.

The glisten of that little victory was taken off by a call from that bushman from *Carte Blanche*. He's seen that goatee freak from Hout Bay's post that we dilute our drinks. I am friendly but firm. Their party nets us a hundred K so I can't tell him to eff off back to Mamelodi or wherever M-Net found him, dusted him off and gave him a pair of Paul Smith specs.

'Don't know where you got that from, pal. We are 100% pure and use only sustainable alcohol.'

He chuckles. Rude.

'But don't worry. You guys are going to have an epic thrash.'

I smell a rat. A big black one that has been mining underground for a week with athlete's foot, halitosis and a septic toe.

THURSDAY 8 DECEMBER 2011

Dad mails. Thirty-one years to the day since John Lennon was assassinated (I was 0). To be assassinated you have to be *big*. If I was shot in New York, it would be just be a normal murder, but if you are assassinated it means you have made it. Or had made it, rather. Mom and Dad love the Beatles.

The Stones to me were bigger. Dad says girls used to queue in the hotel corridors outside their hotel rooms, none uglier than Miss Belgium, waiting their turn.

I just don't like Yoko Ono, not one little bit. Look, it's not racist, it's just that she is the world's top professional widow. That's why she can't get remarried. Then she would lose the title. Mind you, not sure who would marry her. Not with a horizontal vagina.

Tweet:

> **@jasonator069:** great meal@thetestkitchen. Molecular cooking at its best. Luke Dale Roberts #nationaltreasure.

> **@muggsy @jasonator069:** Brydon, what have you become? Do you even know what molecular cooking is?

I see three houses with Greg Bax in his/her mini (car not skirt). *She* is wearing a kaftan. He/she says it's because of the heat. Then don't wear eyeshadow, pal, I think to myself. She is sweating like Sharleen Surtee Richards in a Bombay sauna and we are listening to Foreigner in the mini which the she-man sings along to. 'I wanna know what love is' – and turns round and looks at me as they sing 'and I want *you* to show me.'

I put my hand on the door handle. If she lunges at me, I will, even if we're moving, jump out, roll along the road, jump up and dust my elbow, just like Daniel Craig.

But he doesn't do anything. It's tricky, you know. When you've made it like I have, you get used to living in a certain way. I can't go and live in some shitty old Victorian in Green Point where you can sort of see the sea from the top left corner of the balcony if you crane your neck for 18K a month.

You're not going to get girls flocking back to your spot for the 'original fireplace' or teak floors, or stunning use of space in the backyard. Or the reflection room. I send Mrs Bax back to her office and the drawing board. She squeals that she was working within my budget so I bump him up a bracket.

'I won't get back into your mini for anything less than 22K a month.'

He wears a wedding ring. But I know that sort. He is married to a Cobus who used to be in the Police Dog Unit, but took the package. He is now the country's best British Shorthair breeder. Police Dog Unit to cat breeder. Make up your mind, pal. About everything.

FRIDAY 9 DECEMBER 2011

I have relooked at those legal letters that I got on what historians will call in generations to come Black Monday.

It seems I don't actually have to do anything. There is no ultimatum, no 'if you don't do this, we will arrest you', just an instruction to get out of the house. Which I am working on.

I delete them from my inbox – just seeing them in there is no good for my anxiety. Jordan agrees. Today's proverb: 'He who worries, will worry.' Like it.

I do some load shedding, which hurt like hell after I ordered the Vindaloo at Bukhara last night, fed Sir Alex, I think, and took Megan for a steak down the road. It wasn't a date – we're well past that – but I had a craving for a nice juicy ribeye and it's kak to go for supper alone. So I said she could come.

> **@jasonator069:** great steak at nelsons eye tonite. Still sober enough to floss when I came home. Licked the floss afterwards #mealinitself

Seems some of the twittersphere are grossed out, poor darlings.

SATURDAY 10 DECEMBER 2011

Well, that's the last of the goldfish. Found him floating on the surface in the pond this morning when I went for a pee. I think it may have been starvation, but he seems to have his insides floating out, so I doubt it was that. Maybe old age combined with upset stomach?

This time of year we're doing like three functions a day. Told Ishmael who does our sculptures just to roll out a whole lot of Christmas trees and a few reindeer. Much easier than custom-making for every party. Allah the Most Benevolent and All Seeing does not appear to have a problem with Ishmael making Christian symbols for a bar services solutions conglomerate.

But it means I'm struggling to keep up Red Dot production. Not ideal. There's iceman Kyle, probably now our senior barman, and me sitting in Costa's garage decanting and diluting spirits. Kyle is sworn to secrecy. I can trust him, he went to Wynberg Boys. It may be the school of hard knocks but they breed them tough there, and loyal. I must say – and, please, I don't mean this in the wrong way – he has a six-pack I would kill for.

Sir Alex has shat in the main bedroom on the shaggy carpet and I can't face it. I phone Marvellous Maids, which in my view is an oxymoron of a name. There is lots to do and the only real way is to throw money at the problem.

In the same vein I have got him a dog walker. Some freak who was laid off by the Post Office, an achievement in itself, who comes up in a clapped-out Ford Bantam with a yapping, crapping load of the neighbourhood's most spoilt. To throw in Ferris and Gary Cooper was another R300 a week so I said no. I need them to bulk up for when Costa del Sol comes back, not shed.

SUNDAY 11 DECEMBER 2011

I take the day off – tell the other directors that I need to avoid burnout. Alphonse says he has the perfect product to ensure I don't burn out, but I don't feel like magic mushrooms today – no desire to see a flock of royal blue flamingos in my bath or be chased through Woolworths food by a squadron of goblins in V formation.

Instead I take a classic Cape Town Funday. Go to Clifton Fourth but it seems a bit young, so I pull into my mate Gary's spot above Third, a.k.a. The Hotel Garifornia. At his pozzie we get stuck into a few Heinies and then hit Caprice with the rest of Gauteng.

Slug texts me to ask if I'm going to Reg Hobson's party. NFI. That pleased-with-himself prick is clearly still pissed off that I lost his dog on Camps Bay and that his wife caught me pissing in their sink.

> No mate. Was invited but got 2 other parties on bro. Njoy!!! Beer this week?

> Tks bro. Wasn't expecting u to b invited, just asking cos Lettuce won't go if you going.

Even he calls that frustrated lesbian wife of his Lettuce now. Slug really needs to grow some. Balls not lettuce. On their invitation they wrote at the bottom: 'Stephen (Slug) and Sandi (Lettuce) would like to inform you that this will be an unplugged wedding.' Apparently that means no cellphone pics, tweets, Instagram. What the fuck for? They're not Joost and Amor.

Post a picture of me with James Small, who used to own Caprice, on Instagram.

Gary Baumgarten: careful of burnout.

Talk about a human roadblock. The cops should employ him. He is such a miserable, boring fuck that he will slow anyone down, sober anyone up. The Human Roadblock.

MONDAY 12 DECEMBER 2011

And burnout remains a threat.

Especially when I get this SMS from Kyle:
> Jason, you promised three months ago that I would go onto the same pay scale as Jed and Ross. And you said you would 'sort me out' after I spent after hours helping you dilute booze. Either you square it or I cant guarantee my discretion when it comes to you diluting. Kyle

Wow.

> Kyle, to me this is blackmail. And I am inclined to report it to the SAPS or Carte Blanche, who I deal with all the time. Our @igloo policy is not to react to threats from nor deal with blackmailers, terrorists or extremists. So if you were working for us and you got kidnapped by Al Qaeda, and they wanted a ransom we couldn't pay it even if we wanted to. Plus Jed and Ross are our senior icemen and much more experienced than you. Kr JB

He replies straight away:
> Jason, firstly, you offered to raise my salary, in fact to more than Jed and Ross – I didn't ask you. Secondly, I am not blackmailing

> you – I am just saying to you why should I cover for you and lie for
> you when you won't honour your word to me? Thirdly, when you
> passed out and vomited on the Italian Consul's tennis court, it was
> me who took the rap for you as you said it would be bad for both
> the Brydon and @igloo brands

Honestly, if I wasn't actually diluting I would have phoned the
Scorpions or whatever they are called now and have him locked up
with some oversexed 26ers.

I think by the time the SMS exchange ends, it's fair to say the
relationship may have broken down, based on his last message:

> Look at you Brydon, you a grim little self obsessed perverted little
> fuck, that's who you are. And a criminal – that's what you are, you
> spineless wonder.

You know, I get rubbish from him, but I don't care, I haven't heard
a word from *Carters* so seems that my fear of a trap is unfounded.
Trebles all round. OK, we lose the party (the battle) but win the war.

Oh, and another letter from SLK or whatever Costa's attorneys are
called. I see on their website their firm 'canteen', called Silk, has
its own executive chef, some Austrian hermaphrodite. That's what
Costa is paying for. I am still in the house and he is coughing. Only
one loser here. And it's not me or Mr Shapiro.

As usual the last paragraph is what I skip to – that's the crux. The rest
is their R1,250/minute legal mumbo jumbo.

'Failing which the Sheriff will attend to such eviction at 5pm on
Friday 23 Decmber 2011. He will also attach your movable property
to offset against the costs incurred by our client.'

No problem about my movables. Except the Vespa, I can move that. The rest won't cover the prawn bisque at Silk. But 23 December? The day before Christmas Eve. #haveaheart

TUESDAY 13 DECEMBER

In an effort to mitigate the fallout (and we are expecting nuclear here) of Costa's return, I try to do some damage control. The garden seems to have lost all its greenery and now looks like the Baghdad Botanical Gardens due to a combination of Sir Alex's excavation work and some of the most virulent moles ever encountered.

I call a mole guy. Somehow his ageing Sentra, half-metal, half-duct tape, splutters up the hill. He is also an ex-cop and is called the Moleman. His mission? To exterminate the moles that are breeding like Venda in the garden. I do feel a bit for him – must be tough going from taking on and exterminating cash-in-transit robbers to taking on and exterminating moles. His assistant Bongani is one of those with no hair who has creases in his head. Not sure whether it's a deformity or a tribal thing, but either way it's scary.

When I lived – or rather eked out an existence – in Joburg, our digs had a mole guy whose business was called Moleskin. That to me was much trendier and left you with no doubt as to what was going to happen to those little fuckers.

Anyway I am doing my community best by giving Moleman directions and throwing more acid than there was at Woodstock into the pool to get it to change from sludge green to something more azure, when this Corolla pulls up. Now Corollas might be Big in Bellville and you may only need to change a tissue for 300,000km but they're not big in the City Bowl. Especially ones without headrests. And the guy getting out has a shirt with epaulets. Again, epaulets aren't big in our parts. Unless the Mother City Queer Project theme is WWII. So the freak with the moustache oozes trouble.

'Jason Brydon?' He both asks and states. He is clutching an ominous manila envelope. I scan his waist to see if he has a gun or radio. Just keys and a Leatherman. Bad enough.

I keep quiet and look blank.

Again. 'Jason Brydon.'

I shake my head… Say nothing. But Moleman has other idea.

'That's Jason there, boet.'

I stare back at the fucker. He is unapologetic. 'He's just doing his job, boet. I been on the other side of that fence. Look, he's not coming to arrest you… Not yet.'

As they say, never does a good deed go unpunished. Here I am trying to fix up the Costa Vlissedes Botanical Gardens and I get a subpoena from some prick in a Corolla for my trouble. #justnotfair

I have to appear at the Maintenance Court in Joburg on 10 January. Same day as the Proteas play Sri Lanka in an ODI at Newlands. #evenlessfair

I know Costa is coming back this week. But how do you lease a villa in Cape Town in the middle of December, unless you are Elton John or Graham Norton? Or somebody from *Homeland*.

WEDNESDAY 14 DECEMBER 2011

The domestic crisis continues unabated. Jordan's quote today is from some geezer called George Bernard Shaw. Probably went to Michaelhouse, with a name like that. It's a confusing one in that I'm not sure what she expects me to do:

'Martyrdom: The only way a man can become famous without ability.'

Does she expect the Jasonator to fall on his sword? Or to get necklaced? There is nothing I believe in enough to die for. I'm not Nelson fucking Mandela. Plus I am not brave enough for suicide. I have never seriously considered it. Other than the one time I thought some sloppy chick I had scraped off the floor at Taboo had given me Aids, that night when I snorted Jägermeister. I thought I would rather top myself than weigh 45kg, live on Yogisip and more pills than Madonna, and have bedsores and die from a sneeze.

I figured I could drown myself while surfing: (a) dying while surfing is a lot cooler than lying on the railway in front of the Shosholoza Meyl (the old Trans Karoo); (b) it's not as sore; (c) it's in the budget – given what's going up my nose at the moment recreationally and how much that costs, I don't think I have the funds to OD; and (d) they say drowning is a very peaceful way to go. Apparently even more than ODing. I am not sure how reliable this information can be, in that who can actually tell you unless you go and visit a dreadful lesbian with a hooked nose and tie-dyed pants in her caravan in Noordhoek, reeking of incense. But suicide? It's not me. Bad for the brand. In the '70s it may have been cool, but not any more.

They used to say, back in the day, when you were still allowed to tell jokes: Q: What do you get if you cross a Doberman and a Rottweiler? A: A predominantly white neighbourhood. So, Q: What do you get if you cross a Great Dane with a Boerboel, keep it locked up and let it 'socialise' with some hermaphrodite French Bulldogs? A: Blood.

It seems Sir Alex might be a bit too 'fractious' for Gary Cooper and Ferris. I had to take Ferris to get his lip stitched this morning, this after he has sprayed blood all down the passage and on the spare room curtains. This is his third bit of patching in five days. It's out of control.

> **@jasonator069:** Message to all French bulldogs – if you can't stand the heat, stay away from the Heater. Not right but I seem to be responsible for all my landlords vet bills. #justice4jase

Costa Freakides according to Twitter, is on his way to Athens to fly back. It would be irresponsible of me to rely on Interpol or the SAPS to stop him en route. I suppose that last tweet of mine may just make him do something stupid. Like forget his false goatee or something.

I get hold of Bax. He has two houses on the hotlist. So we're back in the Mini. Right now, I have downgraded *Top Billing*-able to the second-most NB criterion, the most being availability. It must be as close to 'immediate' as can be, as in ideally 5pm today.

I notice the homo estate agent is wearing an IWC watch and it looks real. I am not sure why one would buy a real one when you can't tell the difference with a Thai one at a 100th of the price. But I suppose Greg Bax does have spending power. The moffies all do. You see they don't have to spend money on kids' universities, macaroni cheese, school uniforms, brass band instruments, education policies or Teletubbies, although Bax looks and walks a lot like Dipsy, the lime-green Tubby.

Mind you, that may be changing now with the rate they are adopting Aids orphans and spastics. You can't walk around the pink quarter without a little Zanele hanging on to a pair of them. I suppose it's their way of apologising for starting Aids. Or was it the monkeys in Congo? Or was that Ebola? Not sure – but you get my point.

Anyway we see a place off High Level Road that may do. It has no jacuzzi, no pizza oven, no sound system that you can hear in Fish Hoek, and it doesn't scream 'Fuck Off!' But it has a deck, a pool, a view and remote-control blinds. And a fridge you can programme and lets you know when your yoghurt may be going off. Bax just has to check availability. He says, 'I'm sure we can have you in in a few days.' I point out that I am talking more minutes, not days.

THURSDAY 15 DECEMBER 2011

See a poster for a concert with some chick with an afro calling it AfroPopera. Couldn't think of anything worse – on about three or four fronts.

Dad wants to go to Trennerys for a family holiday for New Year - what's he on? Don't answer, I know. Doesn't he know his daughter is married to a female Bakkies Botha, and is 33; Mom is so neurotic, just mention any of these: Zuma, Telkom, thefts from motor vehicles, farm murders, beetroot stains, Malema, load shedding (whilst she is baking), the price of saffron, the demise of CNA, Winnie, Clicks, garbage workers strike, illiterate policemen, fuchsias that won't grow, E. coli, water restrictions, car guards, Hansie, e.tv soft porn, the N2 minibus taxis, the Williams sisters (and their dad), Nataniël, the budget speech and the ever-rising price of her Gordon's gin and Craven Menthols (Dad says they were named after Doc), Tony

Yengeni (well, you see, he has been caught DUI 100 times and Dad just two and Dad has a restriction). Mention these and she is under her eiderdown.

Judging from Costa's Facebook post about a great meal in Athens this evening, he hasn't left yet. Shew. I wonder if that meal wasn't at a 'little Greek place?' Bahaha. Anyway, I need to know when he heads off to Athens Airport, so I google it just in case he mentions he is somewhere and I confuse it with an ouzeria. Athens International is not called Jackie Onassis International (JOI), as you might expect – it is Eleutherios Venizelos International. Unpronounceable with a couple of those Es written backwards. Ever heard of Eleutherios Venizelos? Nope, me neither, but it turns out he was some prominent Cretan politician. So prominent in fact that I've never heard of him. Not sure what the airport is like, but sure you could buy 20 Stuyvesant, a Coke, *The Star*, a KitKat and play a game of pinball there. Not that I am generalising – lots of Greeks do other things like run strip clubs, produce counterfeit cigarettes, bankrupt the euro, play cards, drive taxis, etc.

But the most important intel is that Costa Plenty is *not* at EVI yet, so I, like Pierce Brosnan as Bond, get to Die Another Day. But Bax must not rest on his adult incontinence nappies yet. I need a cool, cool pozzie tomorrow.

'You have one new voice message.' My standard start to checking in after I ignore a call from some 084 number (who does Cell C?). 'First message.'

'Jason, it's Jeff Jenkins here, Hayley's Dad. Sapphire's grandfather. The Sheriff's office confirms that you have been served your summons. They remember you because apparently you called their server a "sad little fuck". You know what? I actually hope you don't appear because nothing, and I mean nothing, would give me as much pleasure to see you being thrown into a holding cell in your Levi's.'

I don't wait for the voicemail chick to tell me what to push. 9 to save, 7 to delete. 7 wins.

Who still wears Levi's? Come on, Jeff.

FRIDAY 16 DECEMBER 200

Public holiday and @igloo have six, yes, six functions. Ker-ching! Five of them corporates and one for some Pom who was the drummer for Snow Patrol when they first started who now has his own label whose girlfriend is a *Sun* Page 3 Girl and has hired a villa in Camps Bay. He ticks a lot of boxes and I think we have the potential to be friends. We drop our dilution rate for his party – don't want to end up in the *Sunday Times*.

After work Stevie and I go out. It's like the old days – before we made it and became famous. In some ways it was like the old days in that we tried to jump the queue outside a new club in Bree Street called Monolith. We go right to the front of the queue to the red rope. There is some black gorilla with the earpiece and a little creep on the door. His one whole arm is tattooed from wrist to shoulder. The runt is wearing a vest. So you can see his whole 'sleeve', as I think they call it. Honestly, in my opinion, you can only do that if you're the front man for a rock band or the bassist for Kings of Leon or something. Not if you're on the door at Monolith.

I have a few petrols in me so when he tells me we must queue I pipe up, 'What happened to your arm, get caught in the Nashua copier?'

He wheels around. 'What did you say, pal?' He is virtually hissing. And he looks vicious. I sober up 40-45% instantly, it flashes across my mind that he may be one of those cage-fighter types, you know those MMA take-down crack-down smack-down kick-and-bite types. On reflection he looks wiry enough. And scarred enough. Like the Italian generals always recommend when you accidentally stumble on a battle, I hit reverse.

'Not to worry. Just going to the back of the queue,' and I take Stevie's elbow firmly.

But the prick is not having any of it. 'No, what did you say, pal?'

I realise that the Jasonator's in danger of going down. In front of a good crowd of sad cases queuing to go into Monolith. I try to point out that new-age bouncing is more about facilitating entry and defusing than confronting. But he keeps coming. Now he's poking a finger in my (ungymmed this week) chest, each word loud and staccato, 'WHAT, DID, YOU, SAY, PAL?'

Saved I suppose by my native intelligence. 'I was talking to Stevie my mate here, he works for Nashua. I said "Isn't that Carmen, the one you sold the Nashua copier?" And pointed at some scruffy redhead balancing on a pair of Guess shoes in the queue. 'But it's not her.'

It's only when Stevie takes out his ID and business cards to prove that he is a sales manager at Nashua that I am excused my hiding.

Monolith is declared not trendy enough for us and 'run by a bunch of Neanderthals' so we retreat to Aces n Spades.

Stevie is making progress with a poor man's Kim Basinger lookalike – just a bit dikker. But still an 8.3, at least. Lucky fuck, he breathes

Jameson's on me as he tells me to be a sport and be a good wingman. 'She is with some chick she hasn't seen since school, and her mom's got cancer or MND or some shit and she never goes out – I know mate, sniff sniff – but unless you look after Brittany here, my one's not gonna hook up with me. Do this, mate, be a good wingman, and I will tell 3G you must fly business class for your UK trip.'

I take a look at the friend. Oops. She looks a bit backward, eyes quite slit and out of Bluetooth distance from each other, and jaw is a bit recessed – in fact, she looks like there may be just a hint, just a hint of Down's Syndrome. We talking low fives here, maybe even a 4.8. Nowhere near the bracket where the Jasonator has been operating in since he found game and fortune (and some fraud).

But I kind of need Stevie. 'OK, Steve, but it's BA direct, no Air Cameroon or Air Kazakhstan via Vladivostok, business class, and I stay in a hotel near Hyde Park that costs at least 300GBP a night.

'And I take taxis. I never have to go on the tube.'

'But at rush hour the tube is quicker.'

'And much dirtier. Besides I never plan on being in a rush.' I offer my hand. 'Deal?'

He almost shakes my hand off he is so keen. In retrospect, diary, I should have held on for more. But it's done and I'm chuffed. That is until I notice that Miss Potentially A Touch Of Down's has bigger calves than mine. And that's after the Calf Fest of yesterday when I did eight sets of 10 at 150kg plus three drop sets and a super set.

I moan to Steve. 'And I now have to talk to this thing?'

'Not only talk to her, spade her, take her somewhere, take her home, anything. Just so that mine can focus on Stevie Wunda.'

'Cab from Heathrow, no tube.' I order two tequila golds. If I am to do this, let's make it as pain-free as possible. We christen her 'Downers'. Tequila is an upper, they say, and she, literally, is a Downer.

Surprisingly, me and Downers end up having some fun. A few bars in Long Street, the more touristy ones just so I don't bump into mates and I get seen with the girl from the Home. When we walk into a spot I gallantly let her go in first like something out of a Jane Austen novel, but then I hang back a good 30 seconds just to make it clear to the patrons that we are *not* together. By the time we're onto the body shots I think I am wrong about Mongoloid. She is actually starting to look a lot like Kim Kardashian. Or her step-dad. Doesn't matter.

We go back to her place. To my surprise, it's not a place with a matron. It's a normal apartment in Cape Town's biggest dormitory – Vredehoek.

I'm not sure what basis this is on. Are we just in the friends zone? I can do without a coffee. So I get close to her. And ask her the nowhere to hide one. I purr. 'So, is this really happening?'

She lunges me. OK, asked and answered. Upstairs we go.

We're rolling on her bed, various pieces of clothing are coming off. I realise the sheets are kind of squeaking. They are like a kind of plastic. Squeak squelch squeak. The reality hits me. I was right all along about being a Downer. What a downer. I slide off and in one movement hit the floor with my shoulder, roll like Daniel Craig, scoop up my Ted Baker shirt and Fabiani shoes – fuck the socks – only Polos – and am down the stairs and gone.

When I hit the Scirocco I marvel at my escape. What might have happened to me? It's only when I get back home that my heart rate drops below 2000RPM and I think maybe those sheets were something to do with a fetish. Which may have been nice. But I wasn't taking any chances.

SATURDAY 17 DECEMBER 2011

The dictator in charge of North Korea, something like Kim Ping Pong Hung III or something like that, has died. Rex wonders why they, like we're doing with Mandela, are not keeping him alive. It's been a tough year for dictators – Gaddafi, Mubarak from Egypt and now this oke. God has two weeks to call up Mugabe to make it a great year.

Costa Vegetableopolous seems to be stalling in Athens. In that he has not left yet. Which obviously works in my favour, especially given that the guy from Samsung has now declared the double-door fridge that can dispense crushed ice and sparkling water 'BER', which apparently is trade for Beyond Economic Repair. I'm just going to have to say the fridge was fine when I evacuated the property and it's not my fault if it breaks on Costa Idiotiddes' way in from CTI, as we call our airport if you are an FF (frequent flyer). In fact, and here is more Brydon genius, just before he gets back I'm going to put some ice and cold shit in the fridge to prove that it was working.

With Costa Outtacontrol not long before taking off (if Olympic Airlines still do) and thus about to slip through the SAPS cordon, it would be irresponsible not to cast an eye to my transport situation. There is no sport like transport and what message would it send out to the @igloo community and aficionados were I to return to the flat battered, rust experiment of the Golf that has slept on the street since my return to the Mother City. In fact customers would probably flee like the Rushdie family in Mecca.

So I take myself down to Mercedes in Culemborg, which is where Helen should have built the stadium and not in metrosexual Green Point where vuvuzelas are blowing the locals off their Vespas and the fan looting terrifies the local shopkeepers and publicans. But never mind. So I'm not after anything fancy, just looking at the entry-level two-door. I know the sad and limited out there say you should never buy a new car, that I am going to lose a 100K by just driving it off the showroom floor. You know what I say to that kak: LOSER.

Don't you want that feeling – of sinking into the bucket seats and smelling that leather and new-car smell, and knowing that it's all yours? Well, mostly Absa Vehicle Finance's, but you get my drift.

The salesman is, as usual, a charra called Stanley Moodley, oddly enough from Stanger. 'The Stan in Stanger' as he introduces himself. His boss is some bonehead reading *Die Burger* in his office. I think, fuckit, pal, you would move a lot more C-Classes if you shaved your moustache and read *GQ*. Anyway, not for me to say.

That's besides the point: with no xenon headlights, no Bang & Olufsen sub woofers (almost an essential, Stan points out, and I agree), but with sat nav (Cameron Diaz' voice) and Bluetoof (as Naas Botha would call it) and by taking the biggest balloon payment and stretching it over about 45 years, I can just about get an entry-level two-door. As long as the employee strength of the chick on duty at Absa Vehicle Finance is not due diligence.

But with @igloo going like it is, I can afford the repayments, which probably exceed the GDP of Lesotho.

Charcoal. And Stan will throw in a personal number plate. Another Flash of Brydon genius: 1 Met Uys WP

SUNDAY 18 DECEMBER 2011

What a day.

Sir Alex, thank fuck, has been run over. It seems he got out and was knocked over by some old duck in an Austin Apache. Really. How she got up enough clicks to flatten Sir Alex, I don't know. Be that as it may, it is what it is. I hear it happen – the thump and the noise like a live pig having its snout shaved shorter on a Parma ham machine.

I look as upset as I can. I hold him in my arms. I know he's a goner, like in the Westerns, when the blood comes out the mouth or the ear, the game's over, china. I managed to splutter out, convincingly, at the old Oxygen Thief who is empirically more upset than me: 'How fast were you going?'

Neighbours gather around and for once I'm not in their cross hairs. In fact I get a nice hug from the hot mom in 42. (I linger in a bit, breathing in her Anais Anais.)

Of course, I didn't want Sir Alex to die. And I'm probably not as relieved as Ferris or GC, but what kind of life would he have had? I am not ready for the domestic responsibility of pets. And he would have felt that. It's for the best. He never really knew what hit him (well, he would never have seen a 1972 Austin Apache before). And he didn't suffer, give or take a few minutes.

I post on the Book.

> My pride and joy is gone. Sir Alex. I held him in my arms as he breathed his last. Farewell faithful hound. Farwell. Sir Alex May 2011 – 18 December. Gone too soon.#speedkills

My god – the reaction. I couldn't have made it up. About 1,000 likes, 400 comments, 76% from chicks (I counted). So much sympathy. More 'x's than Julio Iglesias.

Not only is this a financial saving and lifestyle preserver, it has other benefits. Kak for the canine, bonus for the brand. But don't tweet or comment anything like that. That, my friends, would just undo all the good work.

Sunday blues – I remember the clanging chimes of *Carte Blanche* doom. I hate Derek Watts. *Carters* used to just give me the blues because it was a Sunday evening. For no real reason. But now I have proper one when Mich sends me a screenshot of a Facebook post from Hayley:

> It's so sad when you have to take your daughter's father to court to pay his basic maintenance.

I call Mich. She uses words like 'disgusted', 'shocked', 'disappointed'. Crikey, she is not my mom, I haven't just taped over the Royal Wedding on the VCR.

But I must admit, this situation is 'brand endangering'.

MONDAY 19 DECEMBER 2011

The thought strikes me that Costa Ekonomicrisis may stick in Athens to have Christmas with his Big Fat Greek Clan. That could

299

be my Shawshank Redemption. Because trying to get Mrs Bax to find a house with immediate availability in Condé Nast's trendiest city in the middle of the season is harder than Oscar Pistorius walking through a metal detector at JFK.

But if he is staying for a Big Fat Greek Christmas, I may have another week. Then again I'm not sure what they worship there. I know they have their own pope with a name like Gregory. It's Greek Orthodox and their Christmas, if they have one, is probably in some odd and meaningless month, like May. I google and see that some of them who follow one calendar (the new one) recognise Christmas on the same day as the rest of the civilised world. Then the rest of the mob who follow the Old Calendar celebrate it on 7 January. Could be even more of a result if he decides to wait in the Land of the Broken Plates (and Economy) chewing on dolmades until then.

I text him:

> Costa, how's it. All looking awesome for your return. Abstinence still abstaining from sabenza. Listen, Boet, are you Old or New Calendar Greek Orthodox. Just want to arrange your Christmas (if that's what you call it) present. BTW, where you guys celebrating? Jase

Doesn't even have the manners to reply.

I keep the pressure on Bax to find me my spot. Bax – long since cured of heterosexuality.

Just to get in the Christmas *gees* my mom SMSes. Yes she SMSes me as the bingo halls of Port Alfred plunge into the 1990s:

> Jason. We are so excited to gave the whole family together for Christmas. When are you arriving? Please drive safely. Dad says

they are trapping by Coega and to remember this is the Eastern Base. [That's predictive text for Cape, I'm guessing.] Leslie and BAC are coming [BAC is what Dad refers to as Lesley's husband – Bladdy Awful Carol]. The done [food, I think] is under control. Abo you bring the booze? Loud mom x

I assume abo is can? Unless that was a Freudian slip.

Mom's not loud. Dad is. So I assume by 'loud' she means love. #thedangersofnokia

TUESDAY 20 DECEMBER 2011

I remember now that I did promised the fogeys I would go home for Christmas. But two things:

Firstly. Have they no appreciation this is Everest season for the @igloo community?

And second. Can I really face a Christmas of Bellingham Grand Cru or the Johannisberger? What sort of name is that? Hardly evocative of Cape vineyards, Cape Dutch architecture and old vats with the winemaker holding the glass up to the slanting sun. It smacks of Rosettenville or Turffontein.

Can I face a Christmas of knitted presents, trifle and Rexy downing Bell's to get over BAC? Mom getting stuck into 50ml of Cinzano.

Hi Mom, will let you know, just got a helluva lot on at work but cant wait xx

301

I can't honestly see myself heading off to the Sunshine Coast. Well, not unless Costa returns. Flights are too expensive now. And I don't think I will give Costa Uphimselfides the ammunition of me having his car in the Friendly Province.

Just then Stan from Stanger rings.

'Hello Jason, Stanley from Mercedes-Benz here, how you blutha?'

'Lekker, Stan, you?'

'Flat out, flat out. Listen, I'm just calling to let you know that Finance have approved your application for your C250. Well done, blutha.'

I'm tempted to ask the guy how the fuck they did that. Don't they do any research? I have that sudden-loss-of-breath feeling. Not out of excitement, but one of rampant anxiety. How will I cope? With those instalments, milk and toilet paper would become luxuries. Wow. But luckily the feeling does not last long. Nanoseconds, in fact. Look, I rationalise, if you are driving a C250 CDI, you're not going to end up in the street, are you? Everything will fall into step after that.

I thank Stan, hit the red button and call Jordan. As usual her wisdom knows no bounds: 'Jason, if you look the part, you will become the part.'

'Thanks, Jordan. I knew I could rely on you.'

'Jase, I haven't received your November payment yet.'

What sort of time is it to ask something like that? Why bring someone down like that? Anyway, I tell her I am in the tunnel and click off.

Maybe I'm going to PA for Christmas. Just as soon as Stan has my charcoal-grey beast licensed and ready.

WEDNESDAY 21 DECEMBER 2011

I collect my charcoal-grey two-door. There can be nothing better to sniff or snort than that smell. My god. There is a bottle of Veuve Clicquot nestling on the driver's seat. I go straight for a cruise through Camps Bay with David Guetta thumping out drowning out the taxis on Main Road. Can anybody see the oke who's just made it? I can.

No more using some Greek fugitive's more common German autos.

May as well strike while the iron is hot. In a while it will go cold, literally. So I post on the Book:

> Its only five days now since I lost my Sir Alex. Life will never be the same again. For those of you that have asked, I have some good days and some not such good ones. Some of you have asked if I am getting another but the answer is and must be no. To me that would be to disrespect his memory. I just feel so vacant. #Gonetosoon #speedkills.

400 likes. Just like that. So we have the long lines out, it's now just time to haul in the bluefin.

I go to Dawesy's Christmas drinks at his spot up the road. There's a friend of Lettuce there called Sarah who is very tidy and gives me a looong hug when she hears of Sir Alex.

Over a Heinie and some hummus on Woolies rosemary crackers, Dawesy asks me why I wrote speed kills in my post about Sir Alex.

'Well, if she was going slower, Sir Alex may still be with us today.'

'Jase, she was 85 going uphill in a 1972 Austin Apache that at best pushed out about 20kW.'

'It's not the point.'

'Truth is, you were not sorry to see him go.'

I look stupefied. Slowly put my Heineken down and walk down to the water feature and stare up at the cable way for a long time, my back to everyone. I was worried it wouldn't work, but sure enough, after a while, I feel a feminine hand on my shoulder. I hope it's Sarah, but it's only Sandy, Slug's (average) wife. She was better in first year varsity, but now her middle order is getting stronger. Out of the corner of my eye I can see Dawesy is getting a bollocksing from Sid, his 'life partner', about being insensitive. I come back and ask for a glass of water. Sarah is looking at me a lot. Now, if only I can find a way to let her find out that that German two-door beauty in the driveway belongs to *moi*.

Dawesy is braaing pork neck and some aubergine thing. What's wrong with the old days of some chops and wors?

But the battle lines are drawn. I bring up my new car ('Is it OK to park there?' so I can point at the Merc.) Stevie pipes up: 'It's like Kenny Kunene's.'

'Kak,' I say. 'Kenny has an E-Class.'

Stevie goes at it and says it's still a BEE car. This is not what I want Sarah to hear. 'No, it's not. Have you ever seen a white driving a Land Rover Evoque?'

Lettuce pipes up with the inevitable: 'Sarah does.'

'I meant black male.'

Well, that starts a whole storm. I am being accused of being sexist *and* racist now, but I wasn't the one who said it was like Kenny Kunene's car. 'It's just a reality, white men don't drive Evoques, straights don't drive Minis, no woman under 70kg drives a Kia SUV and people who wear cardigans drive microbuses. Just facts of life.'

I make some comment about nurses these days being more worried about their Edgars accounts than making people better. Left field, I know, but true. Anyway, and as usual with Dawesy, the whole race thing starts. He accuses me in front of Sarah of being racist.

Stevie points out that they never said thank you for Iscor or Sasol or Eskom.

'Well,' says Dawesy, 'How could they say thank you for Eskom when it doesn't work?'

'It used to. They broke it.'

I am very anxious not to come across as one in front of my Sarah, so make a point of clarifying my position. 'I don't even notice colour.'

And so it goes on.

Dawsey and Slug, laughing so much, spit out some of their Merryweather Midskull Hearty Pale Ale, or whatever up-itself, trendy, artisanal craft beer they're on.

Dawesy: 'So, Jason, you're not a racist?'

'Nope.'

'So would you marry a black?'

'Sies.'

'So you are?'

Oh god, this old chestnut.

'Would you?'

'Yes.'

'Well, you haven't.'

Stevie pipes up, luckily, that the darkest he could go is Christina Storm. That takes all the focus off me.

THURSDAY 22 DECEMBER 2011

Four @igloo functions today and all 'red dots'.

For all Dawesy and his tzatziki-infused, *Mail & Guardian*-reading rubbish, I am a very new South African:

- Voted DA and Cape Independent (ward)
- Been tested – shew (not the best 48 hours of my life)
- Counted (census – easy in Tamboerskloof, trickier in Atteridgeville)
- Got a Bafana shirt (no Protea badge as that's a rip off)
- Save electricity. Pool pump turned off (a.k.a. broken)
- Bought *Funny Money* and *Big Issue*

What more can one do?

> **@jasonator069:** Hout Bay Police Station being guarded by ADT tonight #onlyinmzansi.

FRIDAY 23 DECEMBER 2011

It's so cool staying in Cape Town for this time of year. All the knob locals are off to Hermanus and Plett and have been replaced by those looking for a good time. What a vibe. @igloo flying, Jasonator flying.

Yes, they all ask: 'So where're you going for December, Jase? Arniston?'

And when you say no they react like you have dog faeces running out your nostrils.

'Work, china. Gotta graft.'

In the news today: @igloo does five functions.

Gerald Majola the disgraced former CEO of Cricket SA is diagnosed with stress. After he raided their coffers, of course. Dad, unusually, says we shouldn't blame him: 'It's in his DNA and he learnt it from Hansie who learnt it from Ali Bacher.'

The guy who spilt/poured a drink on Jacob Zuma at the Durban July is being charged with assault. I think if there was ice in the drink you can call it assault, not just for some booze. Unless it was Southern Comfort because it's so sticky.

As the sun sets over the Atlantic I raise a cold Heineken to myself. A well-deserved Heineken. I have made it through. Nobody evicts anyone on New Year's Eve. You would have to be an inhumane member of the Hitler Youth to do that. And then it's the Christmas season and all that and I reckon the sheriffs of Cape Town are all in Langebaan or Hartenbos between Christmas and Easter. Plus who else would look after these two dogs?

Well done, Jase. You stuck to your guns and you won. Another Heinie, please!

SATURDAY 24 DECEMBER 2011

Christmas Eve.

To gym. There's a black American guy who is *massive* benching about 150kg, but he's speaking loudly in his accent just to let us know he isn't one of ours.

I am meant to be settling down to a glass of Riesling and some pork crackling this evening in Port Alfred. As much as I want to blast open the C250's pipes and test it, I can't put myself through the very best of Boney M and two lesbians gifting each other spit.

I know my folks are going to be upset. But that's what folks are meant to do. They forgive, they tolerate. They're not going anywhere.

It may take 14-17 days, but they will get over my no-show. I know I have done lots of things wrong over my fast-lived 30-odd years, and they have always forgiven me. I am guilty probably of: vanity, (petty) theft, sloth, coveting my neighbour's wife (Mrs Fouche from number 17), (technical) fraud, driving drunk (*die appel val nie ver van die boom af nie*), illegal use of narcotics, *dronk op straat*, crimen injuria, possession of pornography, sexual assault (accused but no further investigation because Lisa van Staden was talking rubbish).

I know it's a bit of a list, but there's no murder or treason or anything. No incest. But that was a pretty easy temptation to avoid in the Brydon family. Leslie never laid a finger on me – maybe that was a sign of things to come?

They're just going to have to forgive me for this one. I must say I did feel a bit swak when I was at Café Caprice and saw 16 missed calls from 'Folks Home'. Like Costa, it's tomorrow's problem.

SUNDAY 25 DECEMBER 2011

I do get one early Christmas present in that I see on Instagram Costa and the rest of the oil slick enjoying some traditional Greek Christmas eve sesame baklava somewhere in Athens. So I'm not heading off to The Haven night shelter in my C250 just yet.

I get a bollocksing from Dad. They thought I may have been hijacked and my body thrown off the Storms River Bridge. Or arrested and locked up by some Eastern Cape cop for stepping on the cracks in the pavement. ('They will get you for anything these days, chum, just so they can extract their "lunch" money.') He speaks to me like I'm in Grade 5. Apparently I should have let them know where I was. What they don't seem to appreciate is that I am the CEO of a multi-million rand F&B company – I really haven't got time to worry about my mom's steamed pud.

Still it's probably my worst Christmas since I fell off my three-hour-old Western Flyer 18-speed, broke my front teeth and Dad said we had to wait till the dentists were open because it would cost a bloody fortune on Christmas Day. That was the same Christmas my sister Leslie cried because she got a Barbie doll instead of Ken, which, in retrospect, was another sign of things to come.

I end up getting absolutely totalled on Fanta Browns at an 'Orphans and Jews' party at 3G's. Don't even remember driving home.

It's only when I get up to down a liter of water and piss in the bath (in the interests of accuracy when drunk) that I see the SMS from Costa:

> Happy Christmas, Jason, your last one without a criminal record.

Stunning!

MONDAY 26 DECEMBER 2011

SMS from Leslie:
> You could have let the folks know you weren't going to pitch and then answered their calls They were worried stiff and as a result had an unpleasant Christmas. Leslie x

Reply:
> I am not the reason they had an unpleasant Christmas.

What do you mean?

Never mind.

Then this from Megan:

> You tell me the other night that you have never felt this way about someone, never been so attracted by someone and never been in such a relationship with such a good balance between the mental and physical. Quote. Then I think I may have expected some form of contact over Christmas, even a whatsapp, something. I am meant to be your girlfriend, Jase. Anyway Happy Chistmas x.

What is it with these chicks? A) Megan, you are *not* my girlfriend, you are the reliable stock in my portfolio. And secondly, why do they put 'x's on messages when they are pissed off?

WEDNESDAY 28 DECEMBER 2011

> **@jasonator069:** Not a dry eye in Pyongyang. Dry eyes get you shot. Dramatic grieving gets you a food parcel. #KimJongfuneral

I can't drive a two-door Merc (Slug asks me why two is better than four – surely four is easier – shows what he knows) and not have the iPhone 4S. Just need to double check my old iPhone 4 insurance, so I can chuck it into the docks and claim my iPhone 4S.

Note to self: back it up first.

Mrs Bax claims he has found a place in one of those French avenues in Fresnaye. It's 26 fucking K a month. I can't afford that – not with

Kenny Kunene's Merc outside. But it's available 1 Jan, has a sick view, a pizza oven and a toilet that you can see Lion's Head from.

'Thanks, Greg, how much is the deposit?'

'One month's rent.'

'So all I have to pay by 1 Jan is the deposit? '

'Yip.'

'Let's do it.'

I'm sure when Richard Branson started Virgin Air he didn't sit there in January wondering how he was going to pay October's fuel. Hotel Back Yourself.

'When's the earliest I can get in?'

'Other people move out on the 31st.'

'Can you pay a deposit with a credit card?'

He will look into it. Apparently its unusual.

Acutely worried about Olympic Air and when it flies people in, I ask 'What time on the 31st?'

He will get back to me.

THURSDAY 29 DECEMBER 2011

I go to see the house. I meet Bax there. I can't be seen at Vida with him any more in case people start to twitter.

The wifi for the house key is 'Rich White People'. I like it already. It is amazing. The blinds are remote control and you can see the new stadium from the Weber.

Mel Gibson's ex-wife, Robyn Moore, has been awarded half his $850m fortune in their divorce settlement. I would also sleep with Mel Gibson for that. In fact, I would sleep with Zoomer for that.

Two days to the massive R300K net to @igloo party on the Russian's boat. OMG!!!!!!

And not a tweet or peep from the Greek nor his liquorice all-sorts lawyers. Nothing. Run for the hills. Been stared down and beaten by the Jasonator. See you fellas, drive safe!

FRIDAY 30 DECEMBER 2011

I am at a friend of Megan's dinner in some try-hard Thai place near Kloof Street. Fair enough the chef looks like he comes from the East. I don't know how I didn't say no to this fiasco. It's all her friends. I think it was because I felt bad about Christmas or I wasn't thinking when she phoned to ask or I had sprained my cerebrum or because she mentioned her one friend Nats was going to be there and she is showroom.

Whatever the reason was, I shouldn't have said yes.

It's a room full of conventionally successful types who probably have never lived, never had a credit card declined, or the sheriff of the court come round, or their nostrils so blocked that they just cannot get another thing up there any more. I am sitting next to someone called Clive. Yes, really, Clive. He is an actuary with Old Mutual. And as interesting as the news in Venda. I accept he may earn more than the Free State town of Richmond, but it hasn't bought him a personality. His wife's name is Louise. I reckon at some stage she may have been doable, but a couple of kids at St Andrew's and DSG later and a pad in Kalk Bay, she has lost her spark. Nats is out of talking range. Megan has her hand on my knee, and I honestly feel like breaking it off. If there are any single ones at this table of 16, her hand on my knee is going to send them running.

I go at the tequila. My dad always says of functions such as these: 'If you can't get out of them, get into them.' I am on seven Cuervo golds by the time the starter portion of duck spring rolls arrive. I am trying to stare out some jaundiced creep's wife across the table. You know, I say to myself, 'If she looks at me in the next 10 seconds, she wants me, 10… 9… 8… 7…' But she doesn't. More tequila.

It's hot in the restaurant. And tight. Truth be told, they shouldn't have taken this table of 16. When I slam tequila number nine, I realise there is more chance of a helium balloon staying down. I feel it leave the stomach on the upward path, having been rejected there, through the equally hostile oesophagus and up my throat. I push back violently on the table to launch my dash to the bathroom. But it's too tight. Just too tight. As I push my chair back I hit some German wanker. But a German wanker is not going to stop Jose Cuervo's burst to freedom. I am sweating. Look round and all I see is that Louise's Louis Vuitton handbag. Luckily she has her back (and its fat) turned talking to Megan, so I lean behind the chair and use the bag to dispose of Jose and the duck spring rolls. Amazing to relate, but nobody is any the wiser. I even zip it up to prevent any aroma issues.

That is until the bill came. And I went.

SATURDAY 31 DECEMBER 2011

The Big Day. The Big Party. On – A – Yacht. No chance I will even remember the start to 2012. All I do know is that I am going to be quite a lot richer in the morning. To think, I was once the assistant barman at Royal Port Alfred Gold Club. I now have a Mercedes C-Class and will soon live in Fresnaye.

And I won't be put off by this sort of kak. An SMS from Jeff Jenkins:
Jason, 2012 is going to be a little different for you. In ten days time you are either going to be a lot poorer or in the slammer. Can't wait.

With Costa Halfwittedes imminent, I get Dawesy's Precious to come and give the place a run over. Meant to be there at 8. Swans in at 8.23. Always the same excuse. Taxi/Bus/Train.

I text Dawesy and tell him he has sent me a dud on the BIG day.

He replies:
What do you want them to do – take the Circle line from Khayelitsha, change in Guguletu for the District line, then the Overland to Tamboerskloof?

It's not the point. They know how hard it is to get public transport here, so they must factor it in.

I drop the C250 for a valet and will work one more day out of the Scirocco. Costa won't come back on New Year's Eve. Might as well see in 2012 as another year of Greek recession. Maybe the Interpol thing is also scaring him off.

Thing is, it was never meant to end like this.

The Yacht Party. OMG. There are about 20 chicks there who could have been Miss Iceland if they wanted. Moët et Chandon is regarded as serving Oros instead of orange juice. There isn't any. There is some DJ called Afrojack who apparently used to *pomp*, sorry date, Paris Hilton. There are about 500 people on this ship, nine bars and it's absolutly fucking wild.

I'm climbing into some Grey Goose and Red Bull and some Latvian air hostess, when there's a tap on my back.

There is a bright light in my face, but, hey, I am used to bright lights. It's a chick, of course. 'Are you Jason Brydon?'

'Yes, honey, what can I do for you?'

Then I realise it's that Indian check Devi from *Carte Blanche*. And there's a fucking camera. She is asking, 'Is it true you dilute drinks and swap expensive brands for cheaper ones?'

I'm not faced with a whole range of choice in this situation. I think I realise now that I am more of the flight than fight genre of the species. It sometimes just makes sense. Even if you have your own side of the story you have to make the call that this may not be the right occasion to start getting it across.

I hotfoot it out of there. By the time I'm approaching the Scirocco I think I'm sprinting at 5/6ths full speed. I can feel yesterday's leg presses (200kg eight reps) in my screaming quads.

Not even time to buckle up despite that irritating beep that I've spent the last few months trying to override or break in the Scirocco.

I can't see anything in the rear-view mirror. Sure, I've had a few Grey Geese (is that the plural?) and they say that slows down your motor coordination. But chuck in the fact that I'm moving at speed (Scirocco gear stick in S for sport mode) and have no clue where I am in this 'working' harbour, then yes, there are some ingredients here for things to go peters.

Which they do.

I swing a left past some containers away from any threats I can imagine and put some right foot. Which happens to be the last time the Scirocco's tyres touch tarmac. I am airborne. Briefly. Before being greeted by an airbag and the cold filthy Atlantic.

It's not something out the movies where I have to wriggle free and swim to the surface. The top of the Scirocco is down anyway. Not buckled in so I don't go down with the car. But my iPhone, my iPad, iPod touch and Armani jacket do. Once I realise I am on the surface this thought depresses me. Oh, and of course the car. Which I am now going to have to report stolen.

The water is a sewer, I'm sure, as I now wind my way between empty oil canisters and Steri Stumpies and past Taiwanese fishermen faeces to some old tyres that I haul myself up on. Which is where the spotlight finds me and a grumpy seal.

317

SUNDAY 1 JANUARY 2012

I'm OK but today's *Weekend Argus* isn't. Bottom story on the front page. A nice pic of the Scirocco being hauled out of Duncan Dock, watched by a few natives and a concerned Costa with the headline:

DISGRACED CITY BUSINESSMAN IN BOTCHED SUICIDE BID.

Fuck.

Ctl alt del. Time for a reboot.

ACKNOWLEDGMENTS

Thank you to Neil Ellard and Sean Coetzee for providing limitless material. Jason Brydon is your spawn! And to my mom for encouraging/nagging.

On a more serious note I would like to thank the indefatigable and brilliant Mike Nicol, whose faith is perhaps a little misplaced.

Thanks, as usual, to Shelley Carmichael. Also to Tim Richman of Burnet Media for making this very easy.